THE HUMMINGBIRD WHISPERER

By

Matthew J. Pallamary

Mystic Ink Publishing

Mystic Ink Publishing
San Diego, CA
www.mysticinkpublishing.com

ISBN 13: 979-8-9884998-1-7 (sc)

Library of Congress Control Number: 2024914963
Mystic Ink Publishing, San Diego, CA

Book Jacket and Page Design: Matthew J. Pallamary / San Diego CA
Cover artwork: Matthew J. Pallamary / San Diego CA
Author's Photograph: Matthew J. Pallamary — Robert DeLaurentis / Santa Barbara CA

The Hummingbird Whisperer

And A Little Child Shall Lead Them

Isiah 11:6

ONE

Jeanette Driscoll opened her sparkling blue eyes, stretched out on the bed, and brushed back her long blonde hair before resting her head on her husband Ted's chest. Tall, sandy-haired, and blue-eyed like his wife, Ted's muscular frame complemented her model's figure. Their friends and Ted's colleagues where he worked as head of research and development at Bliss Pharmaceuticals often referred to them as the perfect couple.

"If we're going to bring a kid into the world," she said, "let's create the most perfect one we can."

Ted leaned in to her. "Like Hitler's blond-haired, blue-eyed Aryan boys?"

Jeanette hit him on the shoulder. "Stop it! I was thinking more along the lines of a Jesus, then again, maybe we want a little girl."

Ted chuckled and kissed her. "I'm okay with a blonde-haired, blue-eyed Jesus, especially if he or she looks like their mother!"

"So many choices." Jeanette groaned. "Part of me wishes we could go back to natural selection like our parents did."

"It's a crap shoot with too many unknowns," Ted said with an air of finality. "Aside from that we're both worried about birth defects, delivery complications, or other possibilities for trouble, not to mention the threat and the impact to your health."

"I admit to being a little worried, but part of me craves the idea of nurturing a new life inside of me with all the warmth, connection, and intimacy that comes with it."

Ted caressed the side of her face eliciting a dreamy smile. "I understand that as best as I can from a man's perspective and I know that pregnancy can be exhausting, painful, nauseating, and sometimes flat-out dangerous. If you're pregnant and you stress too much, get sick, or catch some kind of flu or something, you might not be giving our child the best start we can." He ran his hand down over her breasts and followed her sculpted curves down to the softness of her inner thigh. "Not to mention what it could do to your beautiful body."

She giggled when he stroked her thigh and put her hand on his. "Stop it!"

He slid his hand out from under hers and continued his caresses. "Think about the benefits. We can continue having all the sex we want with no interruptions. You might not have the same birthing experience your mother had, but we'll both arrive at our first day of parenthood feeling physically fresh and well-rested, instead of you having been weighed down for months by a parasitic organism that could leave a path of destruction when you birth it. Even in the best case scenario there are possibilities of post-partum depression, hormone imbalances, and other post birth dangers."

"Parasitic organism? That's our child you're talking about. You make it sound so horrible!"

"I'm sorry, honey. I didn't mean it to sound like that. I only want what is best for you and baby. You have to admit, the whole pregnancy thing takes a toll on you. If you take that into consideration and look at the positives, taking advantage of the technological benefits we are blessed with is the best way to go. Everything can be precisely controlled and monitored which eliminates any stress on beautiful *you*, and it ensures the safest, healthiest, most stable environment for our love child to grow in."

They stayed quiet for awhile, then Jeanette sat up and grabbed her iPad from the bed stand. "Let's take another look."

She propped herself up against the headboard, pulled her knees up and put the tablet in her lap, tapping the screen. Ted propped himself up beside her and put his arm around her. A moment later the Fetal Fantasies web site popped up.

Angelic looking baby faces floated up, filling the screen, each framed in baby blue or pink. In the middle of the screen effervescent pulsing pink words dimmed and brightened from a black rectangle along with the gentle throbbing of a tiny heartbeat.

Let Fetal Fantasies eliminate the pain, danger, and discomfort of pregnancy and labor while allowing you the unprecedented blessing of creating your dream child with the special qualities and genetics of your choosing.

Jeanette tapped the pulsing text opening up a new screen.

Fetal Fantasies is San Diego's premier artificial womb facility that brings a novel approach to pregnancy that allows your baby

to grow in an optimally balanced germ free environment inside a transparent growth pod.

Our proprietary technology creates ideal gestation conditions in a temperature-controlled, infection-free womb with a view. A hybrid bioengineered umbilical cord provides oxygen and nutrition as your little bundle of love floats in pharmaceutically pure amniotic fluid that is continually refreshed with precisely tailored hormones, antibodies, and growth factors. Baby waste products are efficiently removed and run through a microfiltered bioreactor that enzymatically converts it back into a steady and sustainable supply of fresh nutrients.

Built in stereophonic speakers ensure that your loved one gets the best possible brain stimulation delivered with binaural beats and direct cranial stimulation, including an ongoing transmission of your heartbeat that your little one can bond to. As baby grows and develops there are options for our recommended classical, or any other music of your choice, as well as your own soothing voice piped in to build and enhance that precious bond.

A video filled the bottom part of the screen. Jeanette tapped the start arrow opening it up into full screen mode.

Brahm's Lullaby played in the background. Technicians dressed in baby blue and pink clean room coveralls, masks, and gloves moved along rows of transparent pods sitting atop active graphical displays, stopping to examine each one. Healthy babies floated inside each pod with electrodes attached to different parts of their bodies. Transparent umbilical cords and other tubes coupled with monitoring devices hung suspended in clear amniotic fluid.

An attractive young couple on a smaller screen in the foreground studied a cell phone screen that matched the graphics on the pod displays while a soothing feminine voice narrated the images and video segments playing out onscreen.

"You can monitor your baby's vitals through the Fetal Fantasy app or tune directly in to sensors in the pod where vital signs are precisely managed allowing strict vigilance over any possible physical defects or genetic abnormalities. Synchronized data on your little bundle of love is only a few taps away on our phone app along with a live HD fetus cam that gives you the ability to scroll through time-lapse video recordings of your child's development from embryo to full gestation.

"Human babies are the most helpless and underdeveloped in the animal kingdom because our brains are too big for the human female

11

hip gap, so they are born with soft, pliable skulls, several months behind other animals developmentally. In a Fetal Fantasy EZ-Womb, there's no such biological limit, allowing parents to experiment with longer gestational periods and healthier more developed babies.

"If this looks and sounds a little impersonal and you think you might miss the feeling of your baby kicking, our haptic suit option can bring that sensation back for any parent that wants it, only when they want it."

An image of the young couple sitting beside each other on a couch wearing VR headsets with wide smiles filled the screen.

"Want to see the beginning of life from your child's point of view? You can with a VR headset that allows you to tune in to a three hundred sixty degree camera any time you like."

The image of the young couple panned back showing them in a comfortably furnished room with a large picture window in the background. A baby floated in a single transparent pod above graphical displays next to a window with an expansive view of a twinkling magical night time cityscape.

"If you're uncomfortable with our standard birth package and are unhappy with the thought of your precious bundle of joy being grown in a four hundred pod baby lab, you can have a rechargeable battery-powered pod installed in your own home."

The narration changed to a male announcer's voice.

"Fetal Fantasies provides the best option for folks who like the idea of a baby but don't want to go through the ordeals of pregnancy and childbirth to get one. Think about it. You might not even need a day off work! Just hold hands with your significant other after a day at the office, head down to the baby farm and dream about life as a parent, or enjoy your special time in the privacy of your own home."

Alternating pink and blue words dimmed and brightened at the bottom of the screen pulsing in time to the gentle throbbing of a heartbeat.

ENROLL HERE FOR OUR FREE
NO OBLIGATION BUILD A BABY WORKSHOP

Ted pulled Jeanette closer. "What do you think, honey?"

"So many choices and options. To be honest, I feel overwhelmed by all of it."

Ted kissed her on the cheek. "We don't have to make any decisions now and we have nothing to lose if we try the workshop."

"I still have lots of questions."

"I'm sure they can be answered at the workshop."

Jeanette remained quiet.

"Nothing ventured, nothing gained," Ted whispered.

Jeanette shrugged and tapped the enroll message.

TWO

Ted and Jeanette joined half a dozen other couples in the spacious sweet smelling lobby of Fetal Fantasies in a large two story mirrored glass building on Torrey Pines Road in La Jolla. Large tropical flowered plants and the gentle burble of water from cascading fountains scattered throughout the atrium created a cool soothing atmosphere.

"Welcome to Fetal Fantasies," a statuesque younger woman with expressive hazel eyes, long brown hair, and a form fitting silk teal dress said when they entered. "My name is Harmony, and it's my privilege to take you on a short tour of our facility before we start the workshop." She gestured toward a mirrored wall that slid open revealing a larger room and waved everybody in.

Floor to ceiling observation windows looked out over an expansive floor where technicians in baby blue and pink coveralls moved along row after row of transparent baby pods on top of graphical displays while Brahm's Lullaby played in the background. Babies in different stages of development floated inside each pod with electrodes attached to their bodies and semi-transparent umbilical cords and other tubes coupled with monitoring devices hung suspended in amniotic fluid. A massive video screen hung above it all cycling through video from the inside of pods, closeup shots, and from other cameras throughout the facility.

Jeanette took Ted's arm and leaned in close, whispering, "It seems so sterile and impersonal."

A moving observation walkway encircled the glass walled enclosure allowing visitors to view the facility from every perspective. Harmony guided them onto it while a pre-recorded male voice spoke from hidden speakers as the group moved around the perimeter gazing down at the baby farm.

"We are living in a moment of super-convergence of a number of technologies that all influence each other," the recorded voice said.

"Affordable sequencing of the human genome allows population-wide phenotypical research to be cross-checked to learn more about how genes express themselves, individually and in concert with one another.

"Artificial intelligence and quantum computing work together giving us the ability to process enormous amounts of data, and its capabilities are rocketing forward daily while gene editing tools give us the ability to edit the genome of living subjects. Our highly trained health care professionals facilitate a more personal and precise approach to customize opportunities for people with specific genetic markers.

"Advanced embryo selection is at the core of our program. Prospective parents will have multiple embryos to choose from, each of which will have its genome fully sequenced so they can choose between offspring from a large database of information. Parents can select against crippling genetic diseases like Down syndrome guaranteeing them a healthy happy child.

"Following our proprietary process new parents can select *for* certain traits as well as against others. Do you want your child to be taller? More athletic, with a greater proportion of fast twitch muscle fibers? What about intelligence? Skin color? Eye color? Would you like to select the genetics for a child with a higher probability of living longer, a child with a higher degree of extraversion, or a more even temperament?

"All of these traits have genetic underpinnings that lets parents choose between dozens of their own biological embryos, so why wouldn't you choose the ones that have the best possible shot at life?

"The disadvantages of having children the old-fashioned way has now become apparent, as smarter, stronger, faster, healthier kids born from selection processes can dominate a range of competitive situations from sport to business to earning capacity. These advantages will multiply with subsequent generations as more and more science is applied to the reproductive process.

"Precision gene editing lets you select multiple options from your pre-selected embryos and allows you to make a number of adjustments before conception.

"The dawn of a new age of superhumans is upon us where a new selected and edited generation will have extraordinary genetic potentials in a wide range of areas."

After circling the perimeter the moving walkway stopped where it had started so everyone could step off. Harmony led them to a classroom where a large flat screen took up one wall with a podium off to its right. Coffee and other refreshments filled a table at the other end of the room. A semi-circle of oversized desks with chairs for two at each one surrounded the big screen. Each desk had a computer monitor at its center displaying a QR Code. Ted and Jeanette found their way to a desk and Harmony went to the podium where she pointed to the QR Code up on the big screen. "You can scan the QR Code on your desk monitors with your cell phone to download the Fetal Fantasies app which will synch to your account here, giving you real time access to all of your information, regardless of your location."

Ted and Jeanette scanned the code and downloaded the app along with the other couples. After a moment the screens on their phones matched the display on the big screen and the desk monitor.

Every screen had a matching graphic display featuring a spot for baby's name at the top which presently said, BABY DRISCOLL. An image of a human body took up the top right quadrant of the screen. Beside it were two rows of menu buttons labeled with selections like sex, eye color, hair color, vocal timbre, physical build, intelligence factor, athletic requirements, and other features. Below that dimmed out across the bottom of the screen were graphs for heartbeat, respiration, blood pressure, EKG activity, immune development, and other factors.

Harmony pointed a remote at the big screen beside her and demonstrated the menu system by hitting a few buttons, showing more detailed choices. "Each menu button on your left has a number of submenus for more detailed selections. Take your time and build your love child the way you dreamed of them. Changes are possible up to the moment of conception, and many can be reprogrammed up to the end of the first trimester."

"So many choices," Jeanette said. "It feels like too many. It makes me feel like I'm playing God."

Ted set down his phone and rested his hand on hers. "Goddess." He grinned. "I feel the same way, but I'm excited about the possibilities. Right now it's just a workshop. We have no commitment. Think of it like taking a new car for a test ride at a dealership."

Jeanette rolled her eyes. "That certainly sounds warm and inviting. I can't help thinking that all of this technology separates me from an intimate nurturing flesh and blood connection between our baby and me."

"While you're making your selections," Harmony said, "I will come around to assist each of you and answer any questions. Happy baby making!"

Ted gave Jeanette's hand a gentle squeeze. "Let's see what kind of angelic love child we can create when we put our minds to it." He kissed her cheek. "Don't forget, we can change whatever we want, wipe it all clean and forget about it, or start all over again fresh."

Jeanette brightened "All right. Let's make an angel."

"Even though I want a boy," Ted said, "I know you want a girl. I could do a lot worse than to have two blonde-haired, blue-eyed beauties in my life."

"I do want a girl," Jeanette said, "but if we started with a boy it would give our little girl a big brother to watch over and protect her." She smiled. "Besides, we can change it if we decide differently later." She tapped a menu button on her phone and selected male. The display on their monitor and their cell phones turned blue.

"Let's stick with the blond hair and blue eyes for now," Ted said.

"Sure!" Jeanette hit two more buttons, changing the displays.

More selections of physical characteristics brought greater detail to the body at the top right of the screens and Jeanette grew more enthusiastic as they selected other attributes. "I'm still not saying I am ready to commit to this," she said, "but if we do, I want to make the most perfect baby possible."

"Of course!"

Harmony joined them at their desk, filling the air with an intoxicating hint of jasmine and lavender. "How is it going, you two? Any questions?"

"So far, so good," Ted winked. "We're having fun, but Jeanette has more questions."

"The ladies always do. That's what I'm here for."

"I have to admit to being fascinated with all of it," Jeanette said, "but I'm still a little uneasy. This makes me feel like I'm playing God and I can't help thinking how this technology separates us from a warm intimate flesh and blood connection between me and our baby."

"Excellent question," Harmony said. "You have been touring a state of the art baby farm so I can understand how it comes across as impersonal. This is what you get with our standard birth package. If you're uncomfortable with the thought of your precious bundle of joy being grown in a lab at a baby farm, you can have a rechargeable battery-powered pod installed in your home. Our deluxe package includes a haptic suit option so you can experience all the mommy feelings you might not want to miss out on at your own chosen times and discretion."

Ted studied Jeanette with an expectant look.

"What about breastfeeding?" Jeanette said. "That's one of the primary bonding experiences between mother and child."

Harmony smiled, showing perfect teeth behind plump lips. "We have options there too. We can supply you with our proprietary nutrient dense formula complete with oxytocin and other supportive hormones. We also have a program that combines special supplements and hormonal injections that allow the mother to have the more visceral experience and physical closeness of breastfeeding their child."

"Think of it," Ted added, looking to Harmony for confirmation. "You can avoid the discomfort of pregnancy and the wear and tear on that beautiful body of yours and you can experience those feelings whenever you want instead of all the time. We can work and play to our hearts desire until the day our baby is born."

Harmony smiled her approval and held up a finger. "And you will avoid post-partum depression and any other post birth complications which will let you embrace and nurture your new born in a fully healthy state."

"That's a lot to think about," Jeanette said.

Harmony nodded. "Yes, it is, so there is no pressure and no time limits. Take all the time you need to decide what is right for you. We're here for any questions or assistance you might need. In the meantime, have some fun." She gestured toward their monitor. It looks like you already have a special child in the making. "Call if you need me."

Harmony stepped away and Ted and Jeanette found themselves consumed in creating their dream child.

THREE

Three months later a tiny fetus floated in a transparent pod above flickering graphical displays over a rechargeable battery-powered pod in a darkened corner of Ted and Jeanette's bedroom in their spacious home overlooking La Jolla Cove. Their cell phones, computers, and iPads all matched the real time readings on the front panel of the unit's display which were all wirelessly connected to the Fetal Fantasies baby farm network through a high-speed fiber optic network.

Inside the see-through womb their gestating infant floated in amniotic bliss with fully formed arms, hands, fingers, feet, and toes. The beginnings of fingernails and toenails were visible and its ears were fully formed. A translucent umbilical cord and other barely visible tubes attached to the infant coupled with monitoring devices that hung suspended in clear amniotic fluid.

Ted and Jeanette cuddled together in the semi-darkness of their room while the pod pulsed softly in the shadowed corner with the faint sound of a muted heartbeat accompanied by the pulsing red glow of vital signs from the unit's display.

"The sound of his tiny heart and the red glow that goes with it makes me feel like I'm in the womb with him," Jeanette said.

Ted squeezed her a little tighter. "We are the womb, honey! Think about it. A see through womb and the sound of that little beating heart and flashing red connects us and makes us part of it every step of the way."

"That's a nice way to think of it."

"And we can communicate with him whenever we want, or play him music from anywhere we want just by picking up the phone."

"I want to name him Theodore after you Ted. We can call him Theo so there's no confusion between the two of you when he gets older."

Ted smiled. "I love it!"

Theo's heartbeat grew stronger over the next few months, filling the room in concert with the red pulsing unit. His fingers and toes became well-defined and his eyelids, eyebrows, eyelashes, nails, and hair were all visible. His teeth and bones had also grown denser, his tiny penis had fully formed, and he had begun to move around.

"Look!" Jeanette said one day, standing in front of the pod. "He's yawning, sucking his thumb, stretching, and making faces. How adorable!"

Ted came closer and put his arm around her, peering into the pod. Baby Theo looked red and wrinkled like a wizened old man and his veins were visible through his luminous skin. "Isn't this great! We get to watch his whole development. We wouldn't get to see any of this detail if he were inside of you."

Theo moved more in the coming weeks and responded to sounds they made when they were in the room as well as changes to the room's light. Ted and Jeanette took turns talking to him through their phones, giggling when they saw him responding to the pod's built in stereophonic speakers.

"He needs some culture," Ted said one day.

"What do you mean?"

He tapped on his phone screen until Pink Floyd's Dark Side of the Moon played through the pod speakers. Theo froze and turned his head to the side as if listening while rocking back and forth with the opening sound of a heartbeat and looked up when the rest of the music followed. As the album progressed, his movements grew more refined while he moved to the beat of the music in a graceful flowing weightless ballet.

"Quick," Ted whispered. "Put on the haptic suit and lie down on the bed. I'm dying to see what you feel."

Jeanette slipped into the suit while the album continued and stretched out on the bed. A moment later her body moved in concert with Theo's as if she were attached to him with strings and he was the puppeteer. "I'm dancing with him," she cried. "I'm dancing with my baby!"

"You're feeling what he's feeling!"

Ted slid into the bed beside her and held her gently. "Now we're all dancing." Ted reached up from behind and caressed Jeanette's enlarged breasts. "Those hormones they have been giving you are working great! Your tatas are looking and feeling very nice!"

She slapped his hand away and giggled, "Stop it! These aren't for you. I have no real physical connection with Theo and I am looking forward to breast feeding him to seal our mother son bond."

"I'm hoping he will be willing to share them at some point. I was here first after all."

They tried different music every day. When they played classical Theo didn't move much and appeared to yawn more, but he always rocked out to Pink Floyd and went into what looked like a trance when they played meditative music from Jeanette's yoga class.

"Everything is so flawless," Jeanette said one day. "He's perfectly formed." She held up her phone to Ted.

His smile went all the way up into his eyes. "The Fetal Fantasy engineers said that our choices of characteristics and attributes in Theo's genetic profile put him in the highest one tenth of a percentile range of anything they have ever seen."

"We're getting close to his birthday," Jeanette said. "We need to pick what day we want that to be."

Ted kissed her on the cheek. "I can't wait."

FOUR

Ted jolted awake to Jeanette's screams in the dark.

"What's wrong?"

She looked at him wide-eyed and Ted realized there were no sounds, no lights, and no signs of life. He reached for his cell phone and saw a blank screen, then Jeanette stumbled across the room. "God, please," she whispered.

Ted jumped out of bed and joined her beside the darkened pod where little Theo floated without movement or any signs of life.

"Please god." Jeanette dropped to her knees, clasped her hands together and started whispering prayers. Ted remained dumbfounded a moment before he dropped down beside her and followed suit.

"Dear God," Jeanette said. "Please save our little Theo. I promise to do anything you ask and promise to serve you with all my heart and soul."

The lights in the room flickered on and off and jumbled graphics danced across the pod's display before the unit thumped back to life. The pod pulsed softly with the sound of a muted heartbeat and the pulsing red glow of vital signs from the unit's display showed normal healthy readings.

Ted and Jeanette leaned in close to the pod and watched Theo yawn and stretch, then to their amazement his eyelids fluttered open wide. Two big bright blue eyes stared back from his wizened wrinkled face taking in Ted and Jeanette with a gaze that seemed to look right through them.

"Wow," Ted half-whispered. "Talk about feeling watched. You and I are going to have to start behaving."

Jeanette let out a long sigh and hugged him around the waist. "I'm so glad he's safe. What the hell just happened?"

"We need to check in with Fetal Fantasies to find out. Let me see if our phones are working."

Theo's gaze followed Ted across the room when he went for his phone.

"It's working!" Ted said. "My phone matches the pod's display."

Theo watched Ted as he returned to Jeanette's side.

"Wow!" she said. "Watch Theo's eyes when I move." She walked back and forth in front of the pod and Theo tracked her movements as if he were watching a tennis match.

"Amazing," Jeanette said. "He's already super aware!"

"Pink Floyd will do that to you."

"Stop it!"

Ted and Jeanette's phones beeped with an incoming text from Fetal Fantasies. Ted tapped his screen and read aloud to Jeanette.

"Alert! Earlier this evening the earth experienced a solar flare that triggered massive black outs and communication disruptions, including some major satellites. Please bear with us and do not request support unless it is a dire emergency. You can rest assured that every available engineer Fetal Fantasies has is working around the clock to restore the system to full viability."

Jeanette rested her hand on the pod and sighed. "Thank God our little Theo is safe."

Ted glanced at the display. "If anything, he's better than ever!"

From that day forward, baby Theo watched their every move whenever they were awake. Often, Jeanette would be involved in another task when the sensation of being watched made the back of her neck tingle. When she turned around to look, Theo's big inquisitive blue eyes locked on hers.

They kept him in the pod for a few days after his programmed birth date as a precaution which also allowed them to pick the time and date of his birth and control the astronomical alignment of his birth sign at the moment of his first breath. Jeanette held back her burgeoning anticipation to cuddle Theo for a full week so he could be born a solid Scorpio on November twelfth at the exact time of a full moon which came at sunrise on that day. Jeanette thought that the timing of it all as the most magical of synchronicities and a true sign from God.

She made everything ready for the new arrival and when the time approached, she and Ted stood before the pod holding hands. Together they watched the display count down to the programmed time of sunrise and at six-thirty on November twelfth, the words BIRTH SEQUENCE INITIATED flashed across the pod's screen.

A hum and the hiss of pneumatics sent the amniotic fluid draining out of ports at the bottom of the pod while the umbilical tube disconnected and the sensors attached to Theo's head and body retracted. The top of the pod slid open with a thump, prompting the infant to clear the fluid from his lungs with a cry, announcing Theo's entrance into the world bathed in the pastel pink and orange hues of a glowing sunrise.

Jeanette picked up the squalling baby, wrapped him in a blanket and held him close while Ted put his arm around her and bowed his head. Theo's blue eyes shone bright and his tiny hands reached for Jeanette's breast.

"I guess it's now or never." She lifted up her blouse and guiding Theo to her nipple.

"He knows what he wants," Ted said. "Can't say that I blame him. Those hormones they gave you made those tatas irresistible if I say so myself."

"Ow!" Jeanette cried when Theo latched on to her nipple. She held him closer. "Take it easy little one," she whispered.

Theo's demand for breastfeeding filled much of his waking moments and when he became cranky and upset the only thing that quieted him was his mother's nursing. When he grew content Theo watched everything they did with wide-eyed attention.

"He never takes his eyes off of us," Jeanette said one day.

"I feel him watching me, then I turn to see him staring right at me, or I should say right *through* me." Ted said. "Sometimes it feels a little creepy."

Jeanette made a dismissive gesture and went over to the crib. "Some of those same thoughts and feelings have crossed my mind, but I ignore them."

Theo reached for her breasts when she picked him up. "He's our little prince," she said snuggling him, "and he's always hungry." She held him to her breast. "I can't wait to get him on solid food so we can give my poor overworked boobs a rest."

Ted stroked Theo's soft golden hair which had grown along with his feathery eyelashes. "You sure are a beautiful boy. I'm glad you got your mother's looks."

Theo turned from Jeanette's breast to Ted, rewarding him with a huge toothless grin.

"Did you see that? He smiled at me. He knows what I'm saying!"

Jeanette chortled. "He hasn't grown enough for that yet, but I can see how it seems that way with the way he looks at us."

Theo's big blue eyes, golden-blond highlights, and plump baby face combined to make him an angelic looking cherub. Friends and strangers seemed to be unnaturally drawn to his beauty. Everywhere they went, people adored him and spoke in hushed deferential tones, bowing when his eyes found theirs with his wide-eyed inquisitive gaze.

"It makes me uncomfortable when they bow down to him like that," Jeanette said to Ted under her breath after a group of people had all acted that way when they saw him.

"Who knows?" Ted answered. "Maybe we did make a little baby Jesus. You have to admit, all the adoration does make him happy. I know every parent feels like their kid is special, but Theo *is* special. If you have any doubt, just look at the way people act toward him. Have you ever seen anyone act that way toward a baby before?"

"I can't say that I have, but I've also noticed that he gets upset when he is not the center of attention."

"Every baby is like that. They are narcissists by necessity and need the attention because they are helpless and totally dependent on us."

"I realize that, but I am his mother and I think he is a little too needy and demanding. It doesn't feel right to me."

FIVE

As the months passed the two sides of Theo's behavior became more pronounced. When everything went his way, he was the happiest, bubbly, smiling, cooing bundle of joy imaginable, but when he didn't get his way, he threw fits until he got what he wanted; Jeanette's breast. Ted jokingly referred to him as Jekyll and Hyde.

For the longest time, Theo's only means of communicating were his smiles and his tantrums and there didn't seem to be anything in between. The more time that passed, the more concerned Jeanette became about the development of his speech, which she felt should have grown faster.

"He's six months old," she said after calming one of his fits with another breast feeding. "He should be babbling and vocalizing more."

"I read that fifteen percent of babies between the ages of eighteen and twenty four months old are late talkers," Ted said. "They say it can be because they are shy or introverted. Most babies say their first word sometime between twelve and eighteen months. Einstein didn't speak full sentences until he was five years old. I have no doubt that Theo's late talking is a sign of his budding genius. Give it a little time."

Nothing had changed by Theo's first birthday, so Jeanette raised the issue when she and Ted took him to the Fetal Fantasies clinic for his first year checkup.

"I'm getting worried," Jeanette said. "According to what I read, his cooing is normal, but he should be babbling more and making longer strings of sounds like ma ma, ba ba, da da. With Theo it's all smiles and tantrums and the tantrums seem to be getting worse."

Doctor Kennedy, a tall, dark-haired lanky man with expressive brown eyes stroked Theo's golden hair. "I admit it's a little unusual," he said, "but still no cause for alarm. There's nothing physically wrong with him. In fact he is the perfect baby." Doctor Kennedy made a slight bow and lowered his voice, speaking in a conspiratorial tone.

"We've been keeping this under wraps because we didn't want to alarm you, so I am telling you this in the strictest confidence. Theo is even more perfect than we might have imagined. He is a *very* special boy."

Jeanette looked at him with an alarmed expression. "What do you mean by that?"

Doctor Kennedy studied her a moment and looked to Ted, then back to Jeanette and let out a deep breath.

"We have held off on saying anything to you because frankly we couldn't believe it ourselves, but we have done analysis after analysis of his DNA and Theo has the honor of being not only the first genetically perfect child that Fetal Fantasies has ever produced, but the first genetically perfect baby the world has ever seen."

"Are you kidding me?" Ted blurted.

Theo cooed, smiled, and kicked his feet.

Doctor Kennedy held up a hand. "We haven't gone public with this and don't plan to out of respect for your family, but my colleagues and the board of directors of Fetal Fantasies have taken a great interest in Theo."

Jeanette shook her head. "No way is our son going to be anybody's guinea pig!"

Doctor Kennedy made a calming gesture. "Precisely! The consensus is to treat him like any other child and not draw any undue attention to him. We will be observing him closely, but only a select few of my colleagues and the board of directors are privy to this knowledge and we plan to keep it that way. In the meantime I'm sure you're giving our sweet little boy plenty of attention, but I think it is prudent for you to step up your game a little bit.

"The best way to encourage Theo to talk is to spend time talking and interacting with him by giving him lots of face time and one-on-one interaction. Children learn language by watching and imitating facial expressions. When he coos, say, Oh, are you happy? Are you sleepy? When he smiles, smile back. You can also narrate what you and Theo do as you do it. For example, say, 'Daddy's changing baby's diaper.' This will help him learn vocabulary. Other things you can do is read a book and point to the pictures on each page, talk about the colors and objects, and sing songs and nursery rhymes. To capture his attention, dance or gently rock him as you sing and act out Itsy Bitsy Spider and Jack and Jill. He will associate movement with words."

"What about his breast feeding tantrums?" Jeanette asked. "My poor boobs are getting worn out."

Doctor Kennedy grinned. "It's time to think about weaning him. The first step will be to put him on a regular feeding schedule instead of giving in to his demands, then you can start feeding him small amounts of baby food and working toward getting him on solid food."

"Thanks for the advice," Ted said. "We'll give it a shot."

"I'm already doing a lot of what you're recommending," Jeanette said, "but I'll be paying even more attention after what you've told us and putting more effort into it. Thank you!"

Ted shook his head. "Genetically perfect? Really?"

"You have a very special beautiful boy there." Doctor Kennedy bowed again. "With all the care you have given him, I'm sure he's developing as beautifully inside as he has on the outside. Rest assured we will be monitoring his development *very* closely." He stroked Theo's hair again, eliciting more coos and a dimpled grin.

Jeanette and Ted came back six months later with Theo. "We're really getting worried, doc," Ted said, "He's eighteen months old and still no change."

"We did everything you suggested," Jeanette added, "but it's still either coos or cries. I'm at my wits end with his tantrums. He should be vocalizing more by now. I'm terrified that something's wrong. Can you imagine what it would be like if he acted this way when he's bigger?"

Doctor Kennedy held up his hands. "We'll run some comprehensive tests and take a closer look at everything to make sure he is still developing normally."

After a day full of tests, scans, and procedures, Doctor Kennedy sat with Ted, Jeanette, and Theo in an examination room looking at a screen that resembled the one on the baby pod.

Doctor Kennedy stood, bowed toward Theo and nodded. "I don't know what to tell you," he said as if addressing Theo. "Sight, sound response, reaction time, visual acuity, dexterity. All on target." He continued nodding. "Bloodwork, pulse, respiration, and other vital signs. All optimal. I can say without reservation that I've never seen a more perfect baby, not only in his physical development, but in every analysis, and every cross-check. All of my colleagues are fascinated with the phenomenon of his genetic perfection and every one of them has done their own independent studies of his genome and physical development, and the consensus is unanimous.

"Theo is a bona fide miracle child who is perfect in every way. We've kept this low key and under the radar following the confidential discretion of my superiors."

Ted looked down at Theo who looked back up at him with innocent blue eyes and a dimpled smile.

"I'll admit that he is running a little behind in his speech development," Kennedy continued, but he should be ready for baby food. Aside from that, physiologically there is absolutely nothing wrong with him." Doctor Kennedy bowed a little lower and stroked Theo's hair while Theo smiled and cooed back at him. "For now the best thing we can do is give him more time. You never know. He might even surprise us when he does speak."

After six more months nothing had changed, and if anything, Theo's tantrums had grown worse. The only thing that seemed to quiet him was breast feeding.

Following Doctor Kennedy's suggestion, Jeanette hoped to break Theo's demand for breast milk by introducing small spoonfuls of baby food, but no matter how many different kinds she tried, Theo clamped his mouth shut and refused, crying until Jeanette relented and breast fed him, the only thing that made him happy.

A week before his second birthday Theo threw his worst tantrum ever. Nothing that they did could console him and the more they tried the worse he got, finally reducing Jeanette to tears. She dropped to her knees, sobbing with her face in her hands while Theo screamed, then she clasped her hands together and started whispering prayers. Ted dropped down beside her.

"Please God," she said, "help our little Theo. We put our faith in technology and maybe we were fools for doing that, but my bigger faith has always been with you. We've done everything we can for him and given him everything he ever wanted. I don't know what else to do." She clenched her hands tighter while tears streamed down her cheeks. "I'll do anything you ask and promise to serve you with all my heart and soul."

"Me too," Ted muttered. "Anything to make the crying stop."

The room went silent. Ted and Jeanette looked up shocked to see Theo standing up in his crib in the corner of their bedroom where the pod had been. His big blue eyes looked brighter than ever before, as if electrified.

He cleared his throat and his little baby boy voice spoke with surreal authority. "I am your creation that you brought into this world. You have been playing God to me by providing for my every need and desire. Your nurturing of me has proven worthy and I am now the center of your universe. You have earned the privilege to bow down, worship, and serve me with everything you have and all that you are for the rest of your lives."

Ted and Jeanette gasped and glanced at each other, then turned to Theo and bowed down to him.

SIX

They looked up again to see Theo plop down on his diapered bottom. His eyes seemed to sparkle as he studied them, once more looking like the two year old that he was. Jeanette held her breath, dumbfounded. Ted took her hand and gave it a gentle squeeze while they both waited in silence for what came next.

Theo smiled through baby teeth, but said nothing more.

"He just spoke," Jeanette whispered.

"Perfectly." Ted squeezed her hand a little harder.

The silence remained while they waited for Theo's next words and the minutes passed with no further utterances. Ted and Jeanette shifted from kneeling and sat back cross-legged, studying their son, who looked from Ted to Jeanette and back again with an expectant look on his face, but no more words or sounds came from him.

Finally Jeanette spoke in a low soothing voice, "Yes, you are the center of our universe. Mommy and daddy love you with all of our hearts and souls."

Theo grinned again and his bright blue eyes grew wider as he lifted his little arms out to Jeanette. She leaned in and scooped him up, hugging him close, then Ted encircled them both with his arms and they remained huddled together for some time before Ted sat back again to see Theo fast asleep in Jeanette's arms. She took him to his crib and gently laid him down, then Ted put his arm around Jeanette and they both stood over Theo watching him sleep peacefully.

After some time, Ted guided her away from the crib into their living room where they sat on the couch speaking in low tones.

"Did he really talk like that in perfect sentences?" Ted said.

"We both heard it."

"We did, but he didn't say anything else."

"Not in words, but for me his open arms said more than words could."

"There is that, and it is one of the sweetest gestures I've ever seen which I admit melts my heart, and I do consider it a privilege to be blessed by having him in our lives, but I'm a little uneasy with his request which sounded more like an order. He throws tantrums until he gets what he wants, then he is as happy as a clam. I love him with all my heart, but are we raising a narcissist?"

"All babies are narcissists," Jeanette said. "You said so yourself. They are unable to take care of themselves and depend on us to meet all of their needs."

"But bow down and worship them?"

Jeanette breathed in deep and let out a long exhale. "I admit, that part is a little disturbing."

"And flawless speech after communicating with nothing but tantrums and smiles?"

"I don't know what to think about that. He's due for his two year check up in a couple of weeks. Should we tell Doctor Kennedy that he spoke and what he said? Even though we both heard it, I still have my doubts."

"I think we better wait and see if he has more to say. The fact that he finally spoke is a miracle in itself, but I don't think it's a good idea to share *what* he said."

Jeanette nodded slowly. "I'm at a loss about what to do and to be honest I'm frightened. Going from tantrums to the authority and sophistication of his language, not to mention its commanding tone." She shook her head. "Of course we will nurture him and provide for his my every need. He's our child and he *is* totally dependent on us. He's right when he says that he is the center of our universe, but to say that we have earned the privilege to worship and serve him with everything we have and all that we are for the rest of our lives? Who's really in charge here?"

Ted put his hand on Jeanette's. "I admit to being scared myself. Shit, if you want to know the truth, I'm terrified! Much of what he says is true. We do have to serve him until he becomes self-sufficient, and in many respects it will be for the rest of our lives. No matter what his age is we will always want what is best for him and will do everything we can to give him the best life possible up to and including college and beyond. That goes without saying."

"Speaking the way he did is surreal enough, but his authority and demand to be worshipped? Have we created our own modern day genetic Frankenstein?"

"Frankenstein was deeply flawed. You heard Doctor Kennedy. Our little monster is perfect in all respects."

Jeanette pulled her hand away. "Don't call him that!"

"Sorry honey, I didn't mean it that way, it's just that…"

"I don't care what he is. He is ours and the product of our own genetics. We brought him into the world and hand picked the qualities we wanted in him. Regardless of what he is or what he might become, we are responsible for his health, happiness, and the best possible life we can give him."

Ted took her hand again. "Agreed. Let's go look in on him to see if he might have anything more to say."

They went back into their bedroom to find Theo lying quietly, gazing up at them with childlike innocence.

"How's our little baby boy?" Jeanette asked, feeling conflicted talking in baby talk after hearing Theo speak using multisyllable words. Theo smiled and cooed, and once again she wondered if it had really happened. She looked to Ted and the concern in his eyes reminded her that he had heard it too.

"Needless to say we were shocked to hear you speak like that," Ted said, addressing Theo like an adult without any hint of baby talk. He felt awkward and conflicted in his own way speaking to a toddler like this and he too had his doubts about what he heard, but as unreal as it was, he hoped for a response that might put his mind at ease. "What you said," he continued, "and how you said it with such sophistication was far beyond anything a child might say for their first words, and to jump from crying and tantrums to fully formed sentences with big words is literally unbelievable. Nevertheless, we do love you with all our hearts and want nothing more than to nurture you and give you everything you need, and yes, you are the center of our universe. We're doing our best to wrap our minds around what you said, especially the part about bowing down, worshipping, and serving you."

Theo looked from Ted to Jeanette and cooed in response.

SEVEN

Ted and Jeanette interacted with Theo in the days leading up to his two year checkup hoping to hear more from him, but other than his cooing, he gave no other responses. When he wasn't scrutinizing them, he stared off into space with a faraway look as if studying something profound that no one else could see. He still had an insatiable thirst for breast milk, but following Doctor Kennedy's suggestion, Jeanette worked toward putting him on a regular feeding schedule which he resisted, but after an extended battle of the wills, he finally accepted the routine and stopped the tantrums. With the passing days his contented behavior and lack of more spoken words rekindled their doubts about whether it had really happened.

"Could it have been a shared hallucination?" Ted said in hushed tones a couple of days before Theo's second birthday when he was scheduled for his two year checkup. He and Jeanette sat together in the kitchen out of earshot of Theo puzzling over what to say to Doctor Kennedy when they brought Theo in for his checkup. "We were under a lot of stress which could trigger something like that. Maybe we should say something to Doctor Kennedy and see what he thinks."

Jeanette shook her head. "Let's keep us out of it. At least his tantrums have stopped, so our focus should be on his delayed speech. Besides, he hasn't spoken a word since."

"If it is in fact really delayed, which we're not sure of, or – shit, I don't know. Something else?"

"What else could it be?"

Ted sipped his coffee. "I've read stories about child prodigies and young kids who say they are reincarnated and give specific details about places and events from the past that there is no way they could have known about."

"I suppose anything is possible, but that whole thing about bowing and worshipping? Where did that come from? That doesn't sound like anything from someone's past life. It sounds like something else and that scares me a little."

"I hate to even think or to say it, but do you think he could be possessed?"

Jeanette's head jerked back as if she had been hit and her words came rapid fire. "No way our perfect child could be any kind of monster like that! Aside from that one time when he spoke, and we're not even sure if that even happened, and now that we've solved the mystery of his tantrums, he's the sweetest baby I've ever seen. How could you even think..."

Ted held up his hands in surrender. "Calm down honey, I'm not implying that we have a demon child or anything like that, I'm just trying to wrap my mind around what happened."

"I'd rather believe it was a shared hallucination than to entertain anything as sordid as that." She huffed. "Other than his unusual speech which we're not even sure of, he has done nothing that could be considered evil."

Ted's phone alarm went off signaling their appointment reminder, prompting them to go into the bedroom where they found Theo sitting up in his crib staring at them with what looked like expectation.

"If I didn't know any better," Ted said lifting him up out of the crib, "I'd think he was anticipating his visit with Doctor Kennedy."

No one spoke on the way to the Fetal Fantasies clinic and Theo remained quiet, looking out the window at the passing scenery from his baby car seat. He stayed that way when they went into the spacious lobby of the Fetal Fantasies building. Doctor Kennedy greeted them in his examining room with a slight bow before ruffling Theo's silky golden hair. "How's our little miracle boy doing?"

Theo looked up at him with a broad grin while the doctor attached sensor patches to his heart, wrists, and other parts of his body that wirelessly transmitted the waveforms, pulses, and numbers of Theo's vital signs to a nearby display.

Doctor Kennedy studied it for a few moments before turning to Ted and Jeanette. "Everything looks great. Have you made any progress on his speech and have there been any more tantrums?"

Jeanette and Ted looked at each other, then back to Doctor Kennedy before Jeanette spoke. "I realized that the tantrums and his delayed speech were signs of his frustration, so I worked toward getting him on a regular feeding schedule. We're still trying to get him to eat baby food. He won't have any of it, but I am happy to report that his tantrums have stopped."

Doctor Kennedy steepled his hands together. "Wonderful! And his speech? How is he doing with that now you've gotten past his tantrums?"

Jeanette looked down at the floor, then looked up, meeting Doctor Kennedy's questioning gaze. A slight tremor crept into her voice when she spoke "Well, um… I'm not sure what to say about…

"Ma Ma!" Theo blurted and clapped his hands. "Da Da!"

Doctor Kennedy beamed and Jeanette's eyes grew wide. Her lower lip quivered and she sobbed while tears ran down her cheeks.

Doctor Kennedy handed her a tissue. "What is it? Are you worried about him not eating baby food yet? I admit, that's gone on a bit long, but now that you have him on a regular schedule I have no doubt that he'll start craving more than your breast milk very soon."

Jeanette took the tissue and dabbed at her cheeks. "It's just that – it's just that…" She glanced at Ted who silenced her with a look.

"It's just that she's overcome with happiness." Ted said speaking rapidly to hide their surprise. He put his hand on her shoulder. "She's worked hard to stop the tantrums and followed your suggestion of talking and giving him lots of one-on-one interaction, reading books, and pointing to the pictures on each page while talking to him about colors, objects, and singing songs and nursery rhymes."

Jeanette nodded and drew in a long trembling breath, wiping away more tears.

Ted gave her shoulder a gentle squeeze. "Needless to say, it's been a stressful time for her, but she's a real trooper and I'm really proud of her."

Theo clapped his hands again. "Ma Ma! Da Da!"

EIGHT

After hearing Theo speak, a delighted Doctor Kennedy bowed and stood up straight proclaiming, "Our little Theo is in excellent health! I guarantee, now that he is beginning to communicate verbally his tantrums will diminish."

"Ma Ma. Da Da" Theo repeated.

Ted hugged Jeanette and kissed her on the cheek. "Our little boy is talking," he whispered in her ear. "Time to celebrate," he said a little louder.

They left the clinic with Ted carrying Theo bouncing on his shoulders singing the ABC song with Jeanette accompanying him while Theo remained quiet. Ted secured him in the baby carrier in the back seat of the car and hopped into the driver's seat to drive them home.

Jeanette turned from the front seat when they pulled out of the parking lot and looked back at Theo. "I'm so proud of you. Can you say more words?" she asked tentatively, once more feeling conflicted talking in baby talk, wondering if he had really spoken that first time in such complex sentences.

Theo stared at her as if looking *through* her, making her feel vulnerable and exposed. She shook off a chill and looked ahead again, hugging herself.

Ted studied him in the rear view mirror and Theo looked to him with the same unsettling expression.

"Hey little buddy," Ted ventured, speaking like an adult without any baby talk. Theo's unchanging expression made him feel awkward and conflicted in his own way, rekindling his doubts about what he had heard with those first words. "I don't know what to think or believe at this point, but you know that your mother and I love you. We'd feel a lot better if you spoke to us so we can communicate better and give you what you want and need."

37

Theo's penetrating look unnerved Ted, triggering unwelcome thoughts of the possibility that his son could be possessed or worse. He broke eye contact and glanced over at Jeanette to see her wiping more tears from her cheek, then he looked back in the rear view mirror to see Theo looking out the window. "Someone's turning two tomorrow," Ted said in an effort to keep the conversation upbeat and positive.

Theo looked from the window and glanced at Ted with what looked like a hint of a smile before turning back to the window.

Ted patted Jeanette on the knee. "And we have lots to celebrate. A healthy miracle baby boy who's learning to speak."

Jeanette crossed her arms over her breasts as if protecting them. "But he still won't eat anything except my breast milk and my poor boobs are so sore."

"I originally planned to invite some friends from work over for the party, but I'm still spooked about how Theo spoke that first time and as the days have passed I'm doubting whether it really happened. We just tried to get him to say more, but he only said Ma Ma Da Da and stopped speaking again, but I'm sure he'll pipe up with more words when he feels ready."

"I find myself wondering if he really said those big words myself, but we both heard it."

Ted glanced in the rear view mirror again to see Theo gazing out the window. "Can you imagine having the house full of people and Theo standing up ordering everyone to bow down, worship, and serve him?"

Jeanette turned and looked back at Theo, who showed no reaction.

She spent the next day nursing Theo on the schedule she had established to avoid upsetting him, doing whatever she could to keep him happy while Ted was at work. When Theo napped she wrapped crayons and paper for coloring, Legos, Tinker Toys, Smurf, Barney, educational video games, a baby laptop, clothes, and gifts their parents had sent along with the ones she had bought. When she finished she baked Ted's favorite carrot cake with cream cheese frosting while making steak, potatoes, and broccoli for dinner. She arranged everything neatly on the dining room table and hung balloons, crepe paper streamers, and birthday banners before Ted came home from work.

When he came home she breast fed Theo and put him in a high chair where he studied the pile of gifts with great interest while Ted and Jeanette ate a quiet dinner. After she cleared the dishes, she brought out the birthday cake with two candles on it and she and Ted sang happy birthday to a grinning Theo, then she held the cake close to him.

"Blow out the candles honey," she said, puckering her lips and blowing toward the cake as an example.

To her and Ted's surprise Theo's eyes grew wide and with a deep breath he blew out the candles.

"Yay!" She said clapping along with Ted.

Theo beamed and awkwardly clapped with them, then she cut slices and dished out cake for her and Ted.

After taking a forkful, Ted rubbed his stomach and looked at Theo. "Yum! Thank you mommy for making my favorite cake for Theo. I have a great idea!" He winked at Jeanette and mixed up a small dab of cake and frosting on the end of his fork and glanced at Theo. "He still hasn't weaned from your breast milk and hasn't touched solid food, but how can he resist this? It's a perfect introduction to solid food and a great way to break him in."

When Ted pressed the fork to Theo's lips he spit out the cake and frosting mash and erupted into a screaming tantrum until Jeanette quieted him with another breast feeding.

Once she calmed him, she and Ted helped him open presents. He examined each one with great fascination, especially the crayons and paper, Tinker Toys, and the baby laptop.

"Come on, birthday boy," Ted coaxed. "Say it one more time for mommy and daddy. Ma Ma. Da Da."

Theo stared at him with a blank expression.

NINE

Ted and Jeanette sipped their morning coffee, each lost in their own thoughts while Theo slept in his crib in their bedroom where his pod had been. They had decided to keep him close by after all the unusual behaviors he had shown them.

"He's quiet this morning," Jeanette said. "He doesn't usually sleep this late."

"He's probably worn out from all the excitement and the gifts he got." Ted fell silent for a moment and a faraway look came into his eyes. "We're all quiet this morning," he added. "I woke up in a bit of a fog."

Jeanette nodded. "I did too. I had the weirdest dreams."

Ted looked up, mild surprise in his eyes. "Me too! They were vivid, but I can't really remember them or put them into words."

"I can't either. It's more like I'm remembering how they made me feel. I know dreams can be bizarre, but they usually happen in situations and settings with other people." She looked up, trying to find the words. "It's strange. These ones *felt* vivid too, but my recall of their visuals is fuzzy. Everything moved fast and seemed to make sense on some deeper emotional level, yet they didn't make sense at all."

Ted nodded. "I vaguely remember dense rapid-fire imagery and a sense of awe that felt and looked – I don't know – alien, as if there were no separation between the imagery and the emotion. I don't know how else to describe it."

"Synesthesia!" Jeanette blurted.

Ted's phone alarm went off meaning it was time for him to go to work at the same moment Theo made waking up noises, so he downed his coffee and went in to say good morning before heading off to his job as head of research and development at Bliss Pharmaceuticals.

Ted picked Theo up from his crib and held him up high. "How's my little man?"

Theo giggled while Ted raised him up and down a few times, then Ted kissed him on the forehead and handed him to Jeanette, giving her a kiss on the cheek.

"Gotta go! We're wrapping up the clinical trials on Trazocodone our antidepressant pain killer today. We have big hopes for this one."

Jeanette kissed him back and lifted her blouse to cuddle Theo to her breast. "See you tonight, honey."

After feeding Theo she sat him by the dining room table in his high chair and arranged his gifts in front of him. "Look at all the new toys momma, daddy, grandpa and grandma got you. Which one do you want to play with first?"

She expected him to grab for the Legos, the Tinker Toys, or the baby laptop, but to her surprise he stretched his arm out toward the crayons and paper.

"Maybe we have a budding artist?" She opened the top of the crayon box and took out a sheet from the package of paper, then she picked up a crayon and drew stick figures, a crude looking house, and a bright yellow sun above it while Theo looked on. "See what mommy did?" She held her picture up and put the box of crayons on the high chair tray along with a fresh piece of paper.

Theo looked up at her and smiled before grabbing a red crayon and drawing on the paper with intense focus while Jeanette watched, happy to see him expressing himself in this way. She sat back to watch him work and to her growing astonishment what she originally thought to be scribbles became a geometric mandala-like pattern. The dawning realization of what she witnessed both amazed and frightened her.

Theo grabbed for a blue crayon and layered a second geometric figure on top of the first, distinct in its own form while adding to and seamlessly blending with the first.

Her heart raced and her throat went dry as Theo layered more geometry on top of the first two figures in different colors, then something shifted inside of her like the piece of an invisible puzzle had fallen into place followed by flashes of her previous night's dream creating a sense of wonder and anticipation that she couldn't articulate.

Theo leaned in and worked intently, finally dropping his last crayon and holding up his drawing with a smile the way Jeanette had.

She took deep breaths and studied it, struggling for something to say, but no words came. Theo reached out toward the package of paper and Jeanette moved as if in a trance handing him another sheet of paper.

Theo went to work again until he completed three sheets of paper with different multicolored patterns and mandalas replete with Platonic solids, Flower of Life patterns, dodecahedrons, and other sophisticated forms. When he finished the last one he held his arms out wide and yawned before nodding off. Jeanette picked him up out of his high chair and laid him back down in his crib where he drifted off to sleep.

Her first impulse was to call Ted to tell him what happened, but she held back, thinking that she didn't want to interrupt his work or panic him. She also thought that the surrealness of what she had seen would be best shared in person so they could puzzle through it together. Like Theo's first words, part of her doubted that it even happened, but the drawings Theo had done were irrefutable proof that it had.

He slept through the rest of the day while Jeanette kept tabs on him with video monitors she and Ted had put in the bedroom and she went in to physically check on him from time to time to make sure he was alright as the day passed. Unable to think clearly, she periodically studied the drawings and busied herself with housework while intermittent flashes of geometric imagery flickered through her mind like muted fireworks. As the day progressed she had a growing feeling that she was on the threshold of something bigger that defied any semblance of rational thought.

Her heart jumped into her throat when Ted came home and she ran to the front door clutching the drawings, anxious to share the strange events of the day.

"You're not going to believe this!" Ted said before she could get any words out. He came through the door holding up his iPad, nearly pushing her aside.

She started to hold up the drawings "I can say the same..."

He held up a hand. "I'm sorry honey, but you have to see this first."

"But..."

He took her by the arm and guided her to the dining room table where he put the iPad down and opened the screen to a crop circle web site, pointing to three complex geometric images that made Jeanette nauseous.

"This is what I saw in my dream!" he said in a monotone.

Jeanette grabbed onto his arm to keep from passing out and dropped Theo's drawings onto the iPad, then she leaned into him while the imagery flooded through her like a bursting dam.

"Ma Ma. Da Da," Theo called out from their bedroom.

TEN

Ted held Jeanette close for a long moment in silence, then he held her by the shoulders and looked into her eyes, seeing her stunned expression reflecting his own astonishment.

Jeanette felt torn between her motherly instinct to run in and embrace her beautiful blond-haired blue-eyed child and the fear that roiled in her gut like an icy snake. *Her* child. *Their* child. They had brought him into the world perfect in every way, except - except what? Nothing about any of this was normal. It felt like the reality of what went on inside of her exceeded anything her brain could handle.

"I felt different waking up from those dreams," Ted finally said, putting words to what Jeanette felt. "Fuzzy, but aware in a strange way, like I was still partially in the dream waiting for something more to happen."

"And it instantly deepened in an inexplicable way when you saw those crop circles just like it did when I saw Theo's drawings."

"And it made me nervous and excited at the same time while everything around me, my office, lab, my life with you…"

"Seemed more dreamlike than ever," Jeanette said, finishing his thought.

He pointed to the iPad and Theo's drawings. "Now seeing them together…"

"Shifted whatever is going on inside of us into something deeper and profound in ways we can't explain or make any sense of," she said.

He nodded slowly.

"Ma Ma. Da Da," Theo called out again.

The sound of his little voice coming from the bedroom combined with the eerie overlapping electronic delay of it coming through the video monitor made her shiver, making her feel like she was an actress in some creepy low budget B horror movie.

Ted gently shook her out of her stupor and took her by the hand, lifting her out of her chair. She leaned against him while he held her by the waist speaking to her in a low voice. "He's our child. We brought him into this world and we are responsible for his well being, and yes, we will serve him with everything we have and all that we are for the rest of our lives."

Jeanette stopped outside the bedroom door, took a long, sobbing breath, and wiped tears from her eyes, then she and Ted went into the bedroom to find Theo standing up in his crib.

He grinned and his blue eyes sparkled as he held his little arms out to Jeanette. In that moment, instinct overcame fear and she leaned in scooping him up, cuddling him close while he hugged her tight, then he reached out to Ted, drawing him into a three way hug and they remained huddled together in a wordless embrace.

"Ma Ma. Da Da," Jeanette whispered.

Theo leaned back and smiled beatifically, but said nothing more, then he hugged them again.

The three of them remained quiet for a long time until Ted's stomach made loud gurgling noises, eliciting a giggle from Theo.

Ted backed away and put his hand on his stomach. "Sorry, I'm starving. I haven't eaten all day."

"Shit," Jeanette said under her breath. "I've been so preoccupied that I totally forgot about dinner."

Ted held up a hand. "Don't worry about it. We can order pizza."

Jeanette breast fed Theo while Ted ordered and set out napkins and plates on the kitchen table.

She rubbed her breasts when Theo finished nursing. "I wish he would start eating solid food. He's teething now which means his little body is ready for something solid. My poor boobs are super sensitive as it is. I don't know how much more they can take."

"At some point he'll have to eat something other than breast milk. He hated the cake. Maybe the sugar was too much for him. We can try a little piece of pizza. He might like that."

Jeanette let out a long exhale. "I wouldn't count on it."

"We won't know unless we try."

The pizza delivery came a short while later. Theo watched with interest as Ted cut pieces for Jeanette and himself and dished it out. After eating a few bites, Ted took a tiny piece from his plate and pressed it to Theo's lips.

Theo scrunched up his face and spit it out.

Ted held his breath anticipating the tantrum that was sure to come, but to his surprise Theo pointed to a bowl of fruit on the counter.

Jeanette's eyes registered *her* surprise and her mouth hung open, then she sprang into action, grabbed a banana and peeled it back, mashing a small piece of it on the end of her finger and putting it to Theo's lips.

He moved his mouth around it with the same puckering motion he suckled her breast with and his little face lit up in a dimpled grin that went from ear to ear.

"My God," she cried. "He's eating real food!"

She mashed up more of the banana and fed it to him with a tiny spoon. After a few bites he pointed to the fruit bowl again.

While Ted looked on dumbfounded she fed Theo small spoonfuls of mashed apple, pear, peach, and strawberries from the refrigerator. Each new taste brought smiles and squeals of joy. When he had enough, Ted and Jeanette sat back and clapped their hands. Theo looked from one to the other and joined them with his own clapping.

In spite of their hunger Ted and Jeanette had all but forgotten about their pizza which had grown cold, but they didn't care and resumed eating it while Theo watched. After gorging himself on a few slices, Ted pushed his plate aside and leaned in toward Theo, bowing forward as he spoke.

"What do your pictures mean?"

Theo studied him as if deep in thought, but gave no response.

"Mommy and daddy want to do everything we can that is the best for you," Jeanette said, speaking in baby talk.

"We just need to know more from you." Ted spoke the way he would to a full grown adult. "Better communication so we can give you what you want. We sincerely want to provide for your every need." He took Jeanette by the hand. "I speak for both of us when I say that we are more than willing to serve you with everything we have and all that we are for the rest of our lives."

Jeanette nodded and looked to Ted. "Even if that means bowing down and worshipping you."

Theo rocked back and forth as if bowing and saying 'Yes' with his whole body while continuing to study them, but no sounds came from him.

"With all the mind boggling abilities we've seen from him and his delayed speech, extended breast feeding time, and other unusual behaviors, I have to admit that I've been worried that he might be some kind of autistic savant or..."

Jeanette let go of Ted's hand and sat back frowning and crossing her arms. "How dare you!" she snapped.

"I didn't mean…"

She covered Theo's little hand with her own and gave it a gentle squeeze. "You heard Doctor Kennedy. Our little Theo is a perfect little boy. We made him that way."

ELEVEN

Jeanette put the crayons and paper in front of Theo the next day hoping he would draw more figures, but he showed no interest in them. Instead, he reached for the Tinker Toys box. She opened it and set him on the floor where she spread out the pieces. Theo examined everything with great interest, then plugged the sticks into the holes of the round joints in different ways and angles, putting them together in an unusual complex configuration with the same intense focus he had shown drawing the geometries, then he fell asleep again, so Jeanette brought him into the bedroom and laid him in his crib where he slept soundly.

She couldn't make any sense of his creation, but she thought that there had to be something to it after Theo had given it so much time and attention. The deep sleep that followed his efforts seemed to confirm her suspicions.

She carefully put the structure in the middle of the dining room table to show Ted when he came home from work, anxious to hear what he might think. Remembering her distraction from the previous day she didn't want to forget dinner again, so she went through the motions of making a casserole while checking the video monitor and peeking into the bedroom to make sure Theo was alright.

While the casserole baked, she spent most of the day sitting at the dining room table staring at the structure and meditating on it puzzling over what it might mean. The only thing she could think of that made any sense was a molecule of some kind, but after the mind blowing experience of the crop circles and geometric drawings and how they affected her and Ted, she struggled to divine any deeper meaning it might hold. After all the other, dare she think *telepathic* connections they shared between the dreams, drawings, and physical manifestation of the crop circles, she thought the idea of a molecule to be too literal. It couldn't be that simple.

There had to be something more to it.

She couldn't wait for Ted to get home to hear what he thought and when he did she met him at the door and hugged him tight.

"What is it honey? Is Theo okay?"

"He's fine." She looked up at Ted and held his gaze, then she took him by the hand and led him into the dining room, holding out her hand like a game show hostess displaying the grand prize. Ted studied it for a moment before his eyes grew wide and his mouth dropped open. "Holy shit!" He walked around the table, examining Theo's Tinker Toy creation from all sides. "I can't believe it. That's a DMT molecule!"

"A what?"

"A Dimethyltryptamine molecule!" He leaned in closer N,N-Dimethyltryptamine to be exact."

"I've heard and read something about DMT, but I really don't know anything about it."

"It's a tryptamine that occurs in plants, animals, and in humans that produces vivid mystical experiences involving euphoria and hallucinations of get this - geometric forms!"

Jeanette hugged herself. "Oh my God."

"It has a long history of prehistoric use by many cultures for ritual purposes, particularly in indigenous shamanic practices throughout the jungles of the Amazon in a brew called Ayahuasca. It can also be inhaled, ingested, or injected depending on its form, and its effects depend on the dose as well as the mode of administration. When inhaled or injected, the effects usually last around five to fifteen minutes. Because of its short term activity they call it the businessman's high. It's also referred to as the spirit molecule."

"I've heard of Ayahuasca."

Ted nodded. "For what it is worth, Psilocin and Psilocybin, the main psychoactive compounds in magic mushrooms are structurally similar to DMT."

"I remember doing those once in college, but it wasn't anything like what we experienced in our dreams. I can't help but wonder. Did Theo somehow make us produce more DMT to give us that experience?"

"After what we've seen from him, I wouldn't discount anything. We both had what seemed like the same dreams, or maybe visions is more accurate. That in itself is uncanny enough, but those drawings he made, then the crop circles that matched them." He rubbed his chin. "I can't help but think that all of this is part of something bigger than us."

"Speaking of thinking and feeling, it's not just the drawings and his Tinker Toy molecule. I feel different, especially since the dreams. I can't put my finger on it, but my thoughts and emotions feel unsettled, like they are shifting as if..."

"We're on the threshold of something more, like we're psychically holding our breath waiting for some kind of breakthrough to happen."

"Exactly! I've had enough breakthroughs as it is, thank you very much. I don't know how many more I can take." Jeanette's voice tremored and she hugged herself suppressing a shudder. "I love Theo with all my heart and soul, but I'm not afraid to admit that he scares the hell out of me."

Ted put his arm around her, drawing her in close and she put her arms around his waist holding him tight.

"Aside from all the mind bending shenanigans he's shown us," Ted said, "you have to admit, now that he's over his tantrums he's the sweetest little boy anyone could ever ask for."

"I hate to say it, but that's one of the things that bothers me the most. I love loving him. He's such a joy in so many respects, but it feels like part of me is being seduced on some level, and for the most part I'm willing, but that whole thing about bowing down and worshipping him and the authority that he said it with in that little voice of his."

"I know what you mean. It was quite a demand."

"More than a demand it feels like an underlying threat of some kind."

"Remember," Ted said. "All babies are narcissists. Of course we're going to serve him with everything we have. We've been doing that all along."

"Under the threat of tantrums I might add. Who's really in charge here?"

"Ma Ma! Da Da!" Theo called out from the bedroom, his voice resounding through the eerie overlapping echo of the video monitor.

TWELVE

In the days that followed Jeanette tried mashed oranges, blueberries, apples, avocados, and more bananas. Theo loved them all. Through trial and error she discovered that he would not eat any processed food which meant only fresh organic foods and he wouldn't eat anything that had added sugar of any kind, or meat.

As more days passed she worked in cucumbers, spinach, carrots, broccoli, Brussels sprouts, kale, green peas, and chard, replacing her now scheduled breast feedings with more solid foods. As his weaning tapered off she worried about fats and proteins, so she fed him quinoa with nut milks, nut butters, and other crushed seeds, seitan, tofu, tempeh, edamame, lentils, and beans. With the passage of time his appetite for solid foods grew and she became more creative mixing nut butters and his favorite fruits with oatmeal sprinkled with nutritional yeast, spirulina, hemp seeds and other healthy garnishes mixed in with his vegetables which included a few solid chunks that he enjoyed chewing on.

His solid food diet progressed until he only required one breast feeding in the morning. During this time he imitated Jeanette's baby talk, making "num num" sounds and he started using two word phrases like "more milk", "good food", "not like", "play toys", as well as simple questions like, "Go bye bye?"

He babbled frequently, imitating both Ted and Jeanette, but he never spoke in front of other adults except for occasional outbursts of his limited vocabulary in front of Doctor Kennedy, which everyone delighted in with lots of hand clapping.

He drew more complex geometries which reflected both Ted and Jeanette's dreams and often triggered recall of dreams they had not remembered until seeing his drawings. Every time he did a drawing it was followed by a long nap, and every time he drew one Ted followed up and found new crop circles that coincided with the drawings and the dreams of the night before.

Theo also built more molecules with his Tinker Toys, among them 5MEODMT, LSD, mescaline, and serotonin. These constructions were always followed by long naps. Jeanette felt sure he would show more interest and do something equally amazing with his Legos, video games, baby laptop, and educational toys or puzzles, but he paid no attention to them or his Smurf and Barney toys.

Other than the drawings and molecules nothing more came from Theo prompting Ted to ask him one day, "Hey buddy? This is great work that you are doing, but I can't help but wonder if you have anything else up your sleeve."

Jeanette gave Ted a playful slap on the shoulder. "Oh Ted! Stop it! Everything he does is a blessing and I have gratitude for everything he does, even if he never did anything more. As long as he's happy and healthy, that's all I really care about."

Ted ruffled Theo's hair. "No argument there honey, but if you ask me, I think there's a lot more going on up there in that little noggin of his." He kissed Theo on the forehead and leaned back, speaking in the baby talk that Jeanette used. "You're holding out on us buddy, aren't you?"

"Ted!"

Theo leaned back, parroting Ted and gracing them with one of his broad baby teeth smiles. He looked from Ted to Jeanette and back again, his blue eyes shimmering with effervescence.

"See!" Ted said. "Look at that mischievous glint! "I'd give my right arm to see what's going on behind those baby blues!"

Jeanette let out an exaggerated sigh and waved a warning finger. "Be careful what you wish for, honey."

Theo fell asleep early that night and Ted and Jeanette soon followed, slipping into a deep slumber until the predawn hours when they both began to dream. In their dreams they shared identical experiences that spooled out in perfect symmetry as if they were watching the same movie together and they felt each other's presence along with something bigger.

Complex imagery came in a growing tide, first rising in a giddy flurry of colors, patterns, and sensations, like a pot beginning to boil before bubbling over into a chaotic rush of thoughts, feelings, and emotions alternating with feelings of certainty and uncertainty.

Colors with hues that defied description bombarded them, unfolding in multihued geometric progressions that could be microcosmic quantum expressions, or unfolding galaxies, until both of their minds spun in a unified whirlwind of kaleidoscopic madness that rocketed them back and forth through alternating fits of terror and amazement shot through with alien feeling symbols, concepts, emotions, thoughts, vistas, and other mixed perceptions.

Throughout it all dense information unfolded through rapidly transforming geometric permutations of colors and patterns. While every one of their senses heightened, they felt transformed in inexplicable ways. What stood out among the palette of sensations was that sound could be seen, color could be heard, and feelings came in hues and colors that defied description.

At its peak Ted and Jeanette both felt as if there was no difference between the infinity expressing itself "outside" of them and the infinity they soared through inside of them.

Everything was one.

Sometimes they felt fully present and aware in two or more places at the same time, often in different times and dimensions.

Their ecstatic visionary states continued to unfold within their minds outside of any sense of three dimensional reality they had any conception of while time and space became fluid, soaring through alien vistas of sight, sound, and feeling while traveling through events of their lives, both good and bad while reliving their emotional content.

Underlying the shared revelation in what felt like a great cosmic truth, they felt their souls connected in an exquisite triad where Theo's "language" spoke with shapes, colors, scents, patterns, abstractions, archetypes, and concepts beyond rationality. Everything unfolded and blossomed in concert with geometric progressions revealing a divine conscious intelligence that permeated all of it in an otherworldly symphony of sight, sound, concepts, emotions and more.

While the tide receded in the aftermath of their psychic storm, they realized that their visions had been directed by sweet incomprehensible alien sounding trills and vocalizations similar to Tuvan throat singing, but at a much higher melodic pitch.

Together they woke from their shared visionary state coming into full consciousness, following the enchanting singing back to its source, the sweet sound of Theo's voice.

THIRTEEN

"What the hell was that?" Ted whispered.

Jeanette's lower lip trembled and her mouth moved but she couldn't speak. Ted wrapped his arms around her and held her close feeling her shiver while the toning continued, then he helped her out of bed. They went to Theo's crib and he went silent the moment they peered in to see him, then he held his hands up giggling with a wide smile. His blue eyes looked preternaturally bright as if energized by an invisible electric current.

Ted froze at the sight of Theo's blazing eyes, struggling with the possibility that he could be some kind of possessed demon baby.

Jeanette took Theo into her arms without hesitation and hugged him while he studied Ted from over her shoulder with angelic innocence.

Theo smacked his lips happily eating fruit and oatmeal for breakfast while Jeanette spoke to him, chattering in nervous baby talk "How's our little boy this morning? Sleep good? Did Theo dream too?"

She looked over at Ted who stared ahead as if studying something far away, drinking his coffee in silence.

"Ted?"

He didn't respond.

"Ted!" She said louder.

He jumped and blinked a few times before looking at her.

"Are you with us?"

Ted shook his head. "Sorry, honey." He sipped his coffee. "I'm here, but I don't think my head is."

"You're not the only one feeling that way," she said.

"I don't know what to think. I admit I'm scared, but I'm also excited. I'm a jumble of mixed thoughts and feelings. To be honest I

53

don't know what to think." He nodded toward Theo who occupied himself with his breakfast, seemingly oblivious to their conversation. "After last night do you really think all that baby talk is going to help him?"

"Yes, I do. It helps him refine and develop his speech."

"Don't you think you should be talking to him like an adult?"

"He's two years old Ted! His language skills need time."

Ted leaned back and crossed his arms. "How many two year olds demand to be worshipped in flawless English?"

She exhaled. "Point taken. It's just that, it's just that – look at him! He's our adorable baby boy and I can't help myself. It feels right and natural."

Ted put his hand on Jeanette's and his voice softened. "But do you really think it's helping him? Helping us?"

"What are you getting at?"

"Last night and this morning proves that he communicates with us in an entirely different way. Something more complicated than simple words. He speaks in geometry, symbols, and god knows what else."

Theo looked up from his oatmeal and smiled, looking from Jeanette to Ted. "Ma Ma! Da Da!"

"It's so cryptic," Ted continued, "yet full of meaning in ways I can't wrap my head around. I wish it was more direct."

"Maybe last night *was* more direct."

He shrugged. "Maybe so, but it seems way beyond me."

She closed her eyes and smiled. "We need to give it more time. Look on the bright side. At least we now know what the Tinker Toys molecules are all about. You have to admit, he is reaching out to us in his own way."

"No argument there. I guess the question is what can we do to reciprocate the way he reaches out? How can we meet him half way? After last night, his geometry drawings, and his Tinker Toy projects - anything we do probably isn't even half way."

"But it's something."

"Agreed, but I don't think baby talk is the way to approach it. He's obviously capable of far more sophisticated communications than that."

"What do you think we should do?"

"Evidently spoken language, at least coming from him, falls short. Maybe we can ask him questions while he is awake. Even though he only says simple phrases, maybe we'll get answers in our dreams? Aside from his demand to be worshipped, his oral communications are still a long way from being well developed, but this dreaming thing - as hard as it is for him to talk to us normally – I don't know - his psychic psychedelic communications are hard for us to understand in their own way."

"It is the weirdest thing, but as dense and incomprehensible as it is, I feel like I'm getting more at deeper levels in ways I can't quite put my finger on."

Ted fell silent and looked down with his hand on his chin, staring into his coffee, then he looked up. "On second thought a little caveat is in order. We should definitely use baby talk when other people are around so we don't draw attention to our unusual situation. That could be dangerous."

"That won't be much of a problem. Theo never makes a sound around anyone else except Doctor Kennedy."

"At some point that will have to happen too, as never talking could also draw attention, especially if he goes around telling everyone to worship him."

"Oh Ted!"

After Ted left for work Jeanette spent the morning bringing different toys to Theo hoping to get some kind of further communication from him, but he showed no interest in any of them. Every time she put something in front of him he turned his nose up at it and pointed to the window whining like a puppy.

"Are you telling me you want to go outside?"

Theo smiled and clapped his hands.

She kissed him on the forehead. "Okay, you win!"

She took him out in a stroller and he smiled, holding his arms out with his hands open to the sunshine.

"My little solar cell," she said pushing the stroller ahead.

Theo waved his arms up and down like a bird and flapped them even faster, growing even more excited when she took him to a park.

She left the stroller by a bench, lifted him out of it, and sat him down in the middle of a playground to see if any of the equipment or other kids playing there caught his interest. He watched the kids running and screaming their excitement for a minute, then looked around at the slides, monkey bars, playhouse, and the rest of the playground equipment before he stood and toddled out of the rubber padded area onto the surrounding grass heading straight for a flower bed. Jeanette followed close behind letting him lead, curious about what drew him away from the play area.

He plopped down in front of a small hibiscus tree and looked up at its bright riot of colors, then he leaned in and gingerly took one in his hand, pulling it to his nose while carefully caressing the flower's petals.

After a few minutes he scooted around the garden repeating his actions with lilies, daffodils, marigolds, and other flowers before spending the longest time with the morning glories and lavender than with the other flowers, gently rubbing it between his palms and pressing them to his face, inhaling deep a few times before putting his hands down.

Jeanette found herself inhaling along with him, catching the calming scent of lavender each time he inhaled, and her vision took on a subtle violet tinge that grew with each inhale and diminished with each exhale. When the sun shone through his fine little boy hair like a golden halo she felt the corners of her mouth turn up into a smile, then he looked up at her with a smile of his own that went all the way up into his twinkling sky blue eyes.

FOURTEEN

"You're not going to believe this," Jeanette said when Ted came home from work that night, meeting him at the door carrying Theo on her hip.

Ted's heart rose in his throat. He took a deep breath and sighed, then set his briefcase down, encircling them both with a hug. "At this stage of the game I don't know what to believe about anything, and I can't say that nothing surprises me." He stepped back taking in Jeanette's glowing expression and Theo's round-eyed innocence. "Our little boy is nothing but surprises."

Theo reached out to Ted. "Da Da!"

Ted took him into his arms and Theo hugged him, instantly calming Ted's racing heart.

"He didn't want to play with any of his toys!" Jeanette blurted, speaking rapid fire. "He literally turned his nose up at them and pointed to the window making the cutest puppy sounding noises."

Ted bounced Theo up and down on his hip. "Slow down honey."

"Sorry." She forced herself to speak in slow measured tones. "Anyway, I took him to the park, thinking he might have fun at the playground, but he had no interest in it or any of the other kids. He went straight to a flower bed and starting with a hibiscus blossom he took it in his hand and pulled it to his nose while fondling its petals. After that he went around the garden doing the same thing like he was introducing himself to lilies, daffodils, marigolds, and other flowers. He spent the longest time with the morning glories."

"That doesn't totally surprise me."

"At the end he spent more time with the lavender than with the other flowers. He rubbed it between his palms, pressed it to his face and breathed in and I swear I smelled it right along with him. When I did he looked up at me with the most adorable smile."

Ted chuckled and held Theo out at arm's length. "Our little nature boy."

Theo giggled and Ted handed him back to Jeanette.

"Why did you say that the extra time with the morning glories doesn't surprise you?"

"Theo's Tinker Toy molecules and our shared dream, or should I say shared visions."

"Go on."

"The seeds of morning glories contain d-lysergic acid amide which can produce effects similar to LSD."

"That makes sense."

After dinner Ted roughhoused with Theo, chasing him around the living room while Jeanette finished up in the kitchen, then he settled back on the couch to watch the news on CNN. Jeanette sat Theo on the floor beside them surrounding him with his toys, hoping he might reveal something new, but Theo stretched out and fell asleep, worn out from playing with Ted.

The television shut off when the sounds and images from a war came onscreen.

"Shit!" Ted said under his breath. He tapped the power button on the remote and the television flashed on and off. He hit it again and got the same result. After trying a few more times he gave up and checked the power cord and cable connection at the back of the flat screen, then he changed the batteries in the remote, but nothing worked.

"So much for that," he said. "There's probably something wrong with the cable or a power glitch of some kind. Can you call the cable company tomorrow and have them check our connection?"

Jeanette picked up Theo and carried him into the bedroom. "Sure babe."

With Theo settled in for the night and the television out of commission, Ted and Jeanette went to bed early and read for awhile before drifting off into a deep sleep that lasted all night until a rose colored dawn filled the horizon.

A low buzzing filled their senses as they dreamed beautiful flowing visions in tandem beginning with soft, exquisite colors and unfolding geometric patterns of blue, pink, and gold neon filigrees that flickered around everything they looked at, all the while fluttering in a heightened sense of consciousness, fully aware of seeing the world through a different set of perceptions.

They flew into high frequency gossamer realities exploding with neon manifestations and felt the ecstatic sensation of their bodies twitching and their heads dipping and nodding under their own volition, separate from any conscious effort on their part. Their hearts swelled when they soared through pastel colored bliss into sublime luminescent realities undercut by an intoxicating mixture of floral essences and their entire beings quivered at a high speed that did not seem possible.

The buzzing grew louder until they awakened to the sound of an insect-like low frequency hum. Feeling themselves vibrating delicately, they hovered together somewhere on the threshold between sleep and waking until Jeanette took Ted's hand, breaking the spell. They both sat up, peering over at Theo's crib where they saw him sitting up cross-legged.

A hummingbird hovered inches from his face.

Startled, Jeanette lunged for the crib, but Ted pulled her back while Theo's body moved with a buzz of its own and his legs flapped faster than what seemed humanly possible.

Toddler and hummingbird fluttered together for the longest time taking turns, alternately bobbing and weaving in a fluid dance while emitting a series of chit chit sounds made up of hummingbird chirps.

Though she knew it couldn't be real Jeanette could have sworn that she saw Theo floating just off the surface of his mattress.

A moment later, the hummingbird darted off, disappearing into nothingness.

FIFTEEN

Jeanette put her hand on her heart and drew in a long, shaky breath. "My God, I thought I was going to orgasm," she whispered.

Ted blinked and shook his head. "I wouldn't believe it happened and definitely would have thought I was dreaming if we both hadn't sat up and seen it."

Theo smiled and stretched languorously, then sank back down onto his pillow and fell instantly asleep.

"The flowers," Jeanette said softly. "Yesterday in the park. The flowers. You should have seen him Ted. The way he interacted with them. The smells. The way the sun shone on him. Now this beautiful vision this morning. This blessing. There's a connection."

Ted propped himself up with pillows and leaned back against the headboard holding her close. "Let's stay quiet for awhile," he said under his breath. "I need a few minutes to let it all sink in."

Jeanette kissed him on the chest and rested her head against it, then they closed their eyes for several minutes, each playing back their visions in their minds while Theo slept.

"Someone once told me that hummingbirds are the nerve endings of God," Jeanette said, breaking the silence.

Ted stroked the side of her face. "Everything about them is high frequency including other forms of perception outside the range of humans and other animals. Even the sparkling colors they reflect radiates high frequency light."

"Do you think that's what we experienced?"

"What do you think?"

"It's almost too much to think about. Part of it frightens me, but it's bigger than that. I can't find the words. It's – it's…"

"Awe."

"That's it!"

Ted snorted. "Do you know what that means?"

"I wish I did."

He kissed the top of her head. "It means we have an awesome son."

"Ted!"

"It's true."

Jeanette called the cable company later that day after Ted went to work and they told her that that the signal was fine going to the house, so she asked them to send out a technician to check the wiring inside the house.

Theo acted restless and she felt fidgety herself so she took him to the park again hoping it might give her more clues about what was happening. Once she lifted him out of the stroller he went straight to the flower bed, repeating his actions from the day before, only this time, after he made his rounds, he stood and held his hands out palms wide remaining stock still like a tiny scarecrow. A single hummingbird darted in and hovered less than in inch between his eyes while others landed on his head and arms transforming him into a miniature Saint Francis.

Jeanette looked around, relieved to see no one else in the park while Theo chittered along with the hummingbirds and then he waved his arms joyously exclaiming, "Picaflor!" while the hummingbirds scattered in every direction, leaving him alone as if they had never been there.

Feeling both curious and inspired, she brought him to a plant nursery where she bought a number of flowering house plants that Theo chose by pointing to them, among them an Amaryllis, Bromeliads, Flame Of The Woods, Flamingo Lilies, a Chenille Plant, Hibiscus, a Lipstick Plant, and a Kalanchoe Plant, all of which had red flowers.

On impulse she also bought hummingbird feeders and on the way out of the store she spotted a book on hummingbirds by the checkout stand, so she tossed it into the cart along with her plants and feeders.

The cable tech showed up later that afternoon while she was arranging the plants throughout the house. He checked the incoming connection, then the connections inside.

"I can't find anything wrong," he said, picking up the remote. He tapped the power button and the television came to life.

Jeanette frowned. "I don't know what to say. It was definitely on the fritz last night."

The technician shrugged. "Works fine now." He made a dismissive gesture. "You probably had a power outage or a spike on the line of some kind. It happens."

SIXTEEN

Bright red Amaryllis flowers greeted Ted in the foyer by the front door when he came home from work that night.

"We're in the kitchen," Jeanette called out.

Ted felt his mood lift when he walked through the house, confirming his suspicions when he saw the other red flowering plants scattered throughout the house. He ended his tour in the kitchen where he found Jeanette feeding Theo quinoa mixed with broccoli, carrots, and tofu.

He leaned in and gave Theo a kiss on the top of his head and kissed Jeanette on the cheek. "Why did you skimp so much when you bought the house plants?"

"Ted! I..."

"Kidding!"

She broke into a smile.

"How's our little flower child?"

"As you can see I took him - no *he* took me shopping today." She pointed to the hummingbird feeders on the counter by the sink. "Those were my idea."

He ruffled Theo's hair and winked at him, eliciting a giggle. "You sure about that?"

"At this point I'm not sure about anything."

"That makes two of us. What's for dinner?"

"Turkey burgers. I have everything ready. I'll cook them as soon as I'm done with Theo."

When she finished feeding him and wiping his face clean, Ted picked Theo up and carried him around the house on his hip while Theo pointed to each plant, reaching out to caress each one in turn.

After dinner Ted played airplane with Theo by holding him up and zooming around the house, then they played with the Tinker Toys, hoping for more molecules. When Jeanette finished loading the dishwasher, the three of them sat on the couch where Jeanette held Theo in her lap.

Ted grabbed the remote and put on CNN to catch up on the news until the sounds and images from a war came onscreen and the television shut off. "Son of a bitch!" he muttered pressing the power button on the remote a few times, but the screen remained black.

"I thought you said the cable guy checked this out."

"He couldn't find anything wrong and said it could be a power outage or a spike on the line of some kind. I watched him turn the TV on and it worked just fine."

Ted put the remote on the coffee table and looked over at Theo who had dozed off in Jeanette's arms.

She rocked him gently and rose from the couch. "Looks like you wore him out with all your play. I'm going to put him to bed."

She came back a few minutes later with the hummingbird book and found Ted sitting on the couch with his arms crossed. "No news and no Netflix for you tonight. Let's see what this hummingbird business is all about. Maybe it will help us understand Theo a little better."

"Sure."

Jeanette flipped open the book to a chapter titled Facts and Figures and scanned the page before reading to Ted. "Listen to this! A hummingbird brain makes up four point two percent of its weight and is proportionally the largest of any bird's. By comparison, our brains are 2 percent of our body weight and hummingbirds can remember every flower they've ever visited. Not only that, they know how long to wait between visits so the flowers have time to generate more nectar. They can even recognize humans, and know which ones can be counted on to refill empty feeders."

"Smart little buggers."

Jeanette nodded quickly. "Though he's only a toddler Theo already knows them. He yelled out 'Picaflor!' at the park. I googled it and it's Spanish slang for hummingbird, especially in Peru."

She picked up her cell phone and tapped the screen. "You're going to love this! In the Andes the *Hawa pacha* is the non-physical level of consciousness thought of as the spiritual, the world unknown to the mind, and the abstract, unknowable, inaudible, incomprehensible, immanent, eternal connection to the source. *Island teqsi*, is the non-physical light that creates and destroys for the eternal existence of the cosmos, represented in the purity of the hummingbird, the only being that Andean myths saw as the face of God in the same golden light, face to face, to become *qori q'ente*; to transmute lead into gold or enlighten and rejoice in the presence of the divine made matter from the island converted to *k'ancha*, to *pacha*, from the spirit of time *pachakamaq*."

Ted frowned. "You're telling me that he's only speaking to us in two word phrases and he already knows Spanish and Andean cosmology?"

"Apparently so." She put her phone down and read from the book again. "Hummingbirds fly forward, backward, hover, and upside-down so fast that we can't see their wings beating between seventy and two hundred times a second and they can reach speeds of up to thirty miles an hour while flying, and sixty miles an hour while diving. Anna's Hummingbirds can move at three hundred eighty five body lengths per second during mating flights which is the highest known velocity attained by any vertebrate."

Ted let out a low whistle. "Wow!"

"They have the highest metabolism of all animals which they need to support the rapid beating of their wings and their heart rate can reach as high as one thousand two hundred sixty beats a minute while breathing two hundred fifty breaths a minute even at rest."

"No shit?"

Jeanette smirked. "No shit! They can outperform humans in distinguishing hues in combinations of ultraviolet and visible light and their vision helps them identity certain flowers because they have a fourth color cone that detects ultraviolet light. Humans only have three color cones that are sensitive to red, green, and blue light. This ability helps hummers find nectar-bearing flowers covered in patterns that humans can't see and they love the color red because their eyes are tuned to the rosy hue with retinas that have a denser concentration of cones that mute shades of blue and heighten warmer shades like red and yellow."

"That's why you bought all red flowering plants."

She smiled. "Hummingbirds see the world in a range of brilliant colors that we can only dream of or see in visions. When the UV hues blend with the ones that humans can perceive, new colors appear."

Ted sat up straight. "That explains what we saw in our dreaming visions."

"Every aspect of the physical and essence of hummingbirds is high frequency, not only in their displays of high frequency color, song, high speed wing hum, and feather trills from their tails, but internally in how they see, hear, metabolize, and burn energy." She looked up at Ted. "Get this! "Other than their bigger hearts, huge lungs, and brains, they are mostly made from air, the elemental defined as the essence of spirit and they are considered masters of air."

"I understand Theo with all his unusual behaviors now and the way he affects us and how he connects with them."

"Unlike our marrow filled bones a hummer's bones are hollow. Even their skulls are filled with passageways for air and their feather shafts are hollow too while the feathers themselves are like strips of Velcro with interlocking barbules for catching air." She held up the book, showing Ted close up pictures of brilliant colored feathers. "Their bodies are also filled with air sacs, which originate in and function in part as extensions of their lungs. Nine of these fill the tiny body of a hummingbird, one pair in the chest cavity, another under each shoulder blade, another pair in the abdomen, one under each wing, and one along the neck making hummers the lightest birds in the sky. The only real mass they have is in their flight muscles which account for thirty five percent of their body weight and their enormous heart constitutes up to two and a half percent of their body weight which is the largest percentage of body weight of all vertebrates."

"Big hearts," Ted added. "We could certainly use more of that in today's world, couldn't we?"

Jeanette closed the book and scooted closer to Ted, putting her arms around his neck, speaking softly. "Maybe that's what Theo is trying to tell us."

"I'd like to think that," Ted said, "but I'm not afraid to admit that sometimes he scares the hell out of me. I mean, he's not norm…"

"No, he's not," Jeanette chided. "He's perfect in every way." She took Ted's hand. "Come on, let's go to bed. You never know. More heavenly dreams could be waiting for us there."

On impulse Ted hit the power button on the remote as he stood and the Netflix logo filled the screen.

SEVENTEEN

"It dawned on me that our little flower child is not only communicating with us in his strange night time psychedelic telepathy, but he's communicating with the hummingbirds in the same way," Jeanette said after she and Ted settled into bed. "Maybe with the flowers too!"

"Don't you think talking to flowers might be stretching things a bit?"

A smirk crept up the side of Jeanette's face. "You're not with him all day like I am. Everything he's done so far stretches *everything*. Who knows what other surprises he might have?"

Ted put his arm around Jeanette and squeezed her shoulder. "I can't argue with you there, honey." He lapsed into silence for a moment before speaking again. "I've been giving this some thought. Even if it doesn't always seem that way to me, I give a lot of weight to your motherly instincts. "I think you're right about using baby talk to help Theo develop his language skills, but I also think we should be talking to him like an adult. We can't dismiss the fact that he communicates with us in a way that is more complex than simple words. He speaks in geometry, symbols, and God knows what else."

Jeanette reached up and put her hand on Ted's. "It's cryptic but it's full of meaning in ways we can't fully understand, but I think it's progressing. We now have a better sense of what the Tinker Toy molecules and his drawings are all about."

"Sort of."

"It's his way of reaching out to us."

"The question is what can we do to reciprocate the way he reaches out to see if we can somehow meet him half way?

"What do you think we should do?"

"At this point spoken language coming from him falls short. Like we talked about before, I think we should be asking him questions while he is awake. Maybe we'll get answers in our dreams. As hard as it is for him to talk to us normally, his dreaming communications are harder for us to understand in their own way."

"As dense and unintelligible as it seems, I think we both feel like we're getting more at deeper levels in ways we can't quite make sense out of."

Ted nodded. "It's a strange feeling."

"I feel and see it all in ways I've never felt before. With my whole being. I'm seeing and experiencing it in my head, but it feels like it's coming from my center. I know it's a contradiction, but at the same time it isn't. Even though the visuals are overwhelming, I have the sensation of feeling it more than seeing it, especially in my heart."

Ted leaned down and kissed her on her chest. "And a beautiful heart it is!"

She squeezed his hand. "Ted!"

They stretched out lying in each other's arms in silence before drifting off to sleep where they dreamed as one. Soft colors and unfolding geometries of blue, pink, and gold filigrees flowed through them while they fluttered through a heightened sense of consciousness into stunning luminescent realities while their essences hummed at an accelerated rate that seemed impossible.

Their hearts opened, blossoming to the point where they feared they might burst, then their visions intensified into increasingly complex spiraling geometries before an instantaneous flash sent them flying through fields of flowers with varied scents that flitted through them in concert with everything they saw, felt, and experienced. Underlying their sensory and emotional overload they felt overpowering sensations of something bigger and more expansive than anything they could ever hope to comprehend.

They woke to the rose colored glow of breaking dawn that filled the room with its soft radiance along with the sweet sound of Theo's melodic trills and vocalizations.

Instead of jumping out of bed, Ted and Jeanette snuggled close in each other's arms, immersing themselves in the aftermath of their visions and the otherworldly sounds permeating the room.

Theo's singing diminished leaving them feeling refreshed and alert. Holding Ted's hand, Jeanette led him to Theo's crib where they found him bright-eyed and smiling.

Theo giggled and raised his arms. "Ma Ma. Da Da."

Ted leaned in and picked him up, then he and Jeanette hugged him close between them.

"Ma Ma. Da Da indeed," Ted said exaggerating Theo's words in a high pitched imitation of baby talk. He tickled Theo eliciting more giggles and held him out at arm's length, speaking normally. "There's a lot more to you than Ma Ma Da Da little man."

Theo clapped his hands.

"Come on, you two," Jeanette said. "Let's get some breakfast."

Ted carried Theo into the kitchen bouncing him on his shoulders and setting him down on a high chair while Jeanette made coffee and started breakfast. "I have to admit to feeling confused," he said. "I love playing with our little boy and he enjoys it, but the strange things he does worries me. Don't get me wrong, I love him dearly, but the Tinker Toy molecules, crop circle drawings, and all this hummingbird weirdness, flowers, his singing and the way it makes me – makes *us* feel, and what we see and experience in the dreaming visions..."

He looked at Theo who studied him intently without making a sound.

Ted shook off a chill. "It's like we're dealing with two different intelligences. I hate to say it, but I can't shake the thought. Do you think it's possible that he could be possessed or something?"

Jeanette slammed a coffee cup down in front of him spilling a little. "Ted!" She kissed Theo on the top of the head and spoke softer. "I don't ever want to hear another word out of your mouth like that."

Theo continued his wordless stare, keeping his attention fixed on Ted.

"I'm sorry babe, it's just that..."

"I've never felt or experienced anything so wonderful as the beauty of those visions he brings us." She stood up straight and looked upward holding her hands to her chest as if praying. "And his singing sounds heavenly - and the way it makes me feel." She took a deep breath and sighed, then leaned in and kissed Ted on the cheek. "I'm sorry I snapped at you honey. I have worries too and I have more questions than answers. I have no idea what is happening with our little boy and with *us* for that matter, but regardless of all the confusion I have – the confusion we *both* have, underneath it all my heart is full."

She went back to the stove and cracked eggs into a bowl. "I can't make heads or tails out of any of it." She beat the eggs with a fork and poured them into a frying pan, scrambling them. "But I'll tell you this. I'm not going to pay much attention to my jumbled up thoughts. I'm going to follow my heart and I suggest you do the same."

EIGHTEEN

Jeanette noticed that Ted was unusually quiet when he came home from work that night. He played with Theo as usual, but he seemed to be going through the motions without his usual enthusiasm.

"How was your day?" she finally asked when he sat down to dinner. "I hope you're not upset about this morning."

He waved his hand. "Sorry babe, it's not that. You're right about following our hearts. I had a tough day at the lab. We have millions tied up in clinical trials for Trazocodone, our new antidepressant painkiller and we've been dealing with Ian Wood from the FDA and his concerns about addiction. Things are coming to a head and today was particularly brutal."

Jeanette went around behind him and massaged his shoulders. "I'm sorry honey."

Ted put his hand on hers. "Thanks sweetheart. It'll all work out somehow. I didn't mean to bring my work home. Let's just relax and stick to Plan A and see what our little flower child might surprise us with. I'm looking forward to posing questions to him like we talked about." He reached out and ruffled Theo's hair eliciting a bright-eyed dimpled smile.

Jeanette gave Ted's shoulders one last squeeze and patted him on the back. "After dinner. I made your mom's favorite casserole."

"Perfect."

Ted played with Theo after dinner while Jeanette finished cleaning up, then she went to the living room where she found them sitting on the couch. She took a seat on the other side of Theo and put her arm up on the back of the couch beside Ted's.

"I know what's wrong with our television," Ted announced. "Watch this!" He tapped the remote and CNN came on. The moment a reporter came on showing scenes of war in the background Ted looked to Theo and the flat screen shut off.

Theo grinned and clapped his hands.

Jeanette smirked and leaned in, kissing him on top of his head, saying in baby talk. "That's my little Flower child!"

Ted tossed the remote onto the coffee table. "Who needs that shit anyway. We have the real entertainment sitting between us. Let's cut the baby talk and ask him some questions."

"He spoke clearly and coherently when he told us that we had earned the privilege to bow down, worship, and serve him for the rest of our lives," Jeanette said. "Those were the first and last multisyllable words he used and he didn't say anything else for the longest time."

Theo looked back and forth from Ted to Jeanette following their conversation like watching a tennis match.

"Until he surprised us in Doctor Kennedy's office with 'Ma Ma and Da Da'," Ted continued. "I'm not expecting anything more than that, but I am hoping for something more when he reaches out to us in our dreams."

"It's like you said. It seems like we have two Theo's. One is our cute little boy who talks baby talk and the other communicates with us in more complicated ways that we can barely understand."

"So we're looking for middle ground. Even though his vocalizations and physical development as a toddler are what we can expect from a two year old, it's clear that what goes on behind his baby blues, regardless of his baby talk, has a much deeper understanding of everything we say and do."

"It's a matter of articulation."

"His mental capacities, and God knows how complex they might be leave his physical development in the dust," Ted said, "but his speech hasn't developed enough to the point of communicating what he really wants to say."

"So he shows us in his actions like the Tinker Toys and drawings and in our dreams where a different set of rules apply, *and* in his interactions with flowers and hummingbirds." Jeanette stroked Theo's head. "Our little Hummingbird Whisperer."

Ted looked down at Theo, meeting his gaze and their eyes remained locked on each other. "Is there any way you can tell us what you are showing us? Any way you can put it into words?"

Theo looked up at Jeanette.

"It looks like you are talking to the hummingbirds the same way you talk to us," she added. "Do you communicate with the flowers in the same way? If so, what is it that they are telling you?"

"Your first words confused us," Ted said. "I've felt nothing but love from you, but to be honest those words contradict your actions. Are you really a narcissist?"

"Ted!"

"It seems like you do your best work in your sleep," Ted went on. "Why is that, and what's up with your diet? You've been one fussy little boy from the very beginning."

"I think that's enough for now." Jeanette patted Ted's arm. "We've asked him a lot of questions and we don't want to overwhelm him."

Ted chuckled. "Who's overwhelming who?"

NINETEEN

In the predawn darkness the following morning Ted and Jeanette experienced a flurry of bright polychromatic visions that intensified before passing like a brief summer rain. Colors and geometries pulsed in intricate pink and teal lacework patterns that flowed in gentle waves on the shores of their consciousness, then an expansive feeling flooded their hearts pulsing in concert with Theo's sweet childlike voice reverberating in their minds, radiating through every fiber of their bodies along with the fantastic blossoming imagery.

Ma Ma. Da Da.

Its quiet power nearly startled them awake.

This is how I speak to you through my physical vessel. It is difficult for me to put what I have to say into words because my communication is more sophisticated than the simplicity of your speech. I am learning to navigate the constrictions of your language with the limited abilities of my developing body. Now that we have established a strong energetic link between us I will continue to communicate with you in this manner to enhance our shared experience within the boundaries of your constrained three dimensional perception.

Fear paralyzed Jeanette making her heart race and her breathing fast and shallow. Ted's heartbeat and breathing rose in tandem, pulsing in unison with hers as if they were one and the same while their eyes moved together in synchronous rapid eye movements.

Breathe slow and deep, Theo's little boy voice continued. *There is no need to fear me. Though I was denied the nurturing warmth of human connection I was conceived in love and I come in love. Breathe deep with me and it will empower our connection.*

The sound of Theo's slow breathing filled their minds and the three of them inhaled and exhaled as one reducing their heartbeats to a gentler rhythm while their rapid eye movements synchronized reflecting the slower pace of their breathing.

You can ask me questions while we are awake and I will do my best to answer them here, but in this shared state of consciousness all you have to do is think them and I will respond to you in turn.

I can't believe this is happening, Jeanette thought.

Me neither, Ted added.

Believe, Theo responded. **What we share here carries great importance for you and for humanity as a whole.**

You want us to believe in and trust you, Jeanette thought, but I'm troubled by those first words you spoke. You told us that we had earned the privilege to bow down, worship, and serve you with everything we have and everything we are for the rest of our lives. Those words and your tantrums to get breast fed led us to believe that you are a dominating narcissist.

It seems like we have two of you, Ted added. One is our cute little boy who talks baby talk and the other communicates with complicated ways that we can barely understand.

As you know, all infants are born narcissists as they come into the world fully dependent on their parents for every need. In my case the need to be breast fed was exacerbated because your reliance on technology disconnected me from the warm nurturing mammalian connection to mother. My constant hunger for breast feeding drove me because I needed the loving Oxytocin connection that I was deprived of during my gestation as well as the superior nutrition it provides and the essence of my loving, nurturing mother.

I can understand that, Jeanette thought. The nutritional part also explains your strict diet of organic, unprocessed foods.

There you have it!

But you expect us to bow down and worship you, Ted thought. How can you say that you come in love and demand that we bow down and worship you. What kind of love is that?

Theo's eerie chuckles sounded both mature and childlike as they reverberated through Ted and Jeanette.

You should bow down and worship me as you should be bowing down and worshipping each other. Sadly humanity has lost touch with the divinity we exist within and this has been intensified by your technological advances which have moved ahead at a rapid pace without you realizing the consequences they bring.

Your over reliance on your intellectual capacities have further separated you from the essence of your heart connection to source. Instead of loving and honoring each other, humanity is intent on destroying itself. The irony of this is that your drive for self-destruction has driven your technological advances more than anything else!

It can't be all bad, Ted thought. What about our medical advances? For example, my company is working on a new antidepressant to relieve pain *and* anxiety. Aren't we doing good by relieving people of them?

On the surface that is a noble intention, but pain and anxiety are symptoms of deeper problems. Relieving people of them does not resolve the source of their wounds, it only covers them over but the wounds only fester below the surface, eventually rising in other forms like hate, suicide, and addiction. Your drugs only cover up and rewire your brains, reinforcing your denial while hiding the real source of the pain. Masking pain does not solve the problems, it only removes the symptoms. The only path back to healing is to face the darkness and the consequences of your trauma instead of masking it. The only way back to the light is through the darkness. There are no shortcuts and there are no magic bullets. Chaos precedes birth and at this point in time and space that is the only true path available to you. Your involvement in pharmaceuticals is one of the reasons I chose you, or better still why we chose each other.

I don't understand Ted and Jeanette thought in unison. Are you saying that you chose us? That you are not our child?

I most certainly am your child. You created the vehicle that brought me into this world. I asked you to serve me, but in truth I am here to serve you. I have much to share.

But how? Jeanette asked. We wanted you. We asked for you. We chose you to be the best that we could imagine.

Perfect! Ted added.

Humanity's intellectual capacities have grown to the point of decoding your origin code, but as with all of your technology, you submerse yourselves within it with no conception of any consequences. Your internet, your AI, your environmental destruction, diseases, and sicknesses are all proof of this.

Unfortunately your thirst, lust, and fascination for knowledge has subsumed your hearts. Though your technology has denied me the warmth and connection of a mother's womb and the subsequent disconnection I have from you, you conceived me in love and passion which serves your nurturing reproductive instincts of survival as a species.

An immaculate conception, Ted and Jeanette thought together.

Though separate, this reunion of your hearts and minds have drawn my essence into existence in this present form so that those with the wisdom to listen and pay attention may be guided on a path into higher energetic realms.

A barrage of questions, uncertainties, and emotions overwhelmed Ted and Jeanette to the point where their thoughts intruded over each other while their eyes jittered faster, nearly rousing them.

I have given you much to consider and my energy is diminishing. I cannot keep this channel open for much longer and your capacity for reception is reaching its limits. I will leave you with these thoughts, which you will find upsetting, but we will continue this dialogue when the energies are in alignment and you have had time to digest and assimilate what I say with greater clarity.

We have so many questions, Ted thought.

More questions than answers, Jeanette added.

An explosive burst of colors, patterns, and geometries filtered through their consciousness and each word pulsed and changed color, form, and emotion within their hearts and minds which they both felt and "heard" with Theo's final words.

The unraveling of your planet is accelerating. Climate disruption has moved from a scientific hypothesis to a governmental priority the world over. Your loving mother's ice caps are melting faster than anyone predicted and you continue to experience your hottest years ever recorded. Record-breaking hurricanes savage your coasts while fires tear through parched hillsides. Your reefs continue to die, species perish, commodities shrink, and a miniscule amount of people own as much half of the world's population combined. Numerous studies have made it clear that these trends are taking you into an agonizing future.

In these times of growing instability old certainties are falling away so it is understandable that people are drawn to political leaders who promise to take you back to more familiar stable times. In two thousand sixteen the United States elected a president who denied the scientific consensus on global climate change and reasserted the old divisions of religion and race while seeking to wall out the world.

In the end, this path will only accelerate your collective unraveling.

Ted and Jeanette jolted awake with a flash while Theo's words resonated through them. Dawn glimmered on the horizon illuminating the wraithlike form of Theo standing beside the edge of their bed studying them with what looked like a fading otherworldly glimmer in his eyes.

"Ma Ma. Da Da," he said before toddling off to his crib where he climbed in and fell into a deep slumber.

TWENTY

"I'm a little concerned about Theo's delayed speech," Doctor Kennedy said when Jeanette and Ted brought him in for his six month checkup on Monday morning. "He was slow to speak to begin with, but I expected more rapid development by this time."

Theo sat on the examination table playing with the doctor's stethoscope.

Ted glanced a Jeanette. "We thought he might be a little slow ourselves, but he is speaking and letting us know his needs."

Kennedy rubbed his chin. "I have had some other lingering concerns, but I don't want to alarm you."

"What are they?" Jeanette said.

"Well, Theo is perfectly healthy in every way. His brain scans show no abnormalities, his bloodwork is perfect, and physically he is the picture of health."

"But?" Ted asked.

"My colleagues and I have been concerned that he might be autistic."

Jeanette gasped. "What?"

Kennedy held up his hands. "It's still too early to tell for sure, but he has been developmentally delayed for a little longer than I am comfortable with."

Jeanette looked to Ted. "He was that way with his speaking, "but he has come around."

"To a point, but he appears to be stalled. There doesn't seem to be any further development. Typically once the words come his vocabulary should be expanding faster than what we have seen so far. How have his interactions with other children been?"

Jeanette remembered taking him to the playground and how he had ignored the other kids and gone straight for the flowers, then she thought about his behaviors at home and how she and Ted kept him isolated from social contact out of fear that his unusual interactions with them could draw the wrong attention.

"To be honest there hasn't been much, but Ted and I are to blame for that. We've kept him at home for the most part, but we'll make more of an effort to socialize him going forward."

"Is it fair to say that his language and his social interactions have been limited, and what about his emotional reactions and eating habits? Would you consider them normal or are they different?"

Jeanette thought about his breast feeding tantrums, his aversion to processed foods, and his preference for natural foods but decided not to mention them. "He eats very healthy. A little fussy sometimes but he has a healthy diet."

"And his sleep patterns?"

Jeanette thought about how he often fell into deep sleeps after activities like his mandala drawings, Tinker Toy constructions, and other communications. "He sometimes falls asleep fast, especially after particular activities."

Kennedy raised an eyebrow. What kind of activities?"

"You know, kid activities. Playing with toys, drawing, outings to the park."

"We can step up his learning," Ted cut in. "We can read to him more, get him out with other kids, make some play dates, and do more educational things to coax him out more socially."

Kennedy looked from Ted to Jeanette and back again, studying them for a long, uncomfortable moment.

"We'll do whatever you recommend," Jeanette said.

Kennedy nodded slowly and clasped his hands together. "Okay, let's give it some more time, but if nothing changes in the next few months, I want him back in for a thorough evaluation, not only by me, but by some of my colleagues who have been studying Theo with me. I want to err on the side of caution, but I also want you to consider the possibility that Theo could be autistic."

Jeanette's eyes grew wide and she bowed her head. Ted put a comforting hand on her shoulder.

"If that turns out to be the case, Kennedy said, "it may not be as bad as it seems. There are varying degrees of autism, and in Theo's case it could be mild, right Theo?"

They all turned to Theo who had been studying them frowning with concentration. He bounced up and down and clapped his hands together when they looked at him, exclaiming, "Ma Ma! Da Da!" He held his hands out to be picked up.

"How are we going to handle this?" Ted said on the drive home."

Jeanette looked at Theo in the rear view mirror and his eyes met hers. "I don't know what to think about this autism stuff."

"As strange as it sounds," Ted said, "I think we can look to Theo for guidance the next time he communicates with us."

A smile lit up Theo's face and Jeanette took a deep breath, feeling some relief.

"I can't help thinking that we have two Theos in there," Ted continued. "Do you think that could be…"

"Don't say it!" Jeanette snapped.

"Sorry, I didn't mean it to sound like that, but I can't shake the thought that there are two Theo's who act very differently. One we need to nurture and protect, maybe even more so after what Doctor Kennedy said, and one who appears to be guiding us, although I'm still confused by what he's told us."

"Me too, but as unnerving as it is, a lot of it makes sense."

Ted chuckled. "As much as any of this makes any sense at all."

Jeanette reached out and took his hand. "Regardless of who or what lives inside our little boy, I'm going to love him with everything I have, no matter what."

Ted squeezed her hand. "All for one and one for all. We're all in this together."

Theo stared out the window and remained quiet for the rest of the ride home while Ted and Jeanette held hands, each lost in their own thoughts.

After Ted pulled into their driveway he leaned in and kissed Jeanette on the cheek, then he turned to the back seat to shake Theo's toe, but Theo was fast asleep and didn't respond. "I need to get back to work. The pressure's on. I'll see you both tonight when I get home."

Jeanette kissed him back, stepped out of the car, and opened the back door. Theo stirred when she picked him up from his car seat and the two of them waved to Ted when he drove away.

She noticed that the amaryllis in the foyer by the front door had wilted when she went in. "Shit," she muttered. "I've been so distracted that I forgot to water it. For that matter I forgot to water *all* of the plants." She set Theo down and he toddled after her as she went to the kitchen and filled up a small watering can. "Mommy needs to give the plants a drink."

Theo ran out of the kitchen ahead of her and waited by the amaryllis where he reached up and stroked the stem and leaves before she could water it.

To Jeanette's amazement the plant rose up like a human waking and stretching until it stood straight, then the red in its flowers brightened into a deeper red.

She gasped and dropped the watering can.

Theo giggled and his eyes grew luminous with a barely perceptible glow.

Jeanette caught her breath and picked up the watering can to water the amaryllis, then trailed behind Theo as if in a trance while he waddled around the house repeating the miracle with all the other plants while she followed, watering each one.

TWENTY ONE

"You won't believe what happened today," Jeanette said, barely able to contain herself when she met Ted by the front door. Theo stood beside her clutching her leg.

Ted reached down and picked him up, holding him high. "At this point I can believe practically anything."

She stepped back and held her hand out toward the amaryllis like a game show hostess presenting a grand prize. "Notice anything different?"

Ted shifted Theo to his hip. "I can't tell for sure, but that plant looks like it's pretty happy."

"Theo has more than a green thumb. He has a Miracle-Gro hand. After you dropped us off this morning I noticed that the amaryllis was wilting, so I got the watering can to give it a drink. When I came back Theo gave it a kind of massage and it perked up, then he went around the house and did the same with all the other plants."

"He did have a magical connection with the flowers and hummingbirds in the park which is why you bought all these red flowering plants."

"Very magical but I had no idea it would be *this* magical."

Ted bounced Theo up and down on his hip. "That's something else we'll have to ask our little miracle worker when he's in his professorial alter ego dream teaching mode. I wish we could communicate with him like that all the time, but it seems like certain conditions have to be met that only he knows. He said something about his energy the last time he opened that channel as he put it. I want to know more about these flower and hummingbird interactions the next time that happens."

Jeanette nodded quickly. "And this autism thing. It worries me."

"Our two Theos."

"I like to think of it as one Theo working in two different ways."

Ted held Theo up high and looked into his eyes, which brightened when they met his.

"Come on," Jeanette said, waving him in. "Dinner's ready."

They ate dinner and went to bed early after Theo dozed off at the table.

Some time after falling asleep Ted and Jeanette became aware of a buzzing sensation that grew into a low frequency hum punctuated by chit chit sounds until they felt themselves vibrating blissfully with their hearts opened until they hovered together on the threshold between sleeping and dreaming.

Colors and geometries pulsed in intricate pink and teal mandala patterns that swept through them as they soared through pastel colored bliss. The expansive feeling in their hearts pulsed in concert with Theo's sweet little boy's voice reverberating in their minds.

Ma Ma. Da Da.

Can you tell us what you are showing us? Ted thought. Is there any way you can put it into words?

It feels like you are talking to the hummingbirds the same ways you talk to us, Jeanette thought. Do you communicate with the flowers in the same way?

Unfolding geometries blossomed into a flurry of colors that morphed into primarily red-hued flowers and other flowers of differing sizes and colors, all outlined in neon filigrees that glowed like bright colors under a black light.

You are seeing what I see when I commune with my picaflors. I see through all of them and they see through me sharing the sacred space of our being in a two way, or better still multiple viewpoints. I see everything through their eyes and they see everything through mine. They are my constant companions that bring me an expanded vision of the world that I can access at any time.

Is it the same with the flowers? Jeanette thought.

Flowers and their sweet essences are some of the highest vibrational energies existing on your planet. Hummingbirds are the next step in moving from the plant into the animal kingdom, which is one of the reasons why they are so closely linked to each other. They share a common vibration at a higher level of interspecies communication.

The radiant visual tour continued while Theo spoke, intertwined with intoxicating floral scents, all of it slowing as they flitted from flower to flower, swimming in each one's unique synesthetic essence of sight, scent, and sound.

For my picaflors, it's all about the flowers, where they are, what they like, how they feel, and what other plants and animals they like. Aside from defending their food for their little ones, The chitters they share are tiny bursts of high frequency joy and excitement.

These visions you bring us are such a blessing, Jeanette thought. I can't tell you how much gratitude I feel toward you for sharing them.

You both are growing into and adjusting to them. These visuals as well as others I have shared constitute a sophisticated heart centered emotion infused language that conveys deeper psychospiritual information that you are receiving at levels that you are barely aware of adding impact to my words which are felt and experienced more than simply heard. The geometries you pass through are a universal language which constitutes a superior method of communication.

Their visions shifted with the sweet sound of trills and vocalizations that came at a higher melodic pitch than Theo's regular voice. Shapes, colors, scents, patterns, abstractions, archetypes, and concepts blossomed into a symphony of sights, sounds, and emotions, then the singing stopped abruptly, bringing them back to the low frequency hum and chit chit sounds and the tapestry of the differing sizes and colors of flowers outlined in glowing filigrees.

I have much to share with you and I know you have many questions for me, but our time in this shared state is limited. Let me end this communication by saying that the high frequency energy of hummingbirds and the essences of flowers are closer to my own which makes it easier for me to communicate with them than with you as you vibrate at a much slower speed than they do.

Please, before we wake, Ted thought. Can you explain why it seems like there are two of you? One is our cute little boy who talks baby talk and who Doctor Kennedy thinks is underdeveloped and autistic and the other one who is speaking now in sophisticated ways that we can barely understand.

It takes a considerable amount of energy to lower my vibration to communicate with you through this limited three-dimensional vehicle, so I have been in and out of it by necessity.

Jeanette's thoughts rushed ahead. Are you saying that you are not our child?

Are you possessing our little boy? Ted asked.

Theo's eerie chuckles tinkled through Ted and Jeanette like wind chimes, calming them. *I am very much your child and as I have told you, you chose me and I have chosen you. I asked you to serve me but I am here to serve you.*

I don't understand, Ted and Jeanette thought.

Sometimes it is necessary for me to vacate for short periods of time to let this little body develop in its own ways, particularly with speaking and language functions. After I perform what you perceive as miracles it is very demanding which

83

is why I have to rest after performing them. Think of it like sleeping and dreaming. Sometimes we are present in dreaming and other times we need unconscious sleep to allow our physical bodies to recharge and heal. During these times I commune with what you might call our ancestors in higher dimensions.

It takes a tremendous amount of energy which taxes this little body, particularly when I am communicating with multisensory sounds and geometries. One way of looking at it is that the higher frequencies that I manifest are more than this precious little body can handle, so it needs recovery time, otherwise I could damage it. In the same way that my body is growing and developing, I have to continually fine tune my alignment with its rapidly changing configurations.

Is that why you appear autistic? Ted thought. Is it permanent?

Will you grow out of it? Jeanette asked.

Do not fear, Theo said calming them. **It is a temporary condition of adjustment which needs to happen for me to come into resonance with this three dimensional form. Rest assured, I will grow into my body and my intellectual capacities will exceed those of my peers. To the external world I will appear stunted in my development. I need the world to perceive me as being autistic for reasons of safety that will become apparent to you, at least for now.**

The first glimmers of pink hued sunlight filtered into the room easing them into wakefulness, both mildly surprised to discover that they were holding hands while Theo slept soundly in his crib.

TWENTY TWO

Jeanette stood by the kitchen window feeling a deeper heartfelt connection than she had ever felt before while watching hummingbirds zipping back and forth to a feeder she had hung. Theo tugged at her pant leg.

"Up Mama! Up!"

She reached down and lifted him, sitting him on the counter beside her so they could watch together. Her breath caught when she spotted a cat crouched on a nearby Adirondack chair ready to pounce on a hummingbird engrossed in feeding. The cat sank lower ready to spring, and in the next moment it turned and crept away as if suddenly changing its mind. She looked to Theo who winked at her.

Inspired by that episode she decided to take him back to the park later that morning and parked his stroller by a bench next to the playground. Though he had shown no interest before, she hoped that seeing other kids playing might get him to socialize some.

He nearly leaped from her arms when she lifted him from the stroller and her heart soared when he bolted toward a group of toddlers, then fear paralyzed her when she saw a mangy German Shepherd bounding toward them from the opposite direction barking savagely, on the attack. Other mothers stood, screaming as the dog closed in.

Theo lurched into the space between the dog and the screeching kids and stood firm, staring at the charging dog. It skidded to a stop inches from him and froze for an indeterminable moment before lowering its head and creeping away the same way the cat had. Mothers rushed in snatching up their children, leaving Theo standing still as a statue until Jeanette scooped him up.

He seemed dazed when she picked him up, but he came out of it when she put him in the stroller where he giggled, saying, "Woof! Woof!"

She rushed him away before any of the stunned parents could ask questions, and breathed in slow and deep to calm her racing heart. "My God, Theo," she said under her breath. "You scared the shit out of me!"

"Woof! Woof!"

"You did the same thing with the cat, didn't you?"

"Meow."

"Wait until your father hears about this!"

Anxious to share the day's events, Jeanette could barely contain her excitement when Ted came home from work, but she sensed his troubled energy when he came through the door. "How was your day?"

He shook his head. "I don't want to talk about it right now. Where's Theo?"

She felt the tension in his shoulders when she hugged him. "He's napping. He had a big day and it took a lot out of him." She followed up with a kiss on the cheek. "I'm sorry honey."

He kissed her. "We can talk about it later. Tell me about our little hummingbird whisperer. I could use a little lift right now." A wry smile crossed his lips. "Pun intended."

She took his briefcase from him and led him to the couch where she stood behind him massaging his shoulders as she spoke. "Theo's connection with hummingbirds and plants is mind boggling enough and he explained how that works in our dreaming visions, but today he surprised me even more."

Ted sat up straighter. "I'm almost afraid to hear."

"I was watching the hummingbirds at the feeder by the kitchen window when he insisted that I pick him up. It felt like he knew what was going to happen and purposely orchestrated how things unfolded. When I looked back at the feeder I spotted a cat about to pounce on an unsuspecting hummer. Right when it was about to spring it suddenly turned and crept away like it changed its mind. When I looked at Theo, I swear to God, he winked at me."

"You think he made that happen?"

"I wasn't sure of what I saw, but his wink answered the question for me. As if that wasn't enough he left no doubt in my mind when I took him to the park later on, hoping he might socialize with other kids there."

"How did he do?"

"Once again it felt like he knew what would happen. He jumped out of my arms when I took him out of the stroller. I thought he was excited when he ran toward a bunch of kids until I saw a mangy looking dog running toward them about to attack." She let out a loud exhale. "Theo stepped between the charging dog and the screaming kids and stared it down. It skidded to a stop inches from him and froze like it hit an invisible wall or something, then it lowered its head and crept away the same way the cat had."

"What did the other parents do?"

"They were screaming more than the kids," Jeanette scoffed. "They all rushed in grabbing their children, leaving Theo standing as still as a statue. I swooped him up and hustled him out of there before they could ask any questions."

"Good move!"

"He's been sleeping ever since we got home so I am sure it took a lot out of him. The way everything happened, first with the cat, then with the dog left no doubt in my mind that he is gradually revealing more and more to us, pushing the boundaries of what we can accept."

"He seems to be leading us on a mystery path." Ted looked up and gave her a lopsided grin. "Though we are his parents I think he's the one in charge and I am not afraid to say that I trust him more with each passing day no matter how strange he behaves." Ted reached up and put his hand on Jeanette's. "I can feel it in my heart."

Jeanette put her other hand on his. "Do you know what he said to me on the way home when I told him that he scared the shit out of me? 'Woof! Woof!' and when I asked him if he did the same thing with the cat, he said 'Meow!'."

Ted chuckled and she felt his mood lighten.

They checked on Theo before dinner and found him sleeping soundly, breathing in long slow breaths.

"Do you think we should wake him?" Ted asked.

"Let him sleep," Jeanette whispered. "I think today's heroics took a lot out of him. Why don't you go relax and watch the news while I make dinner?"

"As long there's nothing about any wars," Ted quipped.

She grinned. "I had a feeling you might be a little down when you came home, so I made your mom's favorite casserole. All I need to do is heat it up. It'll only take a few minutes."

"Thank you, honey."

Theo continued sleeping through dinner so Ted helped with the dishes. "Theo's not the only one who needs rest. I'm really tapped out after today," he said while drying his hands."

"Let's climb into bed ourselves and you can tell me whatever's on your mind. It might be good for you to unload a little unless you don't want to talk about it."

"Sounds good."

After brushing their teeth, Ted and Jeanette checked on Theo one more time before crawling into bed, sitting with their backs against the headboard where Ted put his arm over her shoulder and she rested her head against him.

"What's got you so tensed up, babe?" she said.

Ted snorted. "You know I don't like to bring my work home, but…"

"I appreciate that honey, but we're in this together and when you need to talk, who else can you *really* talk to?"

He kissed her on the top of her head. "We've been – more me than anyone else have been wrestling with government regulatory agencies and things are coming to a head. Bliss Pharmaceuticals has millions tied up in clinical trials for Trazocodone. Our biggest challenge has been sparring with Ian Wood from the FDA over its safety. His biggest concern is addiction. I hate to say this, but the truth of the matter is that any form of addiction, even if it is mild, would bolster the company's bottom line, so many of the board members are pushing hard for this approval. We stand to make tons of money. There have even been whispers of bribes and payoffs."

"I can understand how that would trouble you."

Ted sighed. "I have to meet with the board of directors to sort it all out tomorrow. The irony of it is that I never thought about the profit motive when I took on this project. I was sold on the idea that relieving pain and anxiety were good things, but now after investing so much time and energy developing this drug, I find myself struggling to support it, especially in light of what Theo said. I've thought it all through and he's right, which puts me between a rock and a hard place."

"So when everything is said and done, it comes down to money or your conscience, doesn't it?"

TWENTY THREE

In what had now become an accepted event, Ted and Jeanette experienced bright polychromatic visions full of colors and geometries pulsing within their consciousness coupled with an expansive feeling in their hearts, all driven by Theo's sweet voice reverberating through them in the predawn darkness of the following morning.

Ma Ma. Da Da..

How wonderful to connect with you here again, Jeanette thought. We have been trying to wrap our minds around what our relationship to you is. You seem to be leading us on a mystery path. Though we are your parents I can't help but think that you are the one in charge. I'm not afraid to say that I trust you more with each passing day no matter how strange you behave or how you show things to us, but I am at a loss to understand just who or what you really are.

Theo's wind chime sounding giggles tinkled through Ted and Jeanette before he spoke.

There is no doubt that I am your son and you are part of a group of interdimensional beings connected to humanity throughout your known history and through several other prehistoric cultures. We are here to instruct you in the vibratory nature of the cosmos and the use of sacred geometry to stimulate brain performance and the use of sound to activate psychospiritual experiences.

You have come into this co-creation through your own choices. Nothing was forced on you and everything that you are presented with in this co-creation is an offering which you are free to accept or deny.

I am learning to offer information to you in the form of language, but my primary communications come through vibrational patterns sent to me from other dimensions.

I come in love with the dawning of a new reality. If you are ready to build a new world I invite you to join me on a journey of the heart and mind. Though I am your child conceived in love I am also channeling your elder brothers and sisters you can think of as your ancestors. My race has been with humanity for a long period of your evolution on this earth and we were with you in eons past, even in the

89

forgotten days before any trace of us in your present written history. Our nature is energetic and interdimensional.

*We have also been in contact with Tibetan lamas in the formative period of Buddhism and with other groups. Although we have interacted with some of earths early cultures, we are an intergalactic civilization that spans beyond parts of your known universe.

*We are an ascended civilization who exist within a specific vibratory field, even as you have your own slower energy signature. We vibrate at a faster rate, but we are all part of the mystery of love that holds and binds the universe together.

*We have grown as you have grown, ascending to the One Source and like you we have grown through joy and sorrow. We are a little higher on the spiral of awareness and consciousness than you are which allows us to offer what we have learned as friends, mentors, and fellow travelers on the path that leads back to the remembrance of All That Is.

*We are not saviors and we are not messianic. We want to avoid that projection. We are simply elder brothers and sisters offering our understanding from what we have learned and we offer it freely. In our understanding, the belief that other alien intelligences are going to save you is nothing more than a projection of human unconsciousness. The hope that someone or something will save you, that you will not have to make any changes in yourself, and that you will not have to be responsible is delusional.

*The belief that you can stay in long established patterns of unconsciousness and have something given to you that will transform you without any effort on your part is foolishness. At this point in your evolution there may be alien intelligences that land, but those who count on others to bring in their ascension and elevation without any inner work on their part are going to be sadly disappointed.

*Ascension is a process of self-awareness and mastery on all levels that necessitates bringing all those levels of your existence upward. That is how we see it and how we have done for millennia.

*By offering our aid we do not wish to interfere with any other spiritual helpers and cosmic relationships you may have, nor with any religious beliefs or organizations that might help you..

Together we hope to work with you toward ascension and the evolution of your consciousness.

After a few moments, Ted's agitated thoughts broke through.

I'm having a crisis with my work and I'm at a loss for what to do.

You need to act out of your own volition. My advice is to follow your conscience. It is the voice of your heart. If you take that path there is only one choice.

That is?

*Leave it all behind. If you do that you have to be willing to make great personal sacrifices for the greater good of humanity. Your world is disintegrating *into increasingly divisive polarities. Some will hear you, but most will react in fear and become a danger, but the choice is yours, and the stakes are much bigger than you realize.*

That goes against everything we have worked toward and it could ruin us and the company financially. I have searched my soul and the only thing that remains true is what you are saying. I understand how we have been misguided, but the painful reality is that the bottom line for the company is profit and I can't find it in myself to ruin them as well as the careers of my colleagues and the finances of our investors.

They will find others to replace you.

We could lose everything and I'll never be able to work in the industry again.

There are other healing modalities and other more wholesome natural paths to healing. With the help of our plant family I can assist you in creating your own methods of natural healing as opposed to profit motivated pharmaceutical interventions.

Theo's voice faded into a diminishing echo and Ted and Jeanette awoke to the beginnings of a sunrise.

TWENTY FOUR

"I guess I don't have to ask you how the board meeting went," Jeanette said when Ted came home early from the office and set a box of personal items down on the dining room table where Theo was engrossed in building another mystery structure with his Tinker Toys.

Ted gave a faint smile. "How's our little mad scientist doing?"

Theo continued working without acknowledging him.

"He's been at it for awhile," Jeanette said. "I can't make heads or tails out of what he's making, but I'll bet you can."

Ted studied Theo's work. "So far it looks like another DMT molecule, but I have a suspicion that it's going to be something different."

"Tell me about the board meeting. What did you say? How did they take it?"

A tight smile turned up on one side of Ted's face and he chuckled, pointing to the box. "You can see how they took it right here. What I told them went over like a lead balloon. You should have seen the look on their faces!"

"What did you say?"

"We met to discuss the FDA's concerns which they expected me to refute, but as I listened and thought about what Theo said this morning I ended up siding with Ian Wood and the FDA! The words came out of my mouth on their own accord. It felt surreal, like someone else was speaking them. I could have stopped at any time, but I agreed with everything that came through me, wholeheartedly. On one level it felt effortless, like I was sitting back watching it unfold like a Broadway show." His smile grew. "Better still like a bad sitcom. Even though I was destroying my job and all the years of hard work I put into it, it felt liberating with a freedom I never could have imagined possible.

"I told them what Theo told us, that all of the pain and anxiety that people are experiencing are symptoms of deeper problems and

92

relieving them does not treat the source of the wounds and only covers them over, so the wounds resurface in other forms like suicide and addiction." He snorted. "If looks could kill, I'd be dead many times over and I think I still need to watch my back if you get my drift."

Jeanette's hand flew to her mouth. "My God, Ted!"

"They had security escort me out which was totally inappropriate and humiliating, but their actions reinforced my conviction that I made the right decision. I felt a dizzying sense of freedom when I left the building, like a great weight had been lifted off of me."

Jeanette stood and kissed him on the cheek, then she hugged him while Theo clapped in the background yelling like a cheerleader, "Da Da! Da Da! Da Da! Da Da!"

"I don't know what we're going to do going forward, but right now part of me doesn't care."

Jeanette looked to Theo. "We'll see how the mystery unfolds."

Theo looked from Jeanette to Ted, saying, "Ma Ma. Da Da." He slapped at the empty Tinker Toy box. "Theo wants more toys!" he demanded before going back to work, losing himself in his construction.

Amazon boxes containing three two hundred piece super building Tinker Toy sets showed up at the door the next day. Ted and Jeanette opened the boxes and set them in front of Theo, who poured them all into one pile and went to work, spending equal amounts of time working feverishly, followed with extended periods of deep sleep before beginning the cycle over again, taking up the better part of the next week. Each time he finished a new structure he tapped away on the keyboard of his baby laptop inputting numbers and symbols that spelled out the formula for each one.

At the end of his binge Theo left the dining room table littered with novel molecular constructions of tryptamines, phenethylamines, peptides, and other structures Ted had never seen before, then he fell into the longest sleep they had seen yet.

Ted took pictures of everything, including the formulas Theo had input into his baby laptop. He worked long into the night meticulously copying everything by hand into a notebook as an added precaution and a way to integrate it into his own thought processes. He finished by adding notes, references, and other avenues of research he thought might fill in any gaps he might have as well as questions he wanted to pose to Theo.

Jeanette stirred but didn't wake when he fell into bed some time after two. Hours later when the first glimmer of dawn rimmed the horizon colorful geometric visions came coupled with expansive heart centered sensations that he and Jeanette had come to love.

Theo's reverberating little boy voice chimed through the synesthesia speaking to them in a different timbre. *I know you have many questions, but I don't want to have those discussions now. You need more time for those conceptions I shared to sink in and develop within your subconscious. This morning I want to explain other things to help you understand the greater reality that we share.

*My deeper rest and recovery times are facilitating the advancement of my body, my physiological brain capacities, and their abilities to transmit the higher energies that I am rooted in. My growing aptitude to communicate with you is shifting higher every day as my frequency shifts into more expansive modes of consciousness that allow me to become better at sharing the resonance that we have been cultivating.

*This expansion will broaden your understanding of your true holographic nature and your connection to all that is, bringing greater resources to the work that we do here as you are part of something greater than anything you could have imagined.

You are the Universe incarnate.

We're here in our bodies moving through the world reacting to the perceptions that come to us through our senses, Jeanette thought, but what we experience is limited to the three dimensions we are aware of.

*As soon as I speak, I diminish the greater reality by the limiting confines of words which fall short of something so vast and expansive that it exceeds any conception that your present thoughts and understanding can comprehend. I will try to explain beginning with words before I follow through with something more complex that you might be able to grasp.

Your science has no need to investigate the sun to discover the matter of the solar world. This matter exists in ourselves and is the result of the division of our atoms. In the same way we have in us the matter of all other worlds. You are, we are all universes. Everything inside of us contains everything that makes up the universe. The same forces, the same laws that govern the life of the Universe operates inside of us, so by studying ourselves we can study the infinite universe and just as in studying the universe we can study ourselves.

A flurry of thought, emotion, and geometries flooded through Ted and Jeanette bringing them to the experience of an encounter with a limitless field of bright blinding energy which they intuited as the single energy that composed all existence. In this moment outside of time they understood that all things that existed were pieces of a comprehensive existence that carried with it the sense of an ultimate encounter. Their experience changed into a moving experience of the cosmic tree and the energy became a massive tree of radiant energy suspended in space that seemed bigger than the largest galaxy, and it consisted entirely of light. The core of the tree dissolved and became lost in the brilliant display, but limbs and leaves were visible around its edges and Ted and Jeanette each experienced themselves as one of its leaves. The lives of their family and close friends came to them as leaves clustered close to them on a smaller branch. All the distinguishing characteristics that made them individuals appeared to be variations of a fundamental energy.

They were taken around the tree and shown how easy it was to move from one person's experience to another and they realized that different lives around the world were in essence different experiences the tree was having.

Choice governed all experience.

At this point they became the tree, but they knew that they were not having the full range of its experience, yet each knew themselves to be the single encompassing consciousness and that its identity was their true identity. They experienced it all as a seamless flow of consciousness as well as crystallizations of embodiment so they understood how human consciousness manifests itself in separate forms while remaining unified.

The freedom they felt brought sheer bliss.

As they left the cosmic tree, the intense energy subsided and they found themselves in conscious communication, still fully aware of the surrounding consciousness that enveloped them. As the extreme mental, emotional, psychospiritual energies and imagery receded further, Theo's celestial sing-song voice whispered through them like a sweet summer breeze.

My loving picaflor brothers and sisters will help you understand this and the plants will tell us even more. They have been here much longer than humans or animals, which might lead you to wonder who is really cultivating who?

With their help I promise to give you more glimpses into this sacred connectedness that all humans have the potential to cultivate if they can rise above their fear, hatred, divisiveness, and penchant for destroying everything they come in contact with.

Before they could articulate any further thoughts, Ted and Jeanette awoke to the rose colored glow of the coming day.

TWENTY FIVE

Stunned into silence by the immensity of their experience Ted and Jeanette remained lying in bed immobile for some time until the depth of Ted's breathing told Jeanette that he had fallen back asleep while her mind spiraled.

She slipped out of bed and checked on Theo finding him wide awake with his eyes open making no sound but the gentle whisper of his deep breathing. His eyes locked on hers in silent communication when she peered in on him, somehow expressing more than words could. After a moment of connection he held up his arms and she lifted him out of his crib, holding him close as they crept past Ted who slept soundly.

"I'm not sure how to speak to you after that," she said softly. "You're still my adorable baby boy, but you're also something more than that. Am I talking to my little boy Theo, or – I don't know? Cosmic Theo?"

He giggled when she set him into his high chair and pointed toward the ground. "Baby boy here, Mommy," then he pointed to her heart. "Cosmic Theo there."

She smiled and kissed him on the top of his head, then she made breakfast in silence, letting all that had passed between them find their place within her flustered thoughts and emotions.

They remained quiet while communing silently, finding unspoken comfort in each other's presence until Ted joined them.

"You guys are so quiet I didn't think you were even here," he said, breaking the spell.

"Daddy!" Theo said.

Jeanette blinked as if waking from a trance. "Good morning, honey. Hungry?"

"Starved!"

"Coming right up!"

She went to the stove and cooked sausages, eggs, and toast while Theo and Ted sat together wrapped in their own wordless communion. She brought two plates to the table for her and Ted and a small bowl of fresh strawberries for Theo.

"What are your plans for today?" she said.

Ted rubbed his chin and looked to Theo. "I took pictures of Baby Einstein's models and copied the formulas from his little laptop into my notebook. I'm pretty sure I know what he has in mind, but we'll need to have a discussion around that. I want to do some research before that happens so I have sufficient background data for us to have an informed discussion."

Ted sat with Theo in silence with the two of them studying each other as if in deep conversation while Jeanette cleaned up after breakfast and loaded the dishwasher.

Theo became animated and pointed to the hummingbird feeder outside the kitchen window repeating, "Mommy. Daddy. Out!"

"Okay." Jeanette took him by the hand and headed toward the back door while Ted went the other way toward the dining room.

"Daddy too!" Theo said.

Jeanette looked to Ted who turned around and shrugged. "Why not? Some fresh air might do some good."

Together they went out into the back yard where Theo scurried over to a spot in the middle of the yard where he stood with his arms stretched out and his back to the sun. "Mommy, Daddy, look! Look!"

He made a short series of toning sounds followed by the "chit chit" of a hummingbird's call. Hummingbirds flocked to him resting on his arms and hovering below them, making them look like giant wings while others flew suspended in front of his face forming a beak. Others hovered around him completing the animated form.

He giggled hysterically, looking like a big hummingbird with an exceptionally bright red sparkling iridescence in the place where the eye would be, surrounded by bright flashing reflective green.

The living flickering configuration moved with Theo, gleaming like jewels in the sunlight, the whole mimicking the sum of its tiny fluttering parts. The overall effect looked like a sparkling animatronic character from a Disney theme park.

The hummingbirds all moved in perfect synchrony when Theo turned his head from side to side showing off the bigger figure's gorget at its throat which glittered like a proud knight-in-armor's metallic collar of crimson rainbow-hued brilliance.

Theo made more toning sounds followed by the hummingbird's "chit chit" and the tiny birds flew off, exploding with an iridescent shimmer that looked brighter than Fourth of July fireworks.

Jeanette stared wide-eyed with her mouth open.

After a few beats, Ted said, "I think that was the glimpse of sacred connectedness that Theo promised us."

Theo nodded, grinning and clapping his hands.

TWENTY SIX

"Ma Ma! Da Da!"

Theo clapped his hands while sitting on Doctor Kennedy's examining table after an MRI, EKG, CT, PET, and ultrasound scans as well as a battery of other tests, including a blood panel and genome analysis to see if anything had changed as parts of Theo's three year old birthday checkup.

Kennedy leaned in and peered into Theo's ears with an otoscope to finish his examination, then stepped back shaking his head. Ted and Jeanette sat close by holding hands and mentally holding their breath anticipating what the doctor might say and how they would respond.

Kennedy pulled up a rolling chair and sat across from them with his forehead wrinkled in thought while rubbing his chin, and appeared to come to some inner decision. "It's puzzling. Our little Theo is a miracle child who is perfect in every way and has every indication of being a perfectly healthy three year old. As you know, he is the first genetically perfect child that Fetal Fantasies has ever produced, and is in fact the first genetically perfect human that the human race has ever seen." He paused.

"But," Jeanette said.

Kennedy pursed his lips. "My colleagues and I have studied him with the greatest interest, but I haven't been telling you everything as we have been watching and waiting to see how things have progressed."

"What is it that you haven't been telling us?" Ted asked.

"We've kept this under the radar for some time now following the confidential discretion we have been directed to adhere to by our superiors. We've noticed some anomalies in Theo's chromosomes that are evolving in ways we've never seen creating synaptic connections that are causing unusual reactions in other neuronal clusters."

What do you mean anomalies?" Jeanette snapped. "You've been telling us all along that he's perfect!"

Kennedy held his hands up. "I don't want to alarm you, but there is growing concern and the consensus is that we need to act on it before it progresses further."

Jeanette's hand flew to her mouth. "Oh my God," she whispered.

Ted took her other hand. "In ways you've never seen?"

Kennedy glanced over at Theo who sat immobile staring at him. He took a deep breath before continuing. "In terms of his overall development, I cannot find a single trace of any mutations or abnormalities, yet Theo's lack of developing speech and other indicators all point to a diagnosis of autism. I don't know how much you know about it, but autism is a complex neurodevelopmental disorder that affects individuals differently and is characterized by challenges in social interaction, communication, and repetitive behaviors. It's a developmental disorder that typically manifests in early childhood like we are seeing here."

Jeanette shook her head.

Kennedy held up a finger. "Individuals with autism have unique strengths and abilities. Their experiences can vary, but autistics face challenges in their daily lives that can affect their ability to form and maintain social relationships, communicate effectively, and navigate the world around them. I only see Theo when you bring him in for his checkups, so I don't get to see the big picture. How does he fit in with the profile I just gave you?"

Ted and Jeanette looked at each other and Jeanette spoke up.

"Obviously his speech has been delayed but he doesn't have repetitive behaviors, and I admit that we haven't spent much time trying to socialize him."

The day at the playground when the mangy dog had charged the kids and Theo stepped between the dog and the terrified kids replayed itself in her mind.

Kennedy nodded. "More socialization could be a good thing. He is reaching preschool age, but he has been developmentally delayed in many ways. Have you given any thought to furthering his education going forward? There are special schools for children like him."

Home schooling!

Ted and Jeanette jumped as if shocked and said at the same time, "We'll home school him."

Kennedy blinked and his head jerked back.

Ted and Jeanette glanced over at Theo and saw his dimpled smile.

Kennedy chuckled. "I guess that decision is unanimous."

"We will make more effort to socialize him," Jeanette said. "We just want to see that he's educated the way we think he should be."

"No need to explain." Kennedy reached for his iPad. "I understand. It's a personal choice." He slid his finger down the iPad and scrolled through screens, looking up when he found what he was looking for. "There is something else I would like you to consider."

"What is it?" Ted asked.

"Theo is at the ideal age for an intervention of sorts."

"What kind of intervention?"

"It's a pilot program that Theo is the perfect candidate for. We have had a lot of success using CRISPR technology to edit and target specific genes that make changes to a subject's genetic code to correct specific mutations implicated in autism. By correcting them now we have a good chance of restoring normal function and alleviating behavioral and cognitive symptoms associated with autism and it can produce positive effects on behavior and brain development."

Jeanette shook her head. "But you've told us over and over again that Theo is the first genetically perfect child!"

"That's true."

"So why would you want to alter the genetic profile that we purposely chose?" Ted asked.

Kennedy shrugged. "I'm just sharing the unanimous opinion of my colleagues. Sometimes the devil is in the details. Though we have done as thorough an analysis as possible there may be room for improvement. Think of it like a tune-up that can jump start his development."

Jeanette scrunched up her face. "Jump start? Tune-up? We're not talking about a car here. We're talking about my little boy."

Kennedy waved his hand. "Just hear me out. Editing stem cells and neurons will allow us to focus on a gene called CHD8 that ties mutations to a broad spectrum of molecular and cellular defects. We would use an integrated approach that alters genome regulation, gene expression, neuron function, and connections to other key genes that play a role in autism."

"I'm confused," Jeanette said. "You're telling us that Theo is perfectly healthy with a perfect genome and now you're telling us that this CHD8 gene is faulty?"

"Not exactly, but this gene appears to be the source of autistic problems."

"I still don't get it," Ted said.

Kennedy read from his iPad. "CHD8 mutations make the genome more accessible to regulators of gene expression, which drives aberrant expression of hundreds of genes resulting in molecular defects in neurons that carry the mutation. These defects in neuron function can be thwarted when extra CHD8 is added to the cell. In this case, extra copies of a healthy CHD8 gene without any mutation would be added using a viral vector. Upon differentiation of the stem cells the neurons rescued by the treatment would return to a normal rate of activity and synaptic communication resulting in restored function. The CHD8 mutation will specifically alter other genes that have been implicated in autism or intellectual disability and influence the genes involved in neurodevelopmental disorders."

"So is his CHD8 gene faulty or not?" Jeanette asked.

"We don't know for sure, but it appears to be the source of these kind of problems."

"What if there is nothing wrong with his CHD8 gene?" Ted said.

"Then we would simply be adding a healthy gene to a healthy gene, but from what my colleagues and I have observed, this looks like a worthwhile approach."

"But you're still telling us that Theo is perfect all the way down to his genome," Jeanette said.

Ted held up his hand. "Let me get this straight. This is a pilot program, there are still unknowns, and no one is sure that there is anything wrong with Theo's CHD8 gene. In fact you swear that everything is perfect but you think it is best to add extra copies of it anyway whether there is something wrong with the original or not, and you want to use a viral vector to alter other genes involved in neurodevelopment."

Kennedy nodded. "With all the unknowns we have, I think it is our best shot."

Jeanette opened her mouth to speak and Ted put his hand on her leg, stopping her.

"We appreciate you thinking of us for this pilot program doc, but my philosophy is that if it works, don't fix it, so no thank you."

TWENTY SEVEN

When they drove away from Fetal Fantasies Jeanette turned to look back at Theo who met her inquiring look with one of his own. "That surprised the hell out of me when you spoke in our heads while we are awake, but I guess nothing should surprise us at this point. You are full of them. That last vision of the tree of life shifted everything didn't it?"

Theo winked and graced Jeanette with one of his dimpled smiles and when he "spoke" Ted and Jeanette both heard him in their heads at the same time as if he had vocalized them.

Thank you for declining Doctor Kennedy's offer to manipulate my CHD8 gene. He means well but he's unaware of the bigger forces at work. You created me perfect as I am and the tune-up as he called it would be disastrous to the refinements I am making to this developing body. We have gotten to the point where I can communicate with you more in this waking manner, but you are more receptive in the sleeping state because the synesthetic language that I speak with there is a superior method of communicating. Your experience of the oneness of the cosmic tree of life has facilitated an upward shift in the frequency that we share and opened the door to greater opportunities for communication.

It is imperative that we keep our vocal conversations with baby boy Theo at the illusion of being autistic. As paradoxical as it sounds, the more love we bring into the world, the more dangerous, envious, and hateful people will become. Some will try to silence or control us for exposing the darkness that we bring into the light. These dark forces that you cannot see will bring us greater challenges the more that people become aware of the work we will do, but our inner dialogue with what Mommy calls Cosmic Theo will grow.

I am still struggling to master the developing vocal chords of this little body. I will speak in my little boy voice as much as possible when we talk out loud while my physical body continues to mature, but I will still need breaks when I exert myself communicating so my energies can replenish, especially when my knowledge comes through me from the higher energetic realms of our ancestors.

*Though I still appear as two separate beings, rest assured, I am one and the same. It is simply a matter of time, growth, and adjustment for it all to come into balance.**

Soon after they arrived home Ted and Jeanette "surprised" Theo with a raw vegan chocolate cake made from organic ingredients and natural sweeteners for his third birthday. Both of them wondered if there could be such a thing as a surprise with him because he appeared to not only know what they were thinking, but he often contributed to their thoughts. Theo was genuinely delighted with the cake and the gifts which included video games that required real-time movement to quicken his reflexes and develop more accurate hand-eye coordination. They also gave him more drawing paper, crayons, and exercise dance games that provided added physical benefits.

The doorbell rang when the excitement died down and Ted beamed with an exaggerated smile. "That must be your last surprise. It's not a big deal and I might be more excited about it than you are." He went to the front door and came back escorting a delivery man carrying a bed. At Ted's direction he set it up in place of Theo's crib and took the crib away along with his high chair.

"Theo's growing up," Ted said after the delivery man left. "We should start thinking about setting him up in his own room in one of the spare back rooms."

"Normally I would agree," Jeanette said, "but our relationship and connection between the three of us is far from normal. I think we need to keep him close for awhile to help the dreamwork and that sweet toning he does that brings us all of those magical visions and teachings. When the time *is* right, with Theo's help we can put together a room that fits his needs."

"What do you think, baby Einstein?" Ted asked. "Do you want to stay close to us, or do you want your own room?"

Theo stood from his chair, took Jeanette's hand and pulled her to Ted before taking his hand. Drawing them in close, he wrapped his arms around them and hugged them tight, looking up at them with wide-eyed adoration before ambling off to their bedroom.

"I guess that answers that question," Ted whispered in Jeanette's ear before kissing her.

Later that night when Theo fell into a deep sleep in his new bed Ted and Jeanette climbed into theirs anticipating another synesthetic discussion.

In the predawn hours of that magical time between night and day, words, colors, sounds, and geometries flowed in concert with the expansive heart centered sensations interlaced with Theo's musical chiming voice.

To answer the questions that are bubbling up through your mind, Daddy, we will deal with practical matters during the day with the new communication we have developed, and we will explore the deeper mysteries in this higher frequency communion that we share.

Our love for you has grown beyond what we thought possible and we are open to all you have to share, Ted thought with Jeanette.

They both *felt* rather than saw Theo's expansive grin.

The earth has entered another phase of transformation and what appears to be happening is only a shadow play originating in the deeper levels of consciousness. We are in the midst of an interdimensional struggle between the forces that can liberate human consciousness to its next stage of evolution which you are beginning to experience, and counter forces that strive to contain or control it.

Humanity is at an evolutionary threshold that is being felt in different ways. One of the primary forces is the economic powers that control the global economy by manipulating the press and information systems to create fear which is an ancient method of manipulating human consciousness. When humans are afraid they operate from the reptilian circuitry of their brain resulting in less access to the higher brain centers, a decrease in reason, and an inability to see new possibilities. The present global economic powers have a vested interest in keeping the human race in a lower evolutionary state.

At the monetary level of planetary power, those in control want to remain in control, but the information age is moving the center of control out of their hands, and they are doing everything they can to stop it.

Some of those in economic control of the planet are not who they seem to be. The earth is at a crossing point for galactic and intergalactic intelligence and what happens here will determine future events not only in this galaxy, but in other galaxies as well.

If you collectively pass through this threshold and keep your evolutionary freedom intact you will accomplish great things as a race, but if you are blocked from your advancement by those in power within the religious, social, and corrupt political structures of your society, your race will be imprisoned by the closing of the doors of perception.

Eventually you will free yourselves from this tyranny, but at this point in space and time you have an opportunity to tilt the scales in favor of freedom to usher in an age of worldwide peace that you have never seen before.

The fundamental question facing humanity is whether the earth will become a focus of cooperation and compassion, or a focus of tyranny and limitation?

Some intergalactic intelligences are manipulating the course of events on the earth in the interests of tyranny. They have something to gain through the imprisonment of human consciousness and the human soul. Other intelligences hold the vision of a higher destiny for humanity. We are unable to interfere with your affairs, but we can offer our perspective and our energies to assist you.

*Your greatest weapon against tyranny comes through the harmonic energies of your heart, specifically your open heart. The interference patterns of fear orchestrated by those in power are designed to keep you at a low evolutionary threshold while positive feelings of love, appreciation, and compassion bring you to a higher evolutionary threshold. The more individuals who choose the higher emotional capabilities of human nature, the less effective the interference of this fear on your collective will be.

*Our hope is for you to live in love, appreciation, and compassion for one another so you may bow down, worship, and honor the divinity that lives in each of you. Regardless of what you hear from your chaotic media and those around you, live your life every day as best you can, and learn to grow with these emotions as part of your identity. This will add to the collective atmosphere that counterbalances the interference patterns of fear, and the personal effect will balance your emotional body and bring you increased health and higher evolutionary advances, regardless of what happens to the collective.

*The path of mastery requires the higher pathway even if the collective is moving downward, and whether you recognize yourself as a spiritual master or not, you are, because you are alive in a body localized in time and space during this time of increased pressure.

*You must understand that those who you perceive as tyrants are also masters. What is happening is a confrontation between the masters of life, manifested as open ended evolution, and the masters of death manifesting as close ended evolution. The friction between those who live and strive for higher human destiny and those who live and strive for the limitation and the imprisonment of the human race are complementary evolutionary agents.

*If you demonize those who try to imprison your spirit, then you have fallen into their hands and become their prey. From the higher dimensional aspects of consciousness, this evil is an evolutionary stimulus, for in the world of duality that you exist in, when you have light there is darkness and shadow.

*As you rise to a fuller experience of your mastery you will find yourself in the open hearted harmonics of love, appreciation, and compassion, even to these tyrants. The human capacity to love and cherish each other is one of the most powerful forces in the universe.

*There is another element that relates to the earth as well. Some refer to it as the return of the Cosmic Mother which is also thought of as the balancing of the sun and the moon, the sun being the male fiery energy and its manifestation in the patriarchal society prevalent on the earth at this time.

*The moon represents the feminine, receptive, intuitive connection to the earth and the cosmos. There is an evolutionary shift taking place that will result in a balancing of the masculine and the feminine, and those espousing male dominance will gradually have diminishing numbers.

*These complexities may seem intimidating, but your greatest power is within you and it is a power that can turn the evolutionary tide in your favor. Regardless of how the collective proceeds, it will raise you to higher levels of illumination.

This is the power to love, appreciate, and forgive. Make these a part of your daily life. Your future is not predetermined. It is a swirling mass of uncertainty and possibilities until you make a choice and act, then the forces of the cosmos align with you because you are nothing less than creator gods and goddesses. Know that you are creating your future now, both individually and collectively. There are enough of us on the earth to tip the scales toward a wondrous world of new possibilities.

Theo's angelic voice faded like the diminishing tinkles of a wind chime on the last vestiges of a cool summer breeze as a violet-hued dawn filled the room.

TWENTY EIGHT

Ted and Jeanette sat in the kitchen finishing breakfast with Theo, who sat in a new booster chair.

Ted drained the last of the coffee from his cup and set it down. "I'm still adjusting to not going into work. I don't miss the stress, but I'm getting a little antsy. I don't like the idea of sitting around doing nothing." He ruffled Theo's hair. "How about those more practical matters we were going to talk about?"

Theo slipped down off of his chair and dragged his booster chair behind him, gesturing for Ted and Jeanette to follow him into the dining room where he arranged his drawing paper and crayons in front of him and picked out different colored crayons.

His child's voice filled Ted and Jeanette's minds as if he had vocalized them in normal conversation, only this discussion went on without sound in the external world.

I want to share the teachings of our ancestors in the energetic state we share between sleeping and waking to bring you greater clarity deeper within the three dimensional confines of your day to day existence.

He began drawing diagrams, speaking as he went as if his hands worked independently of his voice while Ted and Jeanette "listened".

It is imperative that you understand. The more love we bring into the world, the more dangerous some people will become. They will try to silence or control us for their own purposes which will bring greater challenges when we least expect it at times of our greatest vulnerability.

"Like Doctor Kennedy's offer to manipulate your genetics," Jeanette said.

Exactly! This inner world we share operates on the principles of integrity and mutual respect.

Theo looked from Ted to Jeanette who both nodded their agreement, then he picked up different colored crayons and went back to his diagrams.

I manifest the guiding voice of our ancestors but you are not obligated to speak what I pass to you unless you are in alignment with what I say. You are under no obligation to act upon anything I suggest. Free will is paramount.

"We're listening," Ted said.

I want to start a clinic with you based on the underlying principles of love and compassion.

He looked up at them to let his words sink in.

*All life is sacred. All beings whether plant, animal, human or otherwise, no matter what form they take deserves respect.

When it comes to a person's health, the whole person, body, mind, and spirit needs to be considered. There is a lot more to being human than limited physical existence. Healing involves more than just the body and mind. An individual's entire being needs to be considered rather than the visible symptoms of their illness.

Theo grabbed a second sheet of paper and continued drawing as he "spoke", expanding the complexity of his diagrams.

The primary focus of our work will be to help others transform their lives with energetic work, special supplements, peptides, and other treatments that we will develop based on my formulas and your knowledge of chemistry, with a focus that envisions all of a person's energetic bodies while supporting the body's innate healing abilities.

Theo dropped his crayons and pushed his papers toward Ted and Jeanette aligning one below the other revealing a crude, but complex diagram showing the interconnections and interactions between humans, plants, and animals, with the plant kingdom shown in green, animals in browns and reds, and humans in combinations of all three colors.

"What do you think we should call this clinic?" Jeanette asked.

Theo grabbed another piece of paper and began drawing again.

How about Temple Nutritionals?

"What made you think of that?" Ted said.

*The human body is a temple and everything that goes into it is an offering to divinity. Together with the knowledge I can access and your chemistry skills we can create remedies and diagnose sicknesses which will raise the vibration of anyone we treat.

Raising their vibration will be reflected back to them by whoever they come in contact with bringing a positive influence on the collective consciousness that will trigger an increase in its frequency.

Theo drew a crude detailed drawing of the human body with lines and arrows indicating measurements pointing to proportions at different points throughout it.

The temple of the human body is laid out with mathematical and geometrical structures that demonstrate how our consciousness resides at the center of our awareness where inner meets outer and spirit meets matter.

"Math and geometry, the language you speak the best!" Ted said.

At the core of this perfection is the number one-point-six-one-eight known as the divine proportion called phi.

The human body is phi-designed throughout, proving that humans were all created using the phi design. Aside from the perfect genome you gave me, Doctor Kennedy and everyone else at Fetal Fantasies are equally fascinated with my body both inner and outer, which is geometrically perfect as well.

Theo traced the length of the body he had drawn along a line through its center with his finger, stopping at its navel where he wrote in the number 1.618 before looking up at Ted and Jeanette to make his point.

When the distance between the navel and the foot is taken as 1 unit, the height of a human being is equivalent to phi.

He drew more lines and arrows adding in the same number pointing to each place, demonstrating as he went.

The distance between the shoulder line and the top of the head and the head length, the distance between the navel and the top of the head, and the distance between the shoulder line and the top of the head, the distance between the navel and knee, the distance between the knee and the end of the foot are all phi.

He looked up and held his arm across his chest pointing to each place as he narrated.

The distance between the fingertip and the elbow, the distance between the wrist and the elbow are also phi.

He pointed at parts of his face indicating different distances.

The width of the two front teeth in the upper jaw over their height is phi. The width of the first tooth from the center to the second tooth is phi as is the length of the face to the width of the face, the distance between the lips and where the eyebrows meet, the length of the nose, the length of the face, and the distance between the tip of the jaw and where the eyebrows meet, as well as the length of the mouth and the width of the nose, the width of the nose and the distance between the nostrils, and the distance between the pupils and the distance between the eyebrows.

The more symmetric the face, the more beautiful it is perceived as being because of phi and it can be defined for both genders and all races, giving power to the mathematical association between beauty and truth.

Every physical attribute of a human being is geometrically definable in three dimensions according to the cosmic laws of geometry. The divine proportion also applies to the fourth dimension of time.

He slid his first drawing aside and using a green crayon he drew a crude rendition of a plant viewed from above showing its leaves spread out in a spiral.

The spiraling leaf pattern follows a sequence called phyllotaxis where each successive leaf grows at the golden angle allowing it to get maximum exposure to sunlight.

Finally, he drew a spiraling ladder that Ted and Jeanette both recognized.

*On a molecular level the DNA molecule is based on phi. It measures thirty four angstroms long by twenty one angstroms wide for each full cycle of its double helix spiral. Thirty four and twenty one are numbers in what you call the Fibonacci series and their ratio approximates phi.

*Not only is the human body a temple, but every aspect of reality that we observe and experience is a temple that reflects the great mystery within us that we are a part of within the great mystery that surrounds us.

These sacred relationships define the guiding principles behind everything that we will do if you are willing.

Jeanette nodded and Ted let out a low whistle. "You've convinced me. Temple Nutritionals it is!"

TWENTY NINE

After the morning full of drawings and explanations Theo went back to their room. Ted and Jeanette studied his drawings after she looked in on him and saw him sprawled across his new bed, fast asleep.

"That was quite a download," Ted said.

"You're not kidding. My brain hurts!"

"We need to give it time to sink in. I'm starting to get a sense of the big picture that Theo is laying out for us."

"I'm glad you are, because I'm feeling kind of lost in it all."

"I am too but I can sense my subconscious sorting through it the way it does when I struggled with problems in the lab. I feel like the answers are floating just out of reach the way dreams are when I try to remember them."

"I know that feeling all too well."

"The best approach is to forget about the problems and let our subconscious do its thing without trying to force anything."

"So if you are not actively working on solving the problem, what do you do?"

"Walks in nature are the best."

Jeanette looked out the window and saw a darkened cloud cover. "I'm not so sure about the weather but we could take Theo for a walk to the park. He loves it and you haven't been with us there yet. I haven't taken him since that dog attack."

Ted followed her gaze to the window. "That's a good idea as long as we don't get rained on and as long as he doesn't call in his gang of hummingbirds. I'm a little worried about getting the wrong kind of attention."

"That's why I haven't brought him since the dog attack, but it's been awhile now and I got him out of there as fast as I could. All those other moms and kids were freaked out so none of them paid much attention to us. We can go after Theo wakes up from his nap."

Ted looked out the window again. "What if we get rained out?"

"That's what umbrellas are for, silly."

Ted answered with a lopsided half smile and looked up to see Theo come out of the bedroom throwing his hands out wide.

"Let's go to the park!"

Jeanette met Ted and Theo by the front door with the stroller and three umbrellas. Ted walked the few blocks to the park carrying Theo on his shoulders while Jeanette pushed the stroller.

No one else was at the park as darkening clouds gathered making the threat of rain look imminent. As usual Theo ignored the playground and ran for the flower beds. Jeanette looked at Ted giving him an "I told you so," look, then she crossed her arms and sat on a bench patting the spot next to her for Ted to sit down beside her.

They laughed watching Theo run through the flower beds like a happy drunk flapping his arms without trampling on any flowers.

Jeanette took Ted by the hand and led him over to the edge of the flower bed for a closer view. They continued holding hands sharing Theo's joy as he stopped to lean in and breathe in the essences of different flowers. Both of them experienced the essence of each flower while inhaling along with Theo, sensing the subtle tinge of each flower's color growing with each inhale and diminishing with each exhale. Theo whispered to each one while caressing their leaves, stalks, and petals like an attentive lover.

"Theo!" Jeanette called out when the first big drops of rain splattered down. "I hate to take you away from all of your..." She looked to Ted and shrugged. "friends? We're going to get soaked if we stay out here. We better get going."

Theo came running out of the flower bed past Ted and Jeanette and climbed up into his stroller. Ted pushed it and Jeanette opened an umbrella when the downpour came. Theo looked back at them with a huge grin and held his arms out spreading his hands wide, stopping the rainfall in front of and to the sides of them like a tiny Moses parting the Red Sea.

A rain free bubble kept them dry and a path appeared in front of them guiding them all the way home.

"I feel like I'm starting to wrap my mind around how to do what Theo is asking," Ted said as they went through the front door.

You are.

Jeanette blinked and glanced at Ted in mild surprise.

The plans that have been gestating within your subconscious are entirely of your own making, but if you will allow me, I would like to merge my thought stream with yours in a collaborative effort.

Ted nodded. "Sounds like fun!"

Theo smiled and looked from Ted to Jeanette. *In case you were wondering Mommy you are always included in our communication. Even though I'm aligning with Daddy for this part of our plans, you are welcome to contribute any thoughts you have.*

Ted went back to the room that served as his home office and retrieved Theo's drawings and the notes Ted had transcribed including the pictures he had printed out of Theo's Tinker Toy molecules of 5MEO, DMT, LSD, mescaline, serotonin, and the novel molecular constructions of other tryptamines, phenethylamines, and peptides that Ted had never seen before.

He brought them all back to the dining room table where he arranged everything in chronological order ending with the notes and drawings Theo had drawn that morning. "We need to set up a self-contained treatment center with a lab that has compounding abilities where we can create Theo's medicines."

"Are there any legal issues that could arise from the FDA or other regulatory agencies that could cause us problems?" Jeanette asked.

"I already have the licenses and certifications to do this from my research work at Bliss, so we're covered there."

Theo drew a crude outline of a working space, making his thoughts known as he scribbled.

With your assistance I can direct the healing work. We need to hide my presence and preserve the illusion of autism to deflect any suspicions of what we are really doing. It will protect you. At some point we will become targets of the dark forces and the more successful we become the greater the danger.

Jeanette frowned. "Do you really think people will want to stop us from helping people?"

Theo looked up from his work, his eyes locking with Jeanette's in an unwavering gaze that looked too adult for his child's face. *It's inevitable. We have to be ready for when it happens. The brighter we shine, the more the dark will try to control or extinguish the light.*

She shook her head. "Unbelievable!"

Theo pushed his drawing in front of them which consisted of a group of squares joined together in a layout with each box labeled, starting from one marked lab at the center surrounded by others designated as hidden observation room, kitchen, treatment room, and reception area. Each room had smaller blocks within it representing a receptionist's desk for the front, work benches in the lab, tables and chairs in the observation room, and an examination table in the treatment room.

Ted and Jeanette studied it for a few minutes before she asked, "How will we be able to afford all this?"

"I have plenty of stock, options, savings, and other investments from all the time I worked at Bliss. If we work and plan smart we should be able to make this all happen."

"And what should we charge for people who come to us and what about health insurance and other considerations?"

Ted looked to Theo.

Whatever they can afford and if they are unable to pay, then we will not charge them for anything.

"A free clinic?" Jeanette said.

Mother nature never asks for anything but love for all the gifts that she gives us. Only humans put a price on what should be free and this has gotten so far out of control that humanity even pays for water, an abundant source of life that falls from the sky and not only gives us sustenance, it covers seventy one percent of the earth's surface.

THIRTY

Ted and Jeanette went to bed that night and fell into a deep sleep feeling their minds overflowing with thoughts and emotions. It seemed like only a few moments passed before the words, colors, sounds, and geometries flowed into their hearts riding the tinkling sound of Theo's wind chime voice. His communication felt like they had seamlessly picked up their waking discussion coming to them from a deeper source that flowed to them from other realms.

*The energetic field of our Mother Earth is morphing, resulting in incremental surges in its power like a wave that rises and falls. The oscillations are minute and it has a profound effect on human consciousness, specifically within your biological experience. Many are experiencing increasing exhaustion and weariness. These symptoms are caused by movements of energies from deep space as they pass through your galaxy and solar system.

*These pulses are caused by the energetic field of the earth responding to the deep energies from space and it is having a conversation with the cosmos which brings catalysts for spiritual evolution.

*Another symptom of the fluctuations within your energetic fields are alterations in how you hold short term memory which is a function of the energies of your nervous system and that of the earth. Your brain processes information through energetic fields of its own structure and is affected by fluctuations in the earth's larger energy field. You might find yourself speaking a sentence and suddenly the words do not come, or you mix up the words from their normal syntax. In some cases this could be signs of brain disorders which are happening within the larger population at an increasing rate. Escalations in collective short term memory faults will lead humanity to novel situations that can be an opportunity or a curse depending on how you work with it.

*It presents the opportunity to see through the mental matrix of your own creation when your mind is unable to continue the way it used to, but it gives you an opportunity to glimpse behind the veil of perception you have created to keep yourselves separated from things you do not wish to see or experience. These are the *unseen manipulators of the members of your collective reality who hold the corrupt economic and political reins of power*

*These are the forces that resist the impulse for spiritual evolution and are invested in continuing their lies through the misappropriation of information in order to control humanity. Their job is getting more difficult because the disturbances of the earth's energetic field creates gaps in the creation of realities projected by the human mind. Those who work to manipulate you have vast resources at their command, but they cannot control the energetic field of the earth.

*The impulses affecting the earth's field comes from beyond their locus of influence. The disturbances of the earth's field will continue to increase over the next several years. Those of you who are sensitive will feel this most intensely. The majority of humanity will be affected by it in ways they are not consciously aware of.

*As energetic beings you can form a conscious energetic relationship with the earth's core by understanding that you are immersed in its energetic field. By going into resonance with the core of the earth you can become energetically stabilized.

*The earth is a conscious being who can reveal herself to you in ways that can't be described. Your culture does not have a language for this and you have been manipulated and controlled to insure that you do not have an awareness of it because it is one of your greatest strengths. I have been exposing you to glimpses of this through synesthetic visons like the one you are presently experiencing.

*By entering into resonance with the core of the earth you become more aware of her as a conscious being and through this link you experience a profound connection within the midst of the evolving chaos.

*When you come to your senses in this manner you are less controllable by the dark forces that control humanity through misinformation, manipulation, and mind control. Forming a direct conscious relationship with the earth's core also allows you to bypass life negating technologies.

*You will be in resonance with the core of the earth simply by knowing it which will impart a sense of stability in the midst of burgeoning chaos and it will awaken your senses by bringing you into a greater conscious relationship to our earth mother allowing you to see through the lies with greater clarity.

*Consciousness can extend instantaneously anywhere in time and space and by extending your consciousness to the galactic core you will stabilize your relationship to the galaxy. When you are in relationship to the earth's core and the core of the galaxy you will be able to ride the waves of energy from deep space with a greater degree of mastery making you less controllable, harder to hypnotize, and you will have the odd experience of waking up while most around you stay asleep.

Your connection to Mother Earth is affected by thought and intention. All it takes to extend your connection into the earth and into the cosmos is the power of your intention.

The colors and patterns ended like someone had turned off a switch when Theo's voice stopped and Ted and Jeanette's eyes opened to the gray light of dawn.

THIRTY ONE

With Jeanette's help and Theo's direction Ted found a modest office building with a storefront on Santa Monica Avenue in Ocean Beach, known as O.B. to the locals. After negotiating a lease they ordered equipment and supplies and furnished a small lab beside an adjoining room furnished like a cozy apartment with a fully stocked kitchen, tables, computers, chairs, and other amenities, as well as a sleeper couch that opened up into a bed. A large one way mirror formed the better part of one wall beside a treatment room where Theo could observe patients without being seen.

One wall of the large storefront had been fitted with shelves and a few small aisles at right angles for over the counter sales of custom made supplements and treatments for common ailments, all based on Theo's nature based formulas.

They filled the other half of the storefront with potted plants, chairs, couches, and a receptionist's desk. A large mural of the Ocean Beach pier seen from Newport Avenue with palm trees in the foreground covered one wall and smaller nature themed prints hung on the back wall.

Once they moved in and stocked the lab Ted spent weeks following Theo's formulas to create unique peptides, ointments, nootropics, salves, ointments, and other organic plant based concoctions. Jeanette busied herself setting up a computer network, email, inventory, and a web page with an online order form for supplements, then she filed for a business license, permits, and other state, city, and county paperwork.

When everything fell into place they had a small celebration with the three of them instead of a grand opening, ending it with Ted hanging a banner above the doorway that said TEMPLE NUTRITIONALS CLINIC - OPEN FOR BUSINESS while Jeanette watched from below, holding Theo's hand.

"Shouldn't we do some advertising to let people know that we are open?" Jeanette said after Ted came down from the ladder and stood with his hands on his hips looking up at the banner.

Theo looked up at them, grinning. "We don't need to. People will come."

"But how will they know if we don't…"

Theo's smile grew wider and Ted smirked.

Jeanette shook her head. "Never mind."

The following morning passed without anyone coming through the door until mid-day when a ragged looking homeless man wearing a tattered trench coat parked his shopping cart full of junk outside the front door and pressed his sunburned face up against the window looking from side to side like a vintage cat clock with moving eyes.

"Shit!" Jeanette muttered. "This is off to a great start. Leave it to O.B."

She held her breath when he pushed open the door and shambled in mumbling to himself before shouting, "Mother fucker! I'm going to kick the shit out of somebody, cut their throat, gut them, and rip their heart out!"

He stopped and stared at Jeanette with bloodshot eyes. The stench of piss and vomit permeated the room. He looked like a scarecrow with a patchy beard, greasy hair that stood up from his head in tufts, and two of his front teeth were missing. His ripped jeans were covered in dark stains and his toes poked out from holes in his worn sneakers.

Her heart rose in her throat when he started toward her until she "heard" Theo's toning in her mind and the man froze as if he had run into an invisible wall, reminding Jeanette of the day at the park with Theo and the mangy dog.

His expression went from anger to confusion, then it became expressionless and his words came softer while he spoke haltingly in measured tones, on the verge of tears.

"I'm so sorry. I'm not right. Not right. I don't know what to do. The voices won't stop. Won't leave me alone."

The fear that gripped Jeanette dissolved into compassion and she found herself sobbing, not knowing what to do. The man dropped down to his knees and looked up at her with wide puppy dog eyes. "Nobody can help me," he whispered. Tears streamed down his cheeks and he put his hands together as if praying while looking down.

Ted came out from the back room and put his hands on the man's shoulders calming him, then he pressed a bottle of pills into the man's hands and slipped a bottle of water into a pocket of his trench coat. "Take one of these every day until they're gone."

The man looked up at Ted and looked down at the bottle. "I don't have any money."

Ted waved his hand. "Don't worry about it."

Curious shoppers drifted in and out for the next few weeks to peruse the shelves of over the counter offerings, but they came sporadically and some days no one came in at all. Online sales trickled in, but they were not much better than what they sold in the store.

A few weeks later a lanky man sporting a neatly trimmed beard and haircut dressed in new jeans, a clean flannel shirt, and expensive walking shoes came through the door holding hands with a stooped over homeless woman with long stringy dishwater colored hair, faded blue flannel pajama bottoms with teddy bears on them, and a blanket wrapped around her neck. She could have been anywhere from mid to late thirties to early sixties. Her rank odor filled the room the moment the door opened and she muttered to herself.

Jeanette puzzled over the pair thinking, an odd couple if I ever did see one.

The man looked from the woman to Jeanette with bright blue eyes full of hope.

"Can I help you sir?"

"You don't remember me," he said in a soft spoken voice, "but I'm Scott. Scott Olsen."

She shook her head. "I'm sorry, I don't. Should I?"

"I came in about a month ago lost and out of my mind and you gave me some pills that brought me clarity for the first time in I don't know how long, and thanks to you I have gotten my life back."

Jeanette's hand went to her mouth and she found herself speechless.

"That was *you?*"

He smiled through perfect teeth. "*Was!*"

She gasped. "I can't believe it."

"Believe it." Scott reached into the top pocket of his shirt and came out with an Alcoholics Anonymous sobriety coin which he proudly held up. "No more crack, fentanyl, or heroin. No more madness!" He slipped the coin back into his pocket and lowered his head. "I hope you don't mind, but I've brought my friend. I think you can help her too."

"Well, I…"

"She's suffering from dementia," Ted said coming in from the back room.

Scott stood up straight and took Ted's hand in both of his and shook it vigorously while tears streamed down his cheeks. "I can't thank you enough for what you did for me. Can you help my friend Patty?" He pulled out a small wad of bills. "I'll pay for her and I'd like to pay for what you gave me."

"I'll tell you what," Ted said. "Instead of paying me, would you be willing to look after her for a bit?"

"What would you like me to do?"

Ted gestured with his head for Scott to bring Patty back to the examination room where Scott helped her sit up on the table.

"She's going to need a little help for awhile."

With Scott looking on, Ted showed him how to apply a salve to Patty's temples. She brightened some with the first application.

Ted handed Scott a large bottle of pills and the container of salve. "She needs to take one of these pills three times a day and you need to rub the salve on her temples the way I showed you here in the morning and at night. Can you do that?"

"Yessir."

"Does she have a place to stay?"

"She has a spot in a shelter."

"Good!"

Scott snapped to attention and saluted Ted. "At your service. Should I bring Patty back when the pills run out?"

Ted winked. "If you feel the need but I don't think you'll have to."

Scott held out the money and Ted pushed his hand away.

"Once Patty gets cleaned up buy her some new clothes."

THIRTY TWO

Scott returned a little over a month later with a barely recognizable Patty clinging to his arm smelling of jasmine. She had a stylish bob cut accented by gold hoop earrings and she wore faded jeans stitched with colorful embroidery, a flower print blouse, and a delicate gold chain around her neck that accented her earrings. Scott put his arm around her and she hugged him tight around the waist, bringing a lump of happiness to Jeanette's throat.

"We don't need anything," Scott said. "We just wanted to thank you for saving our lives. We got financial assistance from the county and we moved in to an apartment together."

Ted came out from the back room and shook Scott's hand, then he leaned in and gave Patty a hug. Scott reached into his pocket and pulled out a wad of twenty dollar bills.

Pay it forward, popped into Ted and Jeanette's heads and Ted pushed Scott's hand back.

"Pay it forward, Scott. Help others the way you helped Patty and that will be more than enough payment."

Scott hugged Patty closer.

"We're more than happy to do that," she said in a rich velvety voice, "but be careful what you ask for."

Ted chuckled, hugged them both, and looked back at Jeanette while Theo's words flowed through both of them and out of Ted's mouth, aligning with his own thoughts and feelings. "We hope you find continued happiness and joy in your hearts and that you spread that joy to those around you and share the love any way you can."

"Bless you," Patty said.

More homeless came in the following weeks and a line began to form outside the door, many of them arriving in wheelchairs and walking out under their own power after a massage with one of Theo's many salves.

Ted brought each one back to the examination room where Theo remained behind the scenes diagnosing the maladies and treatments in telepathy. Online sales picked up, but the expense of helping the homeless who had no money outweighed any income, further draining their dwindling finances.

"We're almost broke," Jeanette said in hushed tones one afternoon when no one had come to the clinic. She and Ted sat in the back lounge while Theo napped on the couch. "I don't know how much longer we can do this and keep paying the bills."

There's no need to worry about finances. The love and generosity we've been giving will come back to us.

Ted blinked and his head jerked back like he'd been hit. He and Jeanette looked over at Theo still sleeping on the couch.

Our connection has grown stronger through the work we share and my abilities are improving along with the increasing mastery of my maturing body. Money is the least of our worries. The more good we do and the more people discover the positive results we are experiencing, the greater the challenges that will be coming our way.

Jeanette frowned. "I'm still struggling with that. It's hard for me to understand how people would want to interfere with something good and positive."

Ted sighed and rested his hand on her back. "Unfortunately it's human nature."

The greater truth is that the human race is motivated by fear, greed, and envy bred and cultivated by the dark forces that struggle to keep everyone buried in ignorance. Some resistance will be directed straight at us and other impediments will be more subtle, coming from places we least expect.

"Like Doctor Kennedy's offer of manipulating your genome," Jeanette said.

Yes, and we haven't heard the last of that. Their attempts to disrupt our work and the loving energy we cultivate will become more brazen and desperate. They see us as an infection to be rooted out.

"Just like they did to me at Bliss Pharmaceuticals," Ted said.

"With all of these dark forces lining up against us," Jeanette said, "is it even worth the effort? Is everything we do going to make any difference?"

One flame can light a darkened room and one spark can burn down an entire forest. In our case, the brighter we burn, the more the darkness will encroach, but the greater the darkness, the brighter the light.

"It's a paradox," Ted added.

Jeanette breathed in and let out a long sigh. "If we continue to shine brighter and the darkness grows stronger and comes from places unseen, what will happen if it overwhelms us?"

When Theo didn't respond Ted and Jeanette looked to the couch. Theo's eyes flickered open and he sat up, looking intently at them.

I don't mean to alarm you but that outcome will be inevitable at some point.

Her eyes grew wide and her mouth dropped open. "You mean we're doomed to failure?"

Ted reached over and put a reassuring hand on her shoulder.

It might look that way on the surface but no matter what happens to us, not only are there bigger forces at work, but we are instruments of love and the forces of the light of the cosmos are on our side. We will be persecuted, but the sparks from the fire of our love will spread to those with open hearts.

They fell into silence both within their minds and without.

Finally, Jeanette whispered, "We're going to become martyrs by sacrificing ourselves."

Theo's blue eyes brightened and everything around them took on soft rose colored hues. *The veil between life and death in this dream that you think of as life is thinner than you might imagine. Our ancestors who speak through me are enhancing our power and perception which will aid us in our times of need in service of the greater good. This blessing is amplified by the love in our hearts that underlies everything we do. Regardless of what transpires, or what path the great mystery leads us down, know that the unconditional love from the source burns through us and the integrity that it engenders will light the way.*

THIRTY THREE

"You're not going to believe this!" Jeanette squealed from the reception area where she sat in front of the computer.

Ted came scrambling out from the examination room. "What is it, honey? Are you okay?"

She pointed at an order form she had up on the computer screen with a shaking finger. "It's an approved credit card transaction. It has to be a mistake."

Ted leaned over her shoulder and stared at the numbers on the screen next to an unused category of the order form.

DONATION: $50,000.00

He frowned and shook his head, then pointed at an icon that said ORDER NOTES. "Click on that."

Jeanette clicked and a note came up.

> Please accept this small token of our appreciation for the miraculous healing work you did in bringing our long lost brother Scott back to our family after we had given up all hope of ever having him back. No high-priced doctors, psychologists, therapists, rehabilitation clinics, treatment centers, addiction specialists, or any other mental health professionals have been able to help him. Every one of them failed where you succeeded and you did it for free with no strings attached.
> Our family will forever be in your debt.
> God Bless!
> Mary Nobles Conrad

Ted let out a low whistle. "Theo was right!"

Theo came out from the back room and stood beside Ted and Jeanette, pulling them in close for a hug. "That's the way love works.

You give it away without expecting anything and it comes back to you in other ways."

Ted picked Theo up and put him between himself and Jeanette and encircled them in a tight hug.

The line of homeless people with shopping carts and wheelchairs outside their door grew longer in the weeks that followed and more donations of varying sizes came in, increasing in proportion to the growing numbers.

Elated by their new found support and burgeoning success, Ted took Theo and Jeanette out for a celebratory dinner at Plant Power Fast Food, Theo's favorite vegetarian restaurant. Theo fell asleep by the time they arrived home, so Ted carried him in to bed and he and Jeanette crawled in to theirs soon after.

Prior to dawn the sweet melodic trills of Theo's toning filled their hearts and minds with expansive thoughts and emotions accompanied by colors, sounds, and geometries in a multilayered synesthetic concert guided by Theo's sweet sounding voice.

*To help overcome your fear of death or any assaults from the darkness coming our way I want to share a glimpse of the realities that transcend the veil between life and death to give you a sense of the vastness that our ancestors reach out to us from. This nonverbal blessing is amplified by the love we share from the source that burns within our hearts and minds to light the way on this path that the great mystery is leading us down.

Above all, remember; fear is contraction and love is expansion.

The mental, emotional, psychospiritual energies and imagery intensified like an evolving map modulated by Theo's singsong voice in an inexplicable multisensory way that swelled Ted and Jeanette's hearts.

*Consciousness is like a gas that will fill any container in the form of that container and it is as ubiquitous as the universe, subsuming and interweaving with the fabric of matter and energy. This fabric is a naturally evolving pattern that the cosmos are woven out of. We can focus on any part of it, minuscule or cosmic, depending on our orientation, environment, expectations, and fears.

*We create reality, often as co-creations, but we are responsible for what we create, whether we are happy or sad. This is our design and we are not alone. We exist as an integral part of all life, including plants and animals that all breathe, pulsate, and vibrate in a multi-level fabric of magnificent designs and patterns that surrounds and enters us, which we are a part of.

*Within this cosmic web there is no other, no subjective and objective, and no duality; just holographic structures for teaching ourselves sacred lessons that we have known but forgotten.

Our ancestors are also our inner Gods, teaching us from the well-springs of unity, intimating, winking, indicating, and speaking to our inner beings with lessons of love, healing, inspiration, and creation so we can enter into the temple of the source where everything is composed of magical crystalline beauty.

Ted and Jeanette felt the sensation of moving forward expanding further into their visions, becoming fully absorbed within them with no differentiation. Multi-hued grids flexed and twisted while carnivals of colorful patterns and beings unlike anything Ted or Jeanette had ever seen peered in followed by arcane hieroglyphs with hauntingly familiar, yet indecipherable aspects. Floating spheres of lambent iridescence descended through diaphanous veils of woven infinity that passed away leaving a poignant feeling of an incomprehensible ache to find the meaning behind it all.

In this place below the surface levels of chaotic, subliminal, purposeful disinformation, we can move toward truth, free from contradictory morals and values. Outside the labyrinths in our minds below our myths and the fragmented communication called language, we can move deeper toward truth. Below our culture and the conditioning embedded in our minds and egos we can penetrate the limits of perception and ride on the energetic impulses at the center of our hard-wired biological construction until we find ourselves at one with the mystery of this ineffable play of joy, creation, and energy.

Source.

The mystic touchstone that heals, renews, and returns us to the beginning. Only those truly seeking self-realization have the courage to pass through all of these veils into the center.

We live in a maze of conditioned responses and conflicting directives because our programmed biocomputer functions to produce a nonstop wash of unconscious noise. Waves of voices, fears, thoughts, plans, and ambitions washes over us constantly and we follow these directives of our mind like robots. We don't think. We are thought by our minds struggling within a swamp of impulses and thoughts that never let us rest.

Our task is to re-emerge from the swamp of forgetfulness and distraction to be reborn in consciousness, but in this rebirth there are no landmarks, limits, boundaries, or road signs. We have to traverse this nether landscape by accessing intuition and observing all that happens guided by this penetrating vision by following our hearts, listening intently for the single true voice that sings out from a unified heart and mind beyond the infernal chorus of conditioned commands and conflicting directives.

At the moment when Ted and Jeanette felt as if they could not withstand any more intensity their surroundings faded.

You have glimpsed the doorways to the personal temple of your own sacredness that opens into the vastness of your personal souls and their intrinsic connection to the universal soul that gives you a transitory experience of this underlying unity of the interconnection of all things. It is a song that rings and reverberates through the lens of the creator to reveal to you that you were born to have this experience of the sacred, the joyous, the beauty, and the blessing of being alive in the arms of the great mystery that lies outside the known, beyond simple logic.

The colors, sounds, geometries, and what remained of their synesthetic overload dissipated into something similar to white noise, leaving behind the melodic trills of Theo's chiming voice.

THIRTY FOUR

Two Black and White San Diego Police cruisers pulled up in front of Temple Nutritionals late one morning and a cop got out of each one. Jeanette watched them as they met at the front door for a brief chat before coming in. A middle-aged heavy set hispanic man with thick eyebrows over wide brown eyes and a bushy mustache came in first. His silver nametag said PEREZ.

A big chested younger cop with muscular arms that strained the seams of his shirt followed Perez in. A few inches taller, his red hair, brush cut, and narrow blue eyes said military, probably an ex-marine. His nametag said COLLINS.

Jeanette stood from her desk. "Good morning officers. Can I help you?"

"We're looking for the manager," Perez said.

Jeanette nodded. "You're talking to one. What can I do for you?"

"We've been watching the activity around here and have had complaints from other businesses about the traffic that comes in and out of here."

"Traffic? I'm not sure what you mean by that. What kind of complaints?"

Collins crossed his arms and rocked back on his heels. "Homeless. We've observed them lining up outside your door and so have your neighbors."

Jeanette frowned and shook her head. "Is there a law against homeless people coming for health and nutritional advice? They are citizens and have rights just like everybody else so I don't understand what the problem is."

"They have been congregating here in growing numbers which arouses suspicion," Perez said, "and they have been seen coming in and walking back out with small packages which gives us reason to suspect that you have been supplying them with drugs."

Jeanette couldn't suppress a short burst of laughter. "You can't be serious."

Collins squinted. "Why would so many of them suddenly be interested in nutrition, and why are more of them coming every day and walking out looking happy? You have to admit, that is pretty suspicious behavior."

Jeanette stifled her anger and held up a hand. "Wait a minute. Let me get this straight. Do you mean to tell me that people are acting suspicious because they look happy?"

Perez glanced over at Collins, then turned back to Jeanette. "If everything is on the level as you say it is, do you mind if we take a look around?"

"Do you have a warrant?" Ted said coming out from the back room.

Collins snorted. "No, but if you want to be uncooperative…"

"We're selling nutritional supplements and homeopathic remedies," Ted cut in, "and everything we dispense here is done under licensing granted by state and federal agencies."

"Can we see them?" Perez said.

"This is ridiculous," Ted said. "You're harassing us because your suspicious that homeless people are coming here and leaving happy. Sure, you can see them."

Perez brightened.

"After you show me your warrant," Ted continued.

Perez's face dropped into a frown, Collins turned red, and Ted glared at them for an uncomfortable moment before Theo toddled out from the back room and looked up at Perez, wide eyed and innocent.

"Hi Mr. policeman!"

Perez broke into a grin and Collins' expression followed as if a switch had tripped a circuit that lit them up in sequence. Perez crouched down. "Hello there, little man," he said in a welcoming tone.

"I'm glad you came by to make sure we are safe," Theo said.

The expression on Perez's face grew softer as if he were a different person. "We're just doing our job and we're happy that you feel that way."

He rose and tapped a smiling Collins on the shoulder. "Come on Steve, everything's under control here." He turned away and headed for the door saying, "You folks enjoy the rest of your day now."

Ted shook his head and he and Jeanette looked to Theo who still smiled.

They're gone now, but that was only the beginning. If not them, others will come.

"You certainly gave them an attitude adjustment," Ted said.

I did, but it's not going to last.

"You stopped them with your mind just like you did with the dog and with our friend Scott." Jeanette said.

It was harder with them. Scott and the dog were operating out of rage while the police were more calculated and directed in their thinking, so my appearance combined with the thoughts and emotions I projected took more energy. They're gone for now but more will be coming.

Jeanette stared down at the floor shaking her head. "They said they were suspicious because homeless people were leaving here happy which is absurd. Can't they see and can't they realize that we're helping people transform themselves?"

That's what concerns me the most.

THIRTY FIVE

More homeless came and the demands on Theo's time and energy grew in proportion making it necessary to move things at a faster pace. The healing miracles coming through him became more apparent with increasing frequency, making Ted and Jeanette wonder if the medicines they had created were even necessary.

With severe cases Theo came out from the observation room and stood behind the person being treated without them being aware of his presence. The first time this happened Jeanette led a stooped over woman with long matted brown hair and a ratty blanket over her shoulders into the examination room. She talked to herself non-stop and smelled like urine and rotting garbage.

Theo put his hands on her back and to Jeanette's amazement her rank odor disappeared while she rose up into a more erect position like the plants Theo had touched. Her head came up the same way the flowers had and her cloudy blue eyes brightened and grew clear.

"Oh my God," she whispered. Tears flowed when she looked from Ted to Jeanette and back again. "The angels have answered my prayers!"

Ted and Jeanette looked at each other feeling as amazed as the woman. They looked behind her to where Theo had been, equally shocked to discover that he was no longer there.

A few days later a man came in in a similar unhygienic state, teeming with lice. Ted and Jeanette kept their distance not only from his stench, but from the infestation. Theo came out from the observation room and stood behind the man who remained unaware of him and put his hands on the man's back. Like the woman, he became rejuvenated and the stench and lice disappeared at Theo's touch, then in the next moment he was gone.

They still prescribed medicines, but the ones who came in suffering in the most incoherent states received hands on treatments followed by Theo requiring deeper sleep and longer naps. In less severe cases Theo diagnosed maladies telepathically to Ted while napping.

While things were in full swing, Doctor Kennedy called to remind Ted and Jeanette of Theo's upcoming annual checkup.

Late on a Friday afternoon Theo sat quietly on an examination table in the Fetal Fantasies clinic after another battery of tests for his fourth year birthday checkup. Ted and Jeanette sat close together on the other side of the room mentally holding their breath anticipating what Kennedy might say.

Kennedy sat across from them studying an iPad with his forehead wrinkled in thought. "Like his last checkup Theo has every indication of being a perfectly healthy four year old and there is no trace of abnormalities, but his lack of developing speech and other indicators including the anomalies in his chromosomes confirm my diagnosis of autism, and as I said before, my colleagues all concur."

Ted and Jeanette looked at each other and Ted spoke up.

"Obviously his speech is still delayed, but he hasn't shown any repetitive behaviors."

Kennedy nodded. "Have you put any more effort into socializing him?"

"We haven't made a lot of effort with other kids," Jeanette said. "We've been really busy getting a new business off the ground."

"But he's a big hit with the adults," Ted added, thinking about all the hands on healings Theo had done.

"Have you given any more thought to the pilot program I mentioned?"

Ted and Jeanette shook their heads no together and Kennedy's brow furrowed deeper.

"I thought you should know that the pilot phase has been very successful. Since we have seen those results from other clinics and laboratories there has been a lot of discussion about making it mandatory."

"Mandatory?" Jeanette said.

Kennedy held up both his hands. "They've developed a new technique using a low voltage electrogenetic interface that can send electrical currents to activate a response in a targeted gene, in this case Theo's CHD8 gene, the one that ties mutations to a broad spectrum of molecular and cellular defects. We're using an integrated approach that alters genome regulation, gene expression, neuron function, and connections to other key genes that play a role in autism."

Ted and Jeanette both shook their heads in a vigorous no again while Kennedy continued reading from his iPad.

They glanced over at Theo and saw him shaking his head no along with them while he spoke in their minds. *That would wipe out all of the psychospiritual connections and programming I have spent this life creating, essentially wiping me clean in a hard reset. Eventually they will force the issue on us. It is inevitable.*

Jeanette put her hand to her mouth while Kennedy continued reading, oblivious to their reactions.

"Electronic and biological systems function in radically different ways and are for the most part incompatible due to the lack of a functional communication interface. Biological systems are considered analog, programmed by genetics, updated slowly through evolution and controlled by ions flowing through insulated membranes, while electronic systems are digital, programmed by updatable software controlled by electrons flowing through wires.

"The two meet in a direct current-actuated technology using this electrogenetic interface to connect the digital with the analog using electric current to activate specific gene responses allowing us to control gene expression by bridging the electronic and genetic worlds." Kennedy looked up from his iPad with an expectant look on his face. "We can precisely edit and target specific genes to stimulate Theo's genetic code to correct any ongoing mutations centered around his CHD8 gene."

"But you still say he's perfect," Jeanette said.

"Yet the autism persists and his behavior and our lab results lead us to believe it is mutating further. By correcting his genome we can most likely restore normal function and alleviate the behavioral and cognitive symptoms he has been exhibiting."

Jeanette shook her head. "I'm sorry, but I still don't understand. All of your tests say that Theo is healthy and perfect and you admit that you can't find any traces of abnormalities."

"But his behavior says differently."

"Maybe he needs more time."

"I might be inclined to agree, but he is now four years old and it's getting a little late in the game." Kennedy snorted. "I don't understand why you are so resistant to this. You should think of it like a tune-up the way they do recalls on cars when they have problems missed in production."

Jeanette scrunched up her face. "You talk like he's a broken piece of machinery."

Kennedy set down the iPad. "He's not a machine, but he *is* a child of technology. In this case, extra copies of a healthy CHD8 gene without any mutation would be added using a viral vector that will return stem cells to a normal rate of activity and synaptic communication, resulting in restored function. The CHD8 upgrade would alter other genes implicated in autism and selectively influence the ones involved in neurodevelopmental disorders."

Jeanette crossed her arms. "I'm sorry Doctor Kennedy, I'm not trying to be difficult here, but I still don't get it. Is Theo's CHD8 gene faulty or not?"

"We don't know for sure, but we think it's mutating and it appears to be the source of these developmental problems."

"What if there is nothing wrong with this CHD8 gene?" Ted said.

"Then we would simply be adding a healthy gene to a healthy gene." Kennedy nodded. "With all the unknowns we are facing, I think it is our best shot."

Ted took Jeanette by the hand and stood, pulling her up alongside him and Theo hopped down from the examination table. "We appreciate all that you have done doc," Ted said, "and we appreciate your concern as well as your thoroughness, but where I come from we have an old saying." He reached out and pulled Theo in hugging him close. "If it works, don't fix it."

THIRTY SIX

After a long day at Temple Nutritionals and a satisfying dinner Ted plopped down on the living room couch beside Theo with Jeanette on the other side of him, and picked up the remote. "Maybe we can find a movie or something so we can forget about work for awhile."

He tapped the on button and froze, still pointing the remote when the local news came onscreen.

"Oh my God, it's Scott!" Jeanette gasped.

I've been expecting this, Theo stated matter-of-factly.

Images of a homeless encampment filled the screen behind a middle-aged conservative looking man at the news desk. Rows of tents lined the street and groups of homeless conversed while others arranged their possessions and pushed shopping carts bulging with large black Hefty bags, clothes, sleeping bags, blankets, and assorted junk.

An announcer's voice said, "News Ten's Sara Johnston is on the scene with a heartwarming story unfolding on the streets of San Diego."

The newsroom cut away to a stylishly dressed red-haired woman with long legs and a pixie cut wearing a tight dress that matched the green of her eyes. She stood holding a microphone at the front of a crowd beside Scott Olsen and a few other people that Ted and Jeanette recognized as former visitors to the clinic.

SCOTT OLSEN – ORGANIZER OF FINDING OUR WAY HOME filled the blue banner at the bottom of the screen.

"Sara Johnston reporting on a small miracle unfolding in the Midway District." She held the microphone out to Scott. "Can you tell us what's happening here?"

A smiling Scott pointed to a panel truck where a group of people handed out food, water, blankets, and other necessities. "All of our volunteers were once homeless themselves, but through the kindness and generosity of others we managed to get our lives back, so we wanted to pay it forward to the community."

"That's an impressive amount of supplies you have there. Where do you get the funding for it?"

Scott looked down a moment and looked up again. "We have some generous benefactors, many of them friends and family who support our efforts. We all know that homelessness is a massive problem especially here in San Diego, not only because of our milder weather, but our closeness to the border with Mexico brings more every day. We realize that we are only making a small difference here, but we are making a difference. We hope that others with more resources will be willing to help not only here, but everywhere else where help is needed."

A toll free number scrolled across the blue banner at the bottom of the screen.

Sara looked directly at the camera which zoomed in on her for a closeup. "Anyone willing to donate or assist with this wonderful program can call the number at the bottom of the screen."

She turned back to Scott and the camera zoomed out. "One last question. What inspired you to start such an ambitious outreach?"

She held out the microphone to Scott.

"Don't say it," Ted said through clenched teeth.

Scott beckoned his helpers closer. "We owe it to the magic, compassion, and healing miracles of Temple Nutritionals in Ocean Beach, the people who gave us our lives back."

"Shit," Ted muttered, "We're going to be swamped."

Sara turned back to the camera. "This is Sara Johnston reporting live for News Ten from the Midway district."

A commercial for SeaWorld followed.

Ted and Jeanette looked to Theo who had fallen asleep.

Jeanette looked at Ted and smirked. "He doesn't seem to be too concerned."

"If I didn't know better, I'd say he planned it."

"I wouldn't go that far, but he did say it was inevitable, so he must have a sense of what's going to happen."

"There's nothing we can do about whatever is going to happen except wait and see. I'm beat and I have a feeling that tomorrow's going to bring more surprises. Let's hit the hay."

Ted picked up Theo and carried him into the bedroom. Soon after he and Jeanette crawled into bed and fell into a deep sleep. When dawn broke the next morning Theo's melodic trills filled their hearts and minds with thoughts, emotions, colors, sounds, and geometries.

The news report with Scott is a catalyst that triggered a new phase of our work so things will be getting more uncomfortable going forward.

We're dedicated to following through on whatever path you take us on, Ted thought.

You're doing a lot of good work and we're happy to be part of it, Jeanette added.

Thank you. When we connect and share energetic space we are one mind that is part of a lineage that comes through me from our ancestors. When I speak they are speaking through me and I surrender to their guidance with no expectations so they can infuse me in a conscious merging of our energies within the same vibration.

I am fully merged with them and pass along the unconditional love that they emanate. In this alignment I surrender myself to the mystery, not knowing where it will lead me or how things will transpire, only that it will turn out how it is supposed to because it is part of something bigger. I accept the outcome no matter how it may appear at that time. It is always headed toward serving the greater good.

That's all we ever wanted, Ted thought. Relieving people of their pain was the motivation that drove me to my drug research.

We are of the same mind, Jeanette thought. I have always supported Ted in everything he has done.

In the difficult times that are coming I would like to speak through you in the same way that our ancestors speak through me to provide guidance. If you are willing the voice of our ancestors can speak through you. It will be your voice as your hearts, minds, and spirits will be in full resonance.

We're more than happy to do whatever is needed, Ted and Jeanette thought.

Though intangible to normal perceptions they felt Theo's smile.

We've already had a visit from the police but that was only a hint of what is to come. Our real threat will come in greater numbers from self identified people who operate through the facade of religion. Though often well meaning they are unconscious puppets that I think of as sleepers in the service of the dark forces that are struggling to exploit the good work we do all in the name of God.

They have convinced themselves that they are in service to the greater good, Jeanette thought.

*It's a classic example of how the dark manipulates their followers in the guise of doing good with a subtle twist of the truth. They believe they are in service to a higher power when they are serving themselves. It's the opposite of what we do. They serve selfishness and we serve selflessness. Their supporters follow their prophets so they do not have to take responsibility for themselves. They honestly believe that the more they give and follow the directives of their prophets, the more saved they become *through their monetary contributions in the misguided belief that their saviors will absolve them of their sins. This fallacy directs their energies outward away from their hearts where the real work needs to be done.*

These sleepers are led by charismatic puppet leaders in service to their prophets, but the reality is that they are out for themselves and have been duped into thinking that the more money they get for God, the greater their reward which is the ultimate self-serving agenda.

So you are saying that these charismatic leaders are in service to their *profits*, as in making money, Ted thought.

Theo's giggles faded like diminishing wind chimes alongside the disappearing colors, sounds, and geometries of their visions while a deep red sunrise crested the horizon.

THIRTY SEVEN

Three black and whites with flashing blue lights greeted them in front of their clinic when they turned the corner off of Sunset Cliffs Boulevard onto Santa Monica Avenue toward Ocean Beach. The line of homeless people now snaked all the way to the end of the block.

"Let the circus begin," Ted said as they drove by, skirting a crowd of reporters, television cameras, photographers, and onlookers, all held back by barricades connected by black and yellow crime scene tape around the front of the building. Two cops stood guarding the front door while others held back the growing crowd. Ted drove around the block and pulled into a parking space behind the building.

"We'll keep Theo out of the limelight," Ted said while unlocking the back door. "Jeanette, you can come out with me, and I'll…" He looked to Theo. "*We'll* do the talking."

Theo hopped up on the chair by the reception desk and Ted and Jeanette went to the front door. "Here we go," Ted said pulling it open.

The two cops guarding the door looked back at them while cameras flashed and the crowd moved in closer to the barricades.

"We'll stay here by the door," Ted said to the cops, "but you can let the reporters in. We'll handle this like a press conference."

An older heavy set cop with a brush cut nodded. "Give me a minute." He took a microphone from his shoulder and had a short discussion, then he waved to the other cops to let the reporters inside the barricade.

Jeanette recognized Sara the red-haired reporter from the previous night's broadcast followed by a cameramen pushing their way to the front of the crowd while being jostled from behind by cameramen from other stations, photographers, and reporters.

She's the one, Theo said in their minds.

Jeanette pointed to Sara and beckoned her forward. Sara's green eyes lit with excitement. She looked behind her and took her cameraman by the hand and pulled him along. Reporters and cameramen from other stations and publications followed, but with the help of the cops, they kept Sara front and center while the others leaned in holding out microphones and snapping pictures. With a nod from Ted, Sara's cameraman switched on his camera and handed her a microphone. She edged in closer to Ted before speaking to the camera.

"This is Sara Johnston on the scene with a follow up report at what is being credited as the source of the Finding Our Way Home phenomenon sweeping Ocean Beach and the Midway District. I'm here with Ted and Jeanette Driscoll, founders of Temple Nutritionals where the homeless have been flocking to experience what are reputed to be miracle cures, all of which have been free of charge. My first question for you Mr. Driscoll is how do you manage to operate and provide care without charging for it?"

Ted cleared his throat and Theo's words flowed through him reflecting his own thoughts. "Our mission here at Temple Nutritionals is to help those in need with natural cures that are abundant in nature." He held his hands out wide. "Our mother earth gives us everything we need freely and abundantly when it is sustainably resourced and properly managed. Like this planet that gives us life we want to follow that example so we are not looking to profit from our work. As a result of our early successes with family members who had been given up as lost to addictions and other mental health issues that drove them to a hard life on the streets, we have some well-to-do patrons who support us out of gratitude for being instrumental in reuniting them with their families."

"And who are these generous supporters?"

Ted wagged his finger. "That is confidential out of respect for their privacy. They don't want attention or praise." He raised his head toward the gathered crowd. "And to be honest neither do we. They simply want to show their gratitude."

"Wow!" Sara said. "That's admirable."

Ted shrugged.

"I understand that you are the former head of research and development at Bliss Pharmaceuticals and that you left a lucrative position there to do this work. How is Bliss connected with the work that you do here? Are they one of your secret sponsors?"

Ted shook his head no. "We have no affiliation with Bliss Pharmaceuticals. What we do here is totally independent of them."

"Can you elaborate a little more on why you left Bliss? I'd imagine they would enjoy having their name connected with such a great community outreach."

"We have no connection to Bliss. I found a new direction I wanted to pursue so we can leave it at that. Temple Nutritionals is an independent entity with no connections or endorsements from any other organizations."

"Temple Nutritionals sounds like it has religious underpinnings. What are your religious beliefs? Do you consider yourself a church?

Ted couldn't suppress his smile from the speed and emotional energy of Theo's response. "Yes."

"So Temple Nutritionals is actually a church like the Hare Krishnas or the Scientologists?"

"Temple Nutritionals is most decidedly *not* a church."

Sara looked to the camera and frowned. "Didn't you just say that you consider yourself to be a church?"

"Temple Nutritionals is not a church. *I* am the church, better still a temple, just like you are. We see the human body as a temple the way the ancients did and we see everything we put into it as an offering to divinity. Not only is the human body a temple, but every aspect of reality that we experience is a temple that reflects the great mystery within us that we are a part of with the great mystery that surrounds us."

Sara's mouth dropped open and her eyes grew wide. "Wow!" Her mouth turned up into a joy filled smile. She looked at the camera. "If everyone is a temple then we wouldn't need any churches."

"That's right! We should all be worshipping each other."

"Wow!" she said again. "What a novel idea. You worship by helping others which is why you don't ask for money. Your treatments are your offering to divinity even if it comes in off the street ragged and dirty."

"That's correct!" Ted pointed toward the line of homeless that led to the clinic door. "Now if you'll excuse us, as you can see we have our work cut out for us."

Sara nodded. "One last question." She turned to the heavy set cop beside Ted. "How is your department dealing with all the extra pedestrian traffic?"

The cop shook his head. "Increasing numbers of homeless are flocking here inundating Ocean Beach with shopping carts, tents, bicycles, and the unsanitary messes they leave behind. We've had a number of complaints and it's created a problem that is straining our resources."

"All the more reason for me to get to work moving them through." Ted turned toward the door and motioned for the first person in the long line of homeless to step into the clinic.

Sara handed Ted her business card. "Thank you for the interview. Please reach out if you feel the need to say more."

THIRTY EIGHT

More donations flooded in after the interview aired as well as requests for more interviews and reporters showed up on a regular basis, but Ted and Jeanette sent them away. Emails and phone calls inundated the clinic and their web page with an escalating slew of offers to be financed, sponsored, and managed by numerous businesses and agencies.

"They're not going to go away," Theo told them one night after dinner. "My communication skills in my growing body continue to develop, but I am still uncomfortable with bigger words and bigger thoughts, so I'll explain it internally."

Theo's dialogue continued seamlessly in Ted and Jeanette's minds without interruption. *The attention that we've gotten was inevitable and the more we refuse it the harder they will try but we have to hold them off for as long as possible. Everything will get more chaotic, and the more attention we get the stronger the forces of darkness will be working to undermine and take control of our work. As the chaos grows multiple sources will swirl around us like a hurricane so finding the protective still point in the center where the real power lies is a necessity. This is the secret to surviving these challenges while restoring ourselves at physical, mental, emotional, and spiritual levels.*

The power of our shared intention creates a third force that is stronger than the forces pursuing their own self centered agendas in the guise of serving the greater good. They will attempt to discredit or take control of our work in the name of God, religion, or some other moralistic or seemingly altruistic motive but they will all be self serving. No matter how it may appear on the surface the work we do has nothing to do with religion. It has to do with the physics of consciousness. They will approach us as friends and advocates who will say they are here to help and when we remain independent of them they will turn on us, but their machinations will become the vehicle that furthers our purpose.

"How will we know?" Jeanette asked.

Theo shrugged and a grin lit his face. "I have no idea."

Ted answered with his own smile. "We'll see how the mystery unfolds."

Theo's eyes sparkled. *I surrender to the mystery not knowing where it will lead me but I know that everything will turn out the way it should so I accept the outcome because I know that it is always in service to the greater good.*

More homeless came in growing numbers. To keep up with the demand Theo diagnosed maladies before their patients came in the door and Ted went through the motions of examining them to keep up appearances. In more severe cases Theo appeared without being seen and did his hands on healing before slipping away when the patient came into full awareness.

Scott Olsen showed up one afternoon and elbowed his way into the clinic's reception area.

Jeanette looked up from her computer when he came in. "We saw you on TV! That's great work that you're doing helping others. It's made things more challenging for us here, but I can't blame you. Between us we are making a difference. What brings you here?"

Scott looked up as if trying to find an answer, then looked down, smiling. "I can't explain it but I got an impulse to come here, thinking that you need help in some way." He held out his hands. "I have no idea how to do that. All I can say is that something urged me to come today." He looked at his watch. "I'm supposed to be here right now."

Jeanette frowned. "I don't know what to tell you except that I hope you're not wasting your time."

Scott turned around and Jeanette looked past him to see two Black and White San Diego Police cruisers pull up in front of the clinic. Collins and Perez stepped out of each one and met at the front door where they looked up and down the block before pushing their way through the waiting crowd.

Jeanette stood from her desk. "Good morning officers. "What can I do for you?"

Perez sighed and rested his hands on his gun belt. "We've had complaints about all the trash your business attracts. The sidewalk is cluttered with abandoned shopping carts, wheelchairs, unsanitary clothes, bedding, and other trash that the homeless leave behind after coming here."

Scott stepped forward. "That's why I'm here."

Perez scowled at him and Jeanette struggled to contain her surprise.

"I'm organizing a crew to return shopping carts to the stores," Scott continued. "We're going to donate anything that is usable to the Salvation Army and clean up whatever else is littering the street."

Perez blinked and Collins narrowed his eyes.

"No need to concern yourselves," Scott went on. "We'll have things cleaned up in the next couple of days."

Collins looked to Perez who continued staring at Scott. Perez opened his mouth as if to say something more but no words came so he shrugged and turned away, saying over his shoulder, "We'll be back to make sure you comply."

"Thanks," Jeanette said to Scott after the door closed. "I wasn't expecting that or your offer of help."

Scott chuckled. "Neither was I, but I guess that's why I came." He reached out and shook Jeanette's hand. "I'll be back with a cleanup crew and a truck to haul things away tonight and we'll come by every night after closing to keep things clean."

"Thank you! That will be a great help."

THIRTY NINE

One afternoon at closing time Ted and Jeanette stood in the reception area watching a pristine black Tesla pull up in front of the clinic followed by a blue Prius. A tall, dark-haired man dressed in a conservative blue suit wearing a red tie stepped out of the driver's side of the Tesla and a woman with a buxom hourglass figure and long impeccably styled blonde hair dressed in a low cut satin dress matching the blue of the man's suit stepped out of the passenger side.

A brown-haired bearded man wearing a red flannel shirt and jeans climbed out of the Prius carrying a large camera, a tripod, and what looked like a large store display. The three of them met in front of the Tesla and conferred for a moment before turning toward the clinic.

"Shit!" Ted moved to lock the front door when Theo's voice stopped him.

Let them in. They're here to put on a show of sincerity where there is none and their intention is to exploit our work to serve their own ends. They go against everything we have manifested, but as I said, the greater the darkness, the brighter the light for those aware enough to see things for what they really are.

Ted looked to Jeanette and could see by her puzzled expression that she "heard" everything Theo said in her mind.

This will be one of our greatest challenges, Theo continued. *The time has come to allow them to swallow us into their darkness. As unpleasant as it will be, by maintaining our integrity they will expose their own hypocrisy which will bring more darkness. It is part of a bigger plan.*

Ted nodded slowly. "Which we don't know what it is, where it will take us, or how it will unfold; only that it will turn out the way it is supposed to."

Ted and Jeanette both felt Theo's broad smile in that strange inner way that felt stronger than normal sensory experience.

Let the games begin.

The man opened the door and held it open for the woman then he stepped in behind her followed by the cameraman.

The man in the suit smiled, showing perfect teeth and held out a manicured hand graced with a large gold diamond and emerald blue topaz gemstone ring. A Rolex adorned his wrist. "Hello, my name is Stewart Alderman." He bowed to the woman while Ted shook his hand. "And this is my wife Carla Nicoletti."

"It's such an honor to meet you," Carla said in a low seductive voice while batting her long eyelashes. Her blue eyes matched her dress and her plump red lips oozed sensuality. A gold, diamond encrusted crucifix drew attention to itself where it nestled within her cleavage. She took Ted's hand and clasped it with both of hers.

"And this is our photographer, René." Stewart held out a hand to the bearded man who was setting up a camera on his tripod.

"We hoped to get a picture commemorating this moment," Stewart said.

"What's this all about?" Jeanette said from behind Ted.

Ted let go of Carla's hand and stepped aside, bowing low holding out his hand toward Jeanette. "This blonde haired beauty is my wife Jeanette."

Stewart stepped forward and took Jeanette's hand in both of his and bent down to kiss it, making Jeanette blush.

"What is this all about?" Ted asked.

Stewart gave another megawatt smile and held out his hand for René to hand him the long poster board. He flipped it around dramatically showing an oversized check for five thousand dollars made out to Temple Nutritionals. "We wanted to make a humble donation to show our support and appreciation for all you do in the name of the lord."

"What's the catch?" Jeanette said before Ted could respond.

"No catch," Carla purred.

"No strings attached," Stewart added. "In fact it is not really from us, we're just the presenters. Please consider it a blessing of unconditional love in support of your healing mission from our prophet Isiah."

Profit! Theo said, emphasizing the it.*We don't need any help from them but we need to play along to see where it takes us.*

Ted struggled to stifle a laugh resulting in a tight smile. "I don't know what to say." He looked over at Jeanette who smiled along with him, knowing that their smiles instigated by Theo's comments were interpreted as gratitude.

"Please excuse my ignorance but other than the bible I have never heard of the prophet Isiah," she said.

149

"He likes to remain behind the scenes and does not want the attention of the public," Carla said. "He has chosen us as his ambassadors for the sacred work he has dedicated his life to."

Ted put his arm around Jeanette pulling her close. "We'd rather work behind the scenes ourselves but the media got wind of our work."

"Praise the lord," Stewart said. "The blessing of the hand of God is evident which is what guided us to you. Would you mind posing for a picture with us to capture the blessing of this moment so we can share it with our flock?"

Ted looked at Jeanette and shrugged.

"Sure. Why not?" she said.

Following René's direction Stewart and Carla posed behind the oversized check on the left in the act of handing it to Ted and Jeanette who stood behind it on the right.

"Thank you," Ted said, "and please thank Isiah for his generosity."

"No thanks necessary," Stewart said, "but we will pass along the message to Isiah." He leaned in and lowered his voice. "Carla and I host the Praise the Lordcast and after seeing the wonderful work you two have been doing we'd be deeply honored to have you on as guests."

"I don't know," Jeanette said.

A wounded expression stole over Stewart's face. "You've already spoken to the media. Your voices on our podcast would bring great happiness and serve as a blessing to our faithful listeners."

Carla lowered her head and put her hands together in prayer and her big blue eyes grew wide in a pleading puppy dog expression. "Don't be afraid to share the magnificent love that you give to the world to those who deserve it the most," she said in a half-whisper. "Please bless us with your presence."

Ted squeezed Jeanette a little closer. "What do you think, honey?"

Go ahead, it's part of the plan. Good job playing hard to get.

Jeanette looked to Ted, then to Stewart, and finally to Carla, "Okay."

"Bless you," Carla said.

She and Stewart bowed low and started for the door with René in tow. "We don't want to take up any more of your precious time," Stewart said as René opened the door for him and Carla. "We'll be in touch with the details."

"I hope we're not making a mistake," Jeanette said after the door closed. "Those two give me the creeps."

They are everything that is wrong with what people think of as serving humanity which is why they are the perfect vehicles for our work.

"It seems like we are using them, which doesn't seem right," Jeanette said.

"Who's using who?" Ted said."

Everything that is going to happen will be because of what they do through their own actions. We will stay in integrity and we won't be adding anything to what they manifest. They will do that on their own which will be colored by their lack of honesty and hidden motives while we will be honest and transparent.

Jeanette sat down on the reception area couch and rested her chin on her hand. "How are we going to do this?" She looked to Theo. "We can't leave you alone, honey, and to be honest I won't feel comfortable without you there either."

Theo sat down beside her and patted her knee. "Daddy is the best person to do the talking because of all his meetings from his old job and you and I will be there to support him." He held up a finger. "Remember, I'm your autistic little boy, so you will be the protective mommy." He tapped his forehead, then his chest. "We will all be involved in the interview together."

Ted sat down beside him. "I can only imagine what's going to come through me."

Theo nodded. "As I grow older more and more people will find out the truth about me."

Jeanette put her hand to her heart. "We need to protect you!"

Theo leaned in and hugged her. "It has to happen but we need it to be revealed as gradually as possible."

"That scares the hell out of me."

Ted reached out and put his arm around Theo and Jeanette. "I don't know what to think about it either but it comes down to trusting in the guidance we have been getting."

Theo leaned back and stretched his arms out behind Ted and Jeanette and pulled them both closer.

FORTY

Ted and Jeanette stood in the doorway to the Praise the Lordcast studio with Theo standing close behind. Ted squatted down next to him and pointed to the cameras, computers, large flat screen displays, and a mixing and editing console all focused on a small stage with four comfortable chairs in an intimate setting. "Wow!"
A huge backlit gold cross glowed from up on a large flat screen behind the chairs. "This is a full on television station."

Stewart looked up from a discussion with Carla and two of their crew on center stage. "Ted! Jeanette!" He strode toward them with his arms spread wide.

"Quite the setup you have here," Ted said.

Stewart beamed. "We consider ourselves to be a twenty first century online church with every phone, tablet, and computer screen that has us on it acting as an intimate chapel for the faithful who watch, listen, and receive the blessings that we bestow on them through the wisdom of Isiah."

"And who is this adorable blond-haired blue-eyed handsome little cherub?" Carla said, coming up beside Stewart.

Theo made a show of pulling back and half hiding behind Jeanette's leg hugging it tight.

She put a protective arm around him. "This is our little boy Theo. He's not used to being around a lot of people."

Theo looked up at Carla wide-eyed.

Carla put her hands on the sides of her face. "Oh my goodness he is an absolute angel!"

Everything about Stewart and Carla looked perfect. Polished shoes, tailored blue suit, gold rings and Rolex complemented by blue-eyed Carla with her matching dress and gold and diamond crucifix conspicuous within her cleavage. Not a hair out of place on either one of them, in fact they seemed to sparkle.

Ted felt underdressed in his jeans and denim shirt.

Stewart shook Ted's hand. "God bless you and thank you for joining us today." He pointed to one of the men he had been speaking with. "You remember René our photographer."

René looked up from one of the cameras by the stage and waved to them.

"We can get a chair and have Theo sit with us on stage," Carla said.

Theo shook his head no and hugged Jeanette tighter.

Jeanette shook her head. "He's not comfortable with a lot of attention." She pointed to the chairs on stage. "You can take away one of those chairs. Theo needs to be close to me." She kissed him on the head. "Ted is our best spokesman. You don't need me there. Ted has a lot of experience speaking from his days as the head of research at Bliss Pharmaceuticals."

"That's impressive," Stewart said.

"Thank you, Ted said. "We don't need to mention that in the interview. The work we do has no connection to Bliss in any way, shape, or form, so we need to keep them out of the discussion."

Stewart pantomimed zipping his mouth shut.

Carla took Ted's hand in both of hers. "Thank you for coming, and god bless" she whispered and did the same with Jeanette.

René and his helper took the empty chair off the set and rearranged the three remaining chairs. Theo and Jeanette sat together in a spot where they could see the stage and the large monitors surrounding it.

Stewart and Carla took the chairs on either side of Ted on the stage while René clipped small microphones to their collars and rearranged the camera angles and adjusted the lighting before going to his spot behind the main camera.

Ted felt awkward when Stewart and Carla closed their eyes and put their hands together in a prayer led by Stewart.

"Thank you lord for honoring us today with the gift of Ted and Jeanette, our brother and sister in the lord's work and for the extra blessing of their beautiful child Theo and for the guidance we receive from your most humble prophet Isiah. Amen."

Profit!

Jeanette suppressed a giggle.

Stewart and Carla opened their eyes and looked up.

"Are we ready?" Stewart said.

René gave them a thumbs up. "We're rolling."

Stewart held up his hands. "God bless you all and thank you for joining Carla and I for a very special episode of the Praise the Lordcast. Today we are blessed to have Ted Driscoll, who along with his wife

Jeanette have founded Temple Nutritionals where the homeless have been flocking to experience what are being called miracle cures."

The studio lights dimmed and an edited version of Ted's interview with Sara Johnston mixed in with her interview with Scott Olsen played on the big screen up on the wall behind the stage. The sequence ended with a still shot of the posed picture of Ted and Jeanette accepting the oversize donation check from Stewart and Carla which remained up on the screen as the studio lights brightened and the video cut back to Stewart giving his trademark megawatt grin.

"Temple Nutritionals is a perfect example of work that we take pride in supporting," he said. "Your donations make you part of the blessing that we can gift to worthwhile causes like this one."

Theo pointed to one of the monitors where a message scrolled across the bottom of the screen with a number and a website to send donations to.

Profit!

Jeanette snorted and tapped his knee. "Stop it," she whispered. Up on stage, Ted smiled in response.

"Thank you for joining us today, Ted. Please tell us about Temple Nutritionals."

Theo spoke through Ted. His words were Ted's and Ted's were Theo's adding to Ted's confidence.

"Temple Nutritionals is based on the concept that the human body is a temple. We specialize in natural remedies that can improve the health and well-being of those we treat."

"I love the idea of the human body as a temple." Carla clasped her hands together and looked up as if praying. "Please, tell us more."

"Ancient wisdom tells us that the human body is a temple. In Egypt The Temple of Anthropocosmic Man at Luxor is laid out in the same proportions as the human body and is considered to be the mathematical and geometrical structure of the Cosmos and its location within human consciousness which recognizes man as the center of the universe. It demonstrates that our consciousness resides at the center of our awareness where inner meets outer and spirit meets matter."

"Praise the lord," Carla half-whispered. "What I'm hearing is that you believe that god is everywhere."

Ted nodded.

"What a beautiful concept!"

"Not only is the human body a temple but we believe that every aspect of reality we experience is a temple that reflects the great mystery both within us and which surrounds us. These sacred relationships are the guiding principles behind everything that we do."

"And your followers?" Carla asked. "They believe the same?"

"We don't have followers."

Carla looked surprised. "But Temple Nutritionals is a church. You have a well-defined canon and you have supporters."

"Temple Nutritionals is not a church. Our mission is to help those in need with natural cures that are abundant in nature." He held his hands out wide and looked to Stewart, then to Carla. "Our mother earth gives us everything we need when it is sustainably resourced and properly managed. In the same way that our planet gives us life, we follow its example. We do not look to profit from our work. As a result of our earlier successes with family members who had been given up as lost we are supported by patrons as acts of gratitude for being instrumental in reuniting them with their families."

Carla frowned. "If everyone is a temple then we wouldn't need any churches."

Steward raised his eyebrows. "So you are not a church, but you are supported by donations."

"We never ask for donations. They are given to us which sustains our work. We don't believe in churches. We believe that everyone is a temple containing individual sparks of divinity. We should all be worshipping each other instead of prophets, icons, and symbols."

Carla squirmed in her chair and made the sign of the cross moving her right hand from her forehead to her breasts and her left to her right shoulder, ending by kissing her crucifix.

"So you worship by helping others," Stewart said, "and you see your treatments as offerings to divinity even if they come in off the street confused, ragged, and dirty."

"Especially if they come in off the street confused, ragged, and dirty. We believe that we are all the keepers of our personal temples which are the portals to the unity and interconnection with all things that bring us the beauty and blessing of being alive in the arms of the great mystery."

"Wow!" Stewart said. "That is very poetic."

"And a beautiful description of our lord," Carla said, once more crossing herself.

The interview continued with Ted fielding questions about their treatments and how their supplements can be purchased on Temple Nutritionals web site. They also discussed Ted's education and chemistry background before the discussion turned to more personal matters which made Ted uneasy.

"Tell us about your beautiful angel Theo," Carla purred.

FORTY ONE

"I understand that you and Jeanette engineered your love child in a Fetal Fantasies growth pod at your home," Stewart said. "From what I can see it's clear that you and your wife made a beautiful angel together."

"Thank you," Ted said. "Like everyone else we wanted a perfect baby and their system let us pick the traits we wanted like sex, eye color, hair color, vocal timbre, physical build, intelligence factor, athletic requirements, and other features. We picked genetics that gave our son a higher probability of living longer and an evenly balanced temperament and we got to choose the embryo with the best chances we could give him."

Carla held her hands over her heart and looked up, eyes wide. "Kind of makes your blonde-haired, blue-eyed little angel an immaculate conception, doesn't it? He's *so* beautiful! Is it true that he is the world's first genetically perfect human?"

Ted jumped like he had been shocked. "Who did you hear that from?"

"I'm so sorry," Carla said. "I didn't know it was a secret. Some of our faithful work at Fetal Fantasies and little Theo's perfect genome has everybody buzzing there."

Before Ted could respond Stewart looked directly at the central camera and René zoomed in for a closeup. "Brothers and sisters, call the number or visit our website at the bottom of your screen to pledge your support to help the Praise the Lordcast spread the word and endorse great works like that of Temple Nutritionals which are done in the name of the lord." He smiled and put his hands together in prayer, then bowed his head with Carla following suit. "Dear lord, thank you for the gift of brother Ted, sister, Jeanette, their beautiful son Theo and for the blessings and wisdom you bring to us through our prophet Isiah, the living manifestation of Christ Consciousness."

Ask them when you can meet him.

Ted sat up straight in his chair. "I was hoping to meet Isiah. He sounds like an amazing man."

"He is anxious to meet you as well. Unfortunately he is out of the country at a distant retreat, but he recorded a video greeting to share with you and our audience."

The studio lights dimmed and sitar music rose to a low level along with the image on the screen behind them that appeared to bloom out of nowhere into an image of a man who looked like Jesus Christ. He wore shimmering lavender satin robes with long brown hair and expressive brown eyes that seemed to plead. He sat in a meditative pose on a large ornate green and gold embroidered pillow adorned with large gold tassels.

"Thank you for joining us," he said in a proper Oxford sounding voice. "I regret that I could not be there with you, but the lord's work has called me to task in a distant place. Please accept my heartfelt apologies." He clasped his hands together. "We are honored by your presence and thank the lord for bringing the blessing that you are to us."

Ted felt an urge to respond until he remembered that the video was prerecorded.

"I received a message from my archangels telling me you would be coming and that you are destined to join our church in a place of honor to serve with us in the name of the lord."

It's nice to be loved, but Isiah not only wants to take over Temple Nutritionals, he wants to exploit me.

Carla let out an exaggerated gasp and Stewart said with a tone of reverence, "I have never seen him accept anyone like this before."

Isiah continued. "My blessed brother and sister Carla will arrange the details and allow you full access to all of the resources we have at our disposal. Working together we can spread your good work further and faster than you can on your own." He made the sign of the cross and looked upward. "Thank you lord for blessing us with the gift of Ted, Jeanette, and their angelic child Theo."

Carla and Stewart put their hands together in prayer and looked up, mimicking Isiah.

"Thy will be done on earth as it is in heaven."

Isiah's image faded into white along with the music, leaving them with his final words.

Stewart beamed. "I can't think of a better way to end an episode of the Praise the Lordcast than a blessing from our prophet Isiah."

Stewart and Carla both made the sign of the cross, the studio lights came up, and René popped up from behind his camera holding an iPad. "That's a wrap. Great job, you guys!" He looked down at the iPad and looked up again, smiling. "We just broke our record for the most donations coming in from a single podcast." He held the iPad in the air. "And they are still coming in!"

Stewart took Ted's hand in both of his and shook it vigorously. "Unbelievable! That went great!"

"We'd love to have you on all the time, " Carla chimed in. "You can be a permanent part of the show." She looked to Jeanette, then to Ted, batting her long eyelashes at him. "That would be one of the biggest blessings we've ever had."

Stewart held his hands up high. "I can see you becoming our online saints." He looked at Theo while he spoke to Ted. "We can bring in more of the faithful to raise a lot more money for the work of the lord. What do you say?" Stewart asked with an expectant look on his face.

"I can't tell you how flattered I am by your offer," Ted said, rising from his chair. "but we have to decline. We have more than enough of our own work to keep up with."

Carla stood up beside him. "I don't think you understand. We're here to help you." She wrung her hands and with a plaintive look said, "Our prophet Isiah, the living earthly manifestation of Christ Consciousness has blessed you with an invitation to take your places, literally sitting at his right hand."

Stewart lowered his voice conspiratorially. "Many believe that Isiah is the reincarnated harbinger of the second coming of Jesus."

"Directly connected," Carla added.

"You and your lovely wife Jeanette are playing the part of spiritual midwives," Stewart continued, "ushering in the Christ consciousness of a new age that our planet desperately needs. You are the Mary and Joseph of our times who brought the first perfect human being into the world."

"As an immaculate conception!" Carla added.

Ted shook his head no and nodded to Theo and Jeanette, who both stood.

Stewart took Ted's hand in both of his, holding tight. "Please don't make the mistake of refusing. You don't see Temple Nutritionals as a church but you are supported by donations. Don't you think incorporating yourself as a church and creating an organizational structure would help spread the word and give you the tax benefits that come with it? We already have the infrastructure and legal paperwork in place and we are willing to put all of it at your disposal."

Ted pulled his hand away and Theo spoke in his mind in concert with what came out of his mouth. "Thank you again for the honor. We really are very flattered by it, but we have no desire to be a church or part of one. Think of us as a no church movement. We want no part in any institutions or organizations. We don't need to change anything. We are already self-sustaining within our present model of operation. We see the human body as a temple, meaning that we all carry our own church inside of us. We are all divinity and the true church of God is inside and around us. It even says so in the bible. The kingdom of God is within."

Theo tugged at Jeanette's hand. "We need to go, honey," she called to Ted. "Theo's getting agitated and it's getting late."

Ted looked Stewart in the eye, shook his hand, and did the same with a teary-eyed Carla before stepping off the stage to join Theo and Jeanette.

"Please reconsider," Stewart said as they headed for the door. "You don't realize what a big mistake you're making."

These last words came out sounding oddly like a threat.

FORTY TWO

Theo turned five the following week and with that came his annual checkup with Doctor Kennedy which Ted and Jeanette dreaded but they didn't want to spoil his birthday, so they took the day off with plans to take Theo somewhere special after his checkup.

He sat on an examination table in Fetal Fantasies after another extended battery of tests by Doctor Kennedy and his associates. Ted and Jeanette stood beside him while Kennedy studied his iPad before looking up and shaking his head.

"As you know, the staff, management, and the board of directors of Fetal Fantasies have an exceptional interest in Theo," Kennedy said. "Out of all the babies we have technologically midwifed into the world, from everything we can assess and volumes of other tests we have been analyzing, Theo's genome has proven to be exceptional in its perfection. There is no other like it and frankly we don't know if we will ever see another one like it. As part of the gene editing procedure we feel it is imperative to clone it so we can preserve it for further study." Kennedy rubbed his chin. "The only fly in the ointment is the molecular defects in Theo's neurons that carry the mutation. We believe we will correct these defects when we add copies of a healthy CHD8 gene and expect the neurons rescued by the treatment to return to a normal rate of activity resulting in restored function. Aside from these indicators we are still puzzling over Theo's lack of developing speech and socialization which supports our diagnosis of autism."

"His speech is improving," Jeanette said, "He's just shy around people and to be honest I don't think he is autistic at all, but I do think he is extremely shy."

Kennedy's eyebrows raised. "Have you made any progress socializing him?"

Ask him about the Einstein syndrome.

What's that? Ted thought, looking to Jeanette who gave a tiny nod.

You're about to find out.

161

The words came from Theo spoken by Ted.

"I'm sorry doc," Ted said. "I hear what you are saying, but you seem to be contradicting yourself. You are telling us that Theo is perfect and you want to clone his genome for further study and you are telling us he is flawed at the same time which makes no sense. Have you ever heard of the Einstein syndrome?"

Kennedy looked surprised.

"Of course you have," Ted said. "It's a developmental disorder where a child experiences a later than the usual onset of speaking, but shows more than average abilities in other non-verbal skills like analytical thinking."

"You think Theo has Einstein syndrome?"

My body and my abilities to use it more effectively are growing rapidly, but it is still not developed enough to be fully functional and in alignment with my true cognitive capacities. Those are still behind my abilities to manifest them. In other words...

"We think Theo's physical development needs more time to catch up with what goes on in his head," Jeanette said, letting Theo speak through her. "He's done some incredible artwork and he's built some amazing things with his Tinker Toys."

"Well, I – I'd really like to see some of that and I am sure my fellow colleagues would like to see that too."

We can't let them see any of my real work with the molecules and geometries but I can make up something else.

"I'll email some pictures of some of his creations," Ted said. "I don't think any tune-ups as you call them are necessary." He ruffled Theo's hair. "What's needed is more time and more patience for our little Einstein."

Theo hugged him and pulled Jeanette into a three way hug, then he broke out in a broad grin and stood up on the table. "I can hear everything you are saying about me," he said, surprising them all. He pointed his finger and accented every word as if admonishing Doctor Kennedy. "Just because I don't talk doesn't mean there is something wrong with me."

Kennedy's face went pale, then in a shocked half-whisper said, "That's the most I've ever heard you say." He brightened. "And it sounded very good. Quite articulate!"

Ted grinned and patted Theo's shoulder. "I'm telling you, our little Einstein is full of surprises!"

Kennedy's smile faded and his expression grew serious. "That's wonderful, but I'm afraid that we are seeing too little too late."

"What do you mean?" Jeanette said.

"Regardless of this late progress, my colleagues and the management of Fetal Fantasies have come to a unanimous agreement. Based on the success of the pilot program the federal government has mandated the CHD8 gene editing treatment as a safety measure to all genetically engineered children under the age of eight to guarantee that they can function normally and eliminate any doubt about their development, and any possible future behavioral and cognitive symptoms."

Jeanette put a protective arm around Theo. "Mandated the gene editing treatment?"

"The pilot phase has been very successful and we all want what is best for our children, especially our little Einstein here."

"Mandatory?" Ted and Jeanette said together.

Ted shook his head. "I don't think so."

We can't let that happen. We have more work to do, but ultimately there will be no escaping it. It will destroy all of the psychospiritual connections I have spent this lifetime creating and it will send me into a deep state of autism. I also understand that as hard as it is to accept, it is part of a bigger plan.

"But he's already perfect," Jeanette insisted. "You said so yourself!" She shook her head. "All of your tests say that Theo is healthy."

"I'm inclined to agree after what I saw today, but this procedure has been signed into federal law." Kennedy sighed. "I don't understand why you are so resistant to it. All we want to do is add extra copies of a healthy gene to insure that Theo can grow at a normal rate of activity and synaptic communication without any further mutations."

"But you have been telling us all along that there is nothing wrong with this CHD8 gene," Ted said.

Kennedy's shoulders slumped and he held out his hands. "We have no choice in the matter. The government will be enforcing it."

Ted shook his head. "I'm sorry but we can't allow that to happen."

Kennedy looked saddened. "It's going to happen anyway so I suggest getting it over with. We can do it today."

"It's not going to happen today or any other day," Jeanette said with an air of finality.

Ted picked up Theo from the table. "Come on, honey," he said to Jeanette. "We need to get going."

He took Theo by the hand and led him to the door with Jeanette following close behind.

"It's the law," Kennedy said, half-heartedly as they left the examining room. "If you don't comply they will take Theo from you and you will be putting yourselves in double jeopardy for child endangerment under California Penal Code Two Seventy Three A as well as under federal statutes."

FORTY THREE

Ted and Jeanette hurried to their car where she dropped into the front passenger seat and slammed the door shut while Ted put Theo in his car seat in the back.

"How dare they try to force us to do their procedure on Theo," she huffed when Ted sat down in the driver's seat.

"No shit," Ted said, "and threaten legal action too. They act like they own him!"

"And they want to clone his genome. No way are we going to let them do that, especially after all they've kept hidden from us. It stinks of eugenics."

"I agree. After all their subterfuge and hidden agendas I'm sorry to say that I don't trust them."

Jeanette shook her head. "It's Huxley's Brave New World all over again! They probably plan to make copies of Theo's genome to start a secret program of selective breeding."

"I hate to say it, but we walked into this when we signed up. Some geneticists view genomic screening and genetic counseling as an extension of eugenics."

"But I don't regret it." Jeanette's voice grew softer. "Theo is the best thing that ever happened to us." She glanced up at the rear view mirror to see Theo smiling back at her.

"I know, honey," Ted said, speaking evenly. "We didn't see this coming. Doc Kennedy always said how perfect Theo is and now they want to mess with his perfection." He chuckled and put his hand on Jeanette's. "Did you see the look on Doc Kennedy's face when Theo stood up on the table and said he could hear everything we were saying about him?"

Jeanette giggled. "It must have shocked the shit out of him."

We kept the illusion of autism for as long as we could until I had to show myself a bit more. My energetic presence is growing into this body which increases my visibility like a brightening light which will continue to attract loving vibrations as well as hidden darker energies.

"Like the proverbial moths to a flame," Jeanette said.

The more I come into my power the harder the forces of darkness will try to diminish the higher frequencies which will only fan their flame and they will try to control it to make it serve their own ends.

Ted looked in the rear view mirror and his eyes met Theo's. "Like our friends from the Praise The Lordcast who want to suck us up into their church."

Jeanette shook her finger. "And don't forget, we were blessed with an invitation to take our places beside the earthly manifestation of Christ Consciousness to make us online saints and stars of the Praise the Lordcast church where we can bring in more of the faithful to raise more money for the work of the lord!" She looked in the rear view mirror again to see Theo looking amused.

Ted looked back at him and Theo looked from Jeanette to Ted and back again and broke into a broader smile, then everyone burst into laughter, lightening the mood.

"They're hard to take." Jeanette said.

It's all part of the plan and it's unfolding perfectly.

Ted rolled his eyes. "But we don't know what the plan is."

All we need to do is follow what happens with our hearts as it unfolds and we will be serving the greater good.

Jeanette waved her hands. "Okay, enough of all that. What's more important than anything else is…" She paused and her eyes grew wide. "Happy Birthday, Theo!" She undid her seatbelt and leaned between the front seats to hug and kiss Theo on the forehead.

Ted reached back and gave Theo's knee a gentle squeeze. "What do you want to do, Sport?"

"Can we go to the mountains? We need to be in nature."

"Mount Palomar?"

"Best birthday present ever!"

"Honey, if it's okay with you," Jeanette said, "I'm going to order more Tinker Toys and anything else you might want."

"I don't want or need anything," Theo said. "You two are the best presents anybody could ask for."

"I'm hoping you can build something like the Golden Gate bridge or other complicated structures to prove to Doctor Kennedy that there's nothing wrong with you," Jeanette said.

"It might buy us some time," Theo said, "but it won't stop what needs to happen."

"I know," Jeanette said, "but that's not going to stop me from giving them a good fight."

Ted shook his fist. "Until the bitter end!"

They took I-15 North and highway 76 East past the Pala and Pauma Casinos to highway S7 and followed route S6 to Mount Palomar where they found a trail leading up to a forested ridge. The moment Ted stopped the car Theo jumped out and bolted for the trail head.

"Come on!" he yelled back. "Let's say Hi!"

Ted and Jeanette looked at each other seeing Theo's joy reflected in each other's eyes. He took her by the hand and led her up the path following Theo who ran ahead.

They heard the melodic trills of Theo's toning and found him in a meadow at the first bend in the trail where he was kneeling before an assemblage of squirrels, birds, racoons, foxes, deer, and two mountain lions surrounding him in a semi-circle, staring up at him with a look that appeared full of an otherworldly intelligence. Other animals crept up behind them as if joining a solemn religious ceremony.

Hummingbirds hovered around Theo's head forming a rainbow colored crown that shimmered with flashes of bright iridescence beneath a sunbeam that lit him like a vibrant fairyland nature prince.

Jeanette gasped and she and Ted stood hugging each other, feeling like they were part of whatever wordless communication they were witnessing.

After a timeless moment Theo bowed low and held his arms out wide, then he stood as if embracing the skies and the animals scattered, disappearing into the surrounding forest.

Theo watched while moving slow and trancelike with a satisfied smile then he ran off toward some trees with more joy than any other kid discovering a new playground would. Everywhere he went he hugged trees, crouched down to sniff flowers, and touch bushes and small plants hiding in the undergrowth. When he stood upright squirrels ran up and down him like he was a tree, eliciting uncontrollable giggles. Other animals appeared with every step he took. A fox came and rubbed up against him like a friendly cat, small shimmering flocks of hummingbirds darted in and out, and a doe and her fawn came in and leaned against him while he patted them.

Ted and Jeanette couldn't find any words to describe their experience, only that it felt similar to the heartfelt synesthesia of their visions in their heightened states of consciousness that they shared between dreaming and waking.

FORTY FOUR

In the weeks following their magical day in the wooded meadow their lives moved like clockwork. The line of homeless people outside of Temple Nutritionals went all the way to the end of the block every morning where the miraculous healings continued. They kept pace by moving through their patients like an assembly line that came in the front door and went out the back where Scott Olsen's crew handed out food and toiletries along with a listing of available shelters, half way houses, job listings, and other offerings. The line was always gone by closing time when Scott's growing crew of volunteers cleaned up the abandoned items that littered the sidewalk, leaving everything pristine so they could repeat the process the next day.

During the evenings Ted and Jeanette took videos and still shots of Theo building a detailed Tinker Toy construction of the Golden Gate bridge as well as other intricate assemblies of hummingbirds and flowers. Jeanette emailed everything to Doctor Kennedy as proof of Theo's abilities, but Kennedy never responded.

"I can't believe how great everything has been going since that silly Praise the Lordcast and Theo's birthday checkup," Jeanette said while preparing to close the clinic for the day.

Ted put a finger to his lips. "Shhh! You'll jinx us."

Theo came out from the back room. "It's the calm before the storm and the next wave is about to hit."

Ted and Jeanette still did a mental double take hearing such refined speech coming from Theo's little five year old voice.

Jeanette exhaled and dropped down on the reception area couch. "Maybe I shouldn't have opened my mouth."

Theo hopped up on the couch and wrapped his arms around her. "You brought it up because part of you can feel what's coming."

"I can hardly wait."

"You won't have to." Theo pointed out the window where a familiar black Tesla pulled up in front of the clinic. Stewart, dressed in

168

his trademark blue suit and red tie stepped out of the driver's side and helped Carla in her color matched satin dress step out of the passenger side.

"Shit!" Jeanette muttered under her breath.

You're about to learn more about human nature from these two. Don't let any surprises they spring on you worry you. It's all part of the bigger plan.

They all stood when Stewart strode up and opened the door for Carla, who strolled in all smiles, batting her eyelashes, her gold diamond encrusted crucifix sparkling from between her breasts. "How wonderful to see you again," she purred, shaking Ted's hand and then Carla's.

Theo made a show of hugging Jeanette's leg and flinching when Carla patted him on the head. "Such an angel," she half-whispered.

Stewart gripped Ted's hand and shook it hard. "Ted! How wonderful to see you. Have you thought over our offer?"

Ted glanced at Jeanette and Theo, who looked up from hugging Jeanette, then he smirked and looked Stewart in the eye. "I told you before that we were flattered by the generosity of your offer." He jerked his thumb back over his shoulder. "But we have more than enough of our own work to do."

Carla wrung her hands together and her eyes teared up, taking on a sad puppy dog look. "But we're here to help."

Stewart took Ted's hand in both of his and squeezed. "Please, don't make the mistake of refusing. We have all the paperwork drawn up to incorporate Temple Nutritionals into the church."

Ted pulled his hand back. "Like I said before, we are a no church movement who see the human body as a temple, meaning we carry our church inside of and around us." He scratched his head. "What part of that do you not understand?"

Stewart put his hands together as if praying and looked down, speaking in a lowered voice. "We were so humbled by the miracles you have created and bowled over by Isiah's acceptance of you and the outpouring of love that he has blessed you with." He looked up at Ted. "You my friend are a living manifestation of a prophecy that is coming true. Isiah is the harbinger of the second coming of Jesus and you and your lovely bride are part of it - not just part of it, you *are* it!"

He took Carla's hand in his and leaned in close to her. "I have to say that we are blessed to have you as the spiritual midwives. You are the twenty first century incarnation of Mary and Joseph who are ushering in the Christ consciousness and we feel blessed to play our part in it."

Jeanette frowned and shook her head. "I have no idea what you are talking about."

"When we first found out about you we had our researchers do an extensive background check after we had you on the show."

"What are you driving at?" Ted said.

"We have many followers, several of which are high level employees and board members of Fetal Fantasies."

Ted and Jeanette felt their hearts jump at the same time.

Stewart smiled. "They shared some highly confidential information with us that you were only recently privy to."

Ted stared at Carla. "We figured that out after it was outed on your show."

"The fact is that your beautiful blonde-haired, blue-eyed little boy is the first genetically perfect child that Fetal Fantasies has ever produced and the management and board of directors have a more than exceptional interest in him, especially his perfect genome which they hope to clone."

"The last thing we need is more attention," Jeanette said.

Carla gasped. "Don't you realize what this means? Your healings are miracles because of the presence of your perfect son who came into this world in an electronic womb without any contact with a human womb. His immaculate conception makes him the second coming!"

Jeanette waved both her hands and shook her head no. "That's the craziest thing I have ever heard."

Stewart crossed his arms and rocked back on his heels. "This means that Isiah is John the Baptist and you, Mother Mary, Jeanette, Ted is Joseph, and little Theo is the Christ child."

FORTY FIVE

Stewart raised his hands and looked up with Carla following suit. "Blessed be," he said. "Christ is born and Christ is risen again. Thank you lord for the guidance through your beloved prophet Isiah and for the blessing of the second coming that you have chosen us to foster."

"Amen!" Carla squealed, raising her hands higher.

We don't need to hear any more of this deranged fantasy. Theo hugged Jeanette tighter and hid behind her, peeking out from around her hip, yelling, "Mommy, they're scaring me!"

Carla froze and Stewart's eyes widened, then he leaned forward, bowing toward Theo. "Don't you understand how special…"

"That's enough!" Ted said.

Jeanette put her arm around Theo who made a show of hiding his face in her side. "It's okay, honey." She stroked his head and glared at Carla. "They're leaving."

Stewart held his hands up in surrender. "Okay. Okay." He lowered his voice. "Ted would you mind stepping outside for a moment?"

Ted looked over at Theo and Carla and Theo gave a tiny nod.

"Sure!" He held his hand out toward the door.

Carla bowed low to Theo and turned away heading for the door with Stewart close behind. Ted followed and looked back over his shoulder, winking at Theo and Jeanette.

"Listen Ted," Stewart said in a conspiratorial voice when they stepped outside. "Our sources at Fetal Fantasies have informed us of your refusal to cooperate with the federally mandated gene editing procedure." He raised his eyebrows. "Isiah has considerable influence and vast resources. With you as a member of our church we can convince the government to grant a waiver for their mandate on religious grounds."

"Your beautiful little cherub is perfect as he is," Carla gushed.

Tell him you want to meet Isiah in person. It will be interesting to see how he responds.

171

"I'm not agreeing to anything here." Ted shook his finger. "But I'm willing to meet Isiah face to face."

Stewart pursed his lips. "Isiah is deeply immersed in a retreat, but we can arrange for a one on one video discussion."

"Video's not going to be good enough," Ted said. "I need to meet him in person."

"That's a bigger challenge. Isiah cannot come to the United States because his visa has expired." He held up a finger. "But you can speak to him face to face."

Stewart patted Ted on the shoulder and nodded to Carla. "We'll be in touch soon." He went and opened the Tesla's passenger door for her and went around to the driver's side winking at Ted before climbing in.

Ted went back into the clinic shaking his head.

"What was that all about?"

"They know about the federal gene editing mandate and claim they can get us a waiver on religious grounds if we are part of their church."

"And now you're going to talk to the *profit* Isiah face to face," Jeanette said, indicating the she had "heard" Theo's inner directions.

"Face to face, but not in person," Ted said. "The story is that Isiah is having problems with his visa."

"It makes me wonder why that would be?" Jeanette said.

"It's hard to know what to believe with all that batshit crazy Jesus, Mary, Joseph, and John the Baptist bullshit."

"You're never going to meet Isiah in person," Theo said.

"Why is that?" Jeanette asked.

Theo giggled. "There is no Isiah."

"What?" Ted and Jeanette said.

"Isiah is an AI generated entity. Stewart and Carla are the only ones who know and now you do. The deeper truth is that everyone who follows Isiah and the Praise the Lordcast are worshiping an A.I. generated program designed to manipulate its followers into sending money to support it. A.I. even made up the story about Isiah being the reincarnated harbinger of the second coming of Jesus."

Ted snorted. "It's the immaculate deception!"

Jeanette burst into laughter, spurring explosive laughter from Ted and Theo.

"And now they want to pimp Theo," Ted said after catching his breath.

Jeanette wiped tears from her eyes "So what are we going to do?"

"Play along to see what else we can learn," Theo said.

"Okay," Ted said. "Then what?"

Theo smiled. "Then we turn them down again."

"What about the forced gene editing and the fact that more and more people now know that you have a perfect genome that tons of doctors and scientists want to clone and experiment with."

Theo's smile grew wider. "We'll see how the mystery reveals itself and we will know what to do in each moment as it presents itself."

"Flying blind," Ted said.

"By instinct," Jeanette countered.

FORTY SIX

Theo and Jeanette sat in the same spot as before off to the side of the stage where they had a full view of the backlit gold cross glowing from the large flat screen behind an overstuffed chair on the stage facing the screen. An elaborately decorated altar sat beneath the screen arranged with flowers, candles, statuettes and other symbols all accented with the lingering scent of sandalwood incense.

Ted studied the setup feeling like he was going to church and talking to the Wizard of Oz behind the curtain at the same time.

We're not in Kansas anymore Toto, he thought.

Stewart and Carla stood at the far side of the stage, their heads bowed in hushed communication before Stewart looked up. "Ted!" He and Carla rushed over to shake his hand. "I can't tell you how excited we are that you're here."

"Isiah is *so* looking forward to meeting and talking with you," Carla said. "And your beautiful family!" She held her hands out and gave Theo and Jeanette an adoring look. "Thank you for coming." She put her hands over her heart and bowed to Theo.

Jeanette nodded hello and Theo scrunched down in his chair.

Stewart and Carla remained somber, speaking in subdued tones with deferential reverence.

"We'll be sitting right back here listening to your personal audience with Isiah, an honor most could never dream of."

"I'm only hearing him out," Ted said. "My mind is already made up and nothing short of a miracle can change it."

Carla smiled dreamily. "Isiah *is* the miracle. You'll see! Once you look into those compassionate brown eyes you will know in your heart that Isiah is the living harbinger of the second coming." She blessed herself and looked at Theo.

"Okay!" Stewart patted Ted on the back and gestured toward the chair up on the stage. "Everything is set up for a one on one chat with Isiah just like you're sitting comfortably at home."

Stewart walked him up to the chair where René attached a tiny microphone to his collar. The studio lights dimmed and sitar music rose. The cross on the screen expanded outward, filling the screen with a golden glow that faded into the image of a benevolently smiling Isiah looking every bit like a compassionate Jesus in shimmering lavender satin robes sitting in a meditative pose on a large embroidered pillow with gold tassels. His expressive brown eyes looked pleading and expectant.

"Thank you for the honor of this conversation, my son," he said in his Oxford sounding voice. "I am honored by your presence and thank the Lord for bringing the blessing that you are to me." He looked up. "Thy will be done on earth as it is in heaven."

Ted "felt" Theo's thoughts inside of him. It felt nice to have them reinforcing his own thoughts, but he didn't feel any need to rely on them. He knew what to say.

"I hope you can find it in your heart to accept the truth that I embody," Isiah said softly. "I have been chosen by the one true father, maker of heaven and earth, to announce to the world the second coming of Christ consciousness."

"I'm not so sure about that."

Isiah smiled. "We have done many hours of research and have deduced that the simple presence of your immaculately conceived Christ child Theo is the source of the miraculous healing power that has made you so successful. That is a huge role for one so young to play." He made the sign of the cross in the air in front of him. "We possess everything you need to call the faithful to our flock in service to the only begotten son of God."

"Thank you, but we don't need any help."

His smile grew. "We hold the solution to all of your problems, particularly the genetic editing mandate that you refuse to accept." He held his hands out wide. "We can make all of that go away. If you look at how this has come about it becomes clear that it is all divinely ordained." His eyes appeared to glitter when he put his hands together and looked up. "All is perfection!"

"Thank you again, but we have chosen our own self-sufficient path."

Isiah made a dismissive gesture. "This will convince you that it is the will of God, written in Matthew eighteen, one through six."

He held up a lavender colored satin bundle and unwrapped a large elaborate leather bound bible embellished with gold book corners and opened it in his lap to read aloud.

"Matthew one. At the same time came the disciples unto Jesus, saying, Who is the greatest in the kingdom of heaven?

"Verse two. And Jesus called a little child unto him, and set him in the midst of them.

"Three, and said, Verily I say unto you, Except ye be converted, and become as little children, ye shall *not* enter into the kingdom of heaven.

"Four. Whosoever therefore shall humble himself as this little child, the same is greatest in the kingdom of heaven.

"Five. And whoso shall receive one such little child in my name receiveth me.

"Six. But whoso shall offend one of these little ones which believe in me, it were better for him that a millstone were hanged about his neck, and that he were drowned in the depth of the sea."

Isiah looked up. "It is written here and clearly shows our role to keep safe and protect your blessed child, Theo. We can guarantee his safety from any harm and resolve any problems so he can go forth and heal in the name of the Lord with the blessing and support of the church to usher in the Christ consciousness of the new age."

Ted looked down and the words came. "My favorite bible verse is Luke seventeen verse twenty one. The kingdom of God, Jesus replied, is not something people will be able to see and point to. Then came these striking words: Neither shall they say, Lo here! or, lo there! for, behold, the kingdom of God is within you.

"Theo, Jeanette and I have no desire to be part of a church. We are self-sustaining and have all the church we will ever need inside of and surrounding us."

A saddened expression stole over Isiah's face and he shook his head. "I fear that the forces of darkness will consume you without our aid and protection. Please, don't make the mistake of refusing the love and protection we offer you. It is written."

"Let me spell it out one last time so there are no misunderstandings. We cannot become or be associated with any churches. If we became a church we would draw followers which goes against what we stand for. The truth lies in each person following their hearts and staying faithful to the inner guidance that has been there all along. No one will find it outside of themselves and no guru or spiritual leader can bring it to them. The best that can happen is for someone else to reflect it back to them from its source which lies in their hearts."

Isiah put his hands together in prayer and looked down. "I will pray that the Lord God has mercy on your misguided soul and that you see the light that I am so you can come to and become one with it and I pray that this happens before the forces of darkness swallow you and yours." He looked up, his brown eyes wide in a beseeching look. "I won't take no for an answer but I will respect the fact that you are considering my offer."

Ted stood. "I said what I have to say so there is nothing more to discuss. Thank you for your generous offer which we will decline." He turned away from the screen and looked to Theo and Jeanette who also stood. "Come on you guys. We have work to do."

FORTY SEVEN

Temple Nutritionals received a hundred thousand dollar donation from the Praise the Lordcast the next day in the name of their prophet Isiah.

"I'm going to email them and turn it down," Ted said.

Of course, but you know that they're going to keep coming. Though it might not seem like it, they are playing their part in the greater unfolding.

Ted dragged his chair closer to the keyboard and typed.

Dear Stewart, Carla, and Isiah,

Thank you for your generous donation but we cannot accept it.

Temple Nutritionals already has everything we need.

Going forward please refrain from instigating any further contact with us.

Thank you.

Ted Driscoll

Ted pushed back his chair and wiped his hands. "That's enough of that."

For now.

A relentless but manageable flow of homeless continued to pass through Temple Nutritionals which kept them occupied.

"I can't believe how smooth everything is going," Jeanette said to Ted while locking the clinic's front door at closing time.

Our biggest challenges are still to come, so enjoy this peace while you can because everything is about to get more chaotic and will be coming at us faster and stronger like birth contractions. It will be a struggle but each wave will make us stronger while guiding us to fulfilling our purpose.

A middle-aged lanky, dark-haired man dressed in a navy blue suit wearing a red tie stepped out of a silver Mercedes in front of Temple Nutritionals the next morning when they opened the front door.

It took a moment before Ted recognized Sidney Sudberg, chief counsel for Bliss Pharmaceuticals. He came in carrying a small leather briefcase which he fished a sheaf of papers from.

"Sidney, great to see you!" Ted said, extending his hand.

Sidney held the papers and briefcase under his arm and gave Ted a brief handshake. "I wish I could say the same, Ted. I never understood why you left the company the way you did but I never wished you any ill will for it. Regardless of your decisions you were always a straight shooter and I respect that so please don't shoot the messenger. If I had my way none of this would even happen but I have to follow orders and serve you this summons and subpoena on behalf of Bliss Pharmaceuticals. They are requesting all of your records as part of their law suit against you for patent infringement and violating your noncompete agreement and your NDA." His shoulders slumped. "I tried to talk them out of it but they are insistent so I had to be the bearer of bad news."

"That's absurd," Jeanette muttered.

Ted made a dismissive gesture. "Don't worry about it, Sid. We have nothing to hide."

Sid's eyes grew wide. "Aren't you worried about what they're going to find?"

Ted patted him on the shoulder. "As I said, we have nothing to hide."

"Okay," Sid said, looking uncertain. "I have to play my part in this but there is nothing personal in any of it from me. It's all business and I have to do what they pay me to do regardless of my personal feelings."

"No worries, Sid."

Sid sighed. "Thank you for understanding and if it is any consolation I hope you prevail."

"We will," Ted said, a little too quickly.

Sid shook his hand again and nodded to Jeanette before turning around and heading for the door.

"Shouldn't we be hiring a lawyer?" Jeanette asked after the door closed.

Theo came out from the back room. "We don't need a lawyer to speak the truth. We have nothing to hide. Our purpose is to serve the greater good so we have guidance that is way ahead of anything a lawyer can come up with. People will be discovering more and more about me as time passes which will create even bigger challenges for us but it is all a process of learning and discovery for everyone involved."

Ted crossed his arms and shook his head. "It's going to be a ton of work getting all those records together."

"No it won't," Jeanette said, brightening. "I have it all organized on our web site that they can download to their heart's content. We even have all of your scanned notes and the pictures you took of Theo's formulas, his Tinker Toy molecules, and the geometries he drew."

"It might not seem like the best way to do it," Theo said, "but this will be a big step in getting our work out into the world so others can benefit from it. Bliss Pharmaceuticals will try to block that from happening because they want to profit from our work by claiming it as their own and they will do everything they can to discredit us so they can take us over and turn us into a money making machine that benefits them and their stockholders."

Ted snorted. "It doesn't sound any different from the Praise the Lordcast."

Theo smirked. "It isn't."

FORTY EIGHT

The honorable judge Victor Villaseñor tapped his gavel and sat up straight in his chair at the judge's bench in The Superior Court of San Diego County. Heavy set, his salt and pepper shaggy hair, bushy mustache, and goatee made him look like a conquering conquistador. "At the request of Sidney Sudberg, chief counsel for the plaintiff Bliss Pharmaceuticals we're here for a pre-trial consultation with the defendants Temple Nutritionals to try and settle matters without going to trial. If we have to go to trial we will establish the ground rules for written requests, oral depositions, and the discovery phase, as well as assigning trial dates."

A plump dark-haired court reporter sitting at a desk to the left of the judge's bench tapped away at her stenographic machine.

Ted sat alone at a table across from the judge's bench on the left side opposite another table to the right with three attorneys sitting behind it; Sidney Sudberg Chief Counsel, Kayla Lithgow, a conservatively dressed petite blonde with a bob cut, and Bill McBride, a tall balding gray-haired man also dressed in navy blue with eyes that matched the color of his hair.

Jeanette sat in the first row behind Ted on the other side of the railing with her arm around Theo.

Judge Villaseñor cleared his throat. "I see that the plaintiff is well represented, but I don't see any representation for Temple Nutritionals. Where is your attorney, Mr. Driscoll?"

Ted stood. "I'm representing myself, you honor."

Villaseñor squinted. "Do you think that is a wise choice?" He looked down and read from something on his desk. "California Civil Code Section thirty four twenty six point one includes a definition of trade secrets that protect a broad definition of information. Civil penalties can include monetary damages or an injunction to prevent further violations of the agreement including copyright infringement, breach of fiduciary responsibility, and violations of intellectual property. This includes drawings, computer codes, programs, formulas, and business techniques. You can also be held liable for punitive damages, legal fees, and other costs associated with this lawsuit. Additionally criminal penalties can bring significant incarceration time so I will ask you again, do you think that it is a wise choice to represent yourself without an attorney?"

Ted looked down shaking his head, then looked up. "I know. I know. A man who is his own lawyer has a fool for a client. Call me crazy but I have nothing to hide. I have broken no laws and I am confident that truth will prevail here in our justice system."

Judge Villaseñor chuckled. "Thank you for the vote of confidence. I hope that the truth will prevail here too."

Sidney stood. "If it pleases the court, out of respect for the value of the court's time, in a show of good faith, the board of directors of Bliss Pharmaceuticals have authorized me to offer a settlement of ten million dollars to cease and desist operations and turn all products and formulas made by Temple Nutritionals over to them."

"We've already done that," Ted said."

"I'm not talking about what we subpoenaed."

"Actually we are. Everything we gave you is in the public domain under a Creative Commons Attribution-Noncommercial four point zero International License that requires reusers to give credit to the creator. It also allows reusers to distribute, remix, adapt, and build upon the source material in any medium or format. Only noncommercial use of our work is permitted which means work not intended for or directed towards commercial advantage or monetary compensation."

Sidney looked wide-eyed before blurting, "Do you mean to tell me you are giving *all* of it away?

"For anyone who can use it."

"Isn't that a bit presumptuous when the patents and copyrights of those very same properties are being questioned here as part of this lawsuit?"

Ted shrugged. "They are not in any of Bliss Pharmaceuticals' archives or patents. I move that we subpoena all of *their* records like they did ours which will prove my point."

Sidney sat down and Kayla Lithgow the petite blonde lawyer, stood. "So if none of your products fall under Bliss patents you must have registered patents of your own.

Ted shook his head. "We have no patents. We believe that everything should be given freely and have made it all available to anyone who wants it on our website for the taking. Look it up!"

The court fell silent for a moment before the judge spoke.

"In all my years on the bench that's the first time I've ever heard anything like that."

"Your settlement offer is moot at this point," Ted said to Kayla, "but a donation of that size to the homeless would be a nice community outreach gesture for Bliss Pharmaceuticals."

"Your honor," Kayla said. "As my colleague stated it is the patents and copyrights of these properties that are being questioned in this lawsuit, not their value."

"So it's clear that reaching a settlement is off the table," Judge Villaseñor said, "which means we can move ahead with trial preparations. I'll have my clerk give you my instructions regarding protocol, rules for written requests, depositions, discovery, and any other relevant details and my clerk will add the trial dates to my calendar so we can begin voir dire." The judge looked directly at Ted. "Any questions?"

"No sir."

Villaseñor nodded. "Good luck, son."

FORTY NINE

Ted, Jeanette, and Theo sat together in their hidden lounge at the clinic having breakfast before opening the next day.

"My mom always said that the wheels of justice turn slowly," Jeanette said.

Ted set his coffee cup down. "She was right. This is going to drag out. It'll be a couple of months before jury selection gets started and the trial could go on for weeks or longer after that." He looked to Theo. "I don't have the slightest clue about how to select a jury."

"It's not going to matter in the bigger scheme of things," Theo said. "It's only the start of this part of our adventure. We're going to have a lot more to deal with than Bliss Pharmaceuticals, the Praise the Lordcast, and the federal gene editing mandate from Fetal Fantasies."

"I thought we were pretty final in our reply to the church," Jeanette said.

Theo ate the last strawberry from his fruit bowl. "That was not as final as you think. Their A.I. profit Isiah has a lots of influence and practically unlimited resources."

Ted stood and went out to the reception area to open the front door. "I figured as much. In the mean time we have people to help. I don't know about you two but I'm ready to get this show on the road. We can't let these other issues interfere with our work."

Jeanette picked up their dishes and brought them to the kitchen. "Even if that is what they are trying to do."

With Ted out of the room, Theo continued speaking internally to keep him in the conversation. *All of their manipulations will only fan the fires of our work and bring us more attention which as unpleasant as it seems will end up serving us when it all comes together.*

"I wish I had your confidence," Jeanette said.

You do whether you know it or not so don't let all of these greedy fear-based entities distract you from our true purpose because they are going to keep coming at us faster and faster and in greater numbers.

"I can hardly wait."

You won't have to. We'll have another visit from an old friend of dad's later today.

Ted opened the front door to the usual line of homeless with junk-laden shopping carts, wheelchairs, and bicycles. Jeanette came out from the back and took her place at the reception desk.

Later that morning she popped her head into the treatment room between patients. "There's a Ian Wood on the line. Says he knows you. He wants to know when is the best time to come talk to you. He says it's important."

"Tell him to come at closing time."

"Got it!"

A black Ford Escape with US Government license plates pulled up when Ted went to lock the front door at closing time. Ian Wood, a heavy set brown-haired man with a neatly trimmed Van Dyke beard stepped out, waving when he saw Ted.

Ted let him, locked the door behind him, and gestured toward the couch in the reception area. "Hi Ian, You're the last person I expected to see."

He's exactly who I expected to see.

Ian shook Ted's hand. "I don't understand how it has come to this, then again you shocked us all when you flipped and agreed with our concerns about safety and addiction in the process. That was career suicide, especially with all the board members pushing for approval and all the money tied up in it." He gave a half-smile. "Though I thought it insane you have my respect for taking a stand. Ballsy move!"

Jeanette came out from the back room and joined them while Theo stayed out of sight.

"Hi honey," Ted said. "This is Ian Wood from the FDA."

"I remember you talking about him when you were trying to get the Trazocodone approved." She gave Ian a quick nod. "What can we do for you?"

"As I was telling Ted I don't know how it has come to this, but I suspect that it is tied to the failed Trazocodone approval."

Ian took a deep breath and exhaled. "Temple Nutritionals is now under investigation by the FDA. I'm sorry that I am the one leading the investigation because I respect you but I have to follow my orders."

Ted shrugged. "We have nothing to hide."

Ian shook his head and handed Ted a search warrant. "This is no doubt retaliation for sabotaging their approval and I understand that you are also being sued by them, so in their eyes this investigation not only puts more pressure on you but they feel it can add to their case against you."

Ted studied the warrant. "That's fine. Like I said, we have nothing to hide."

"I'll do my best to make this as painless as possible."

"Everything you need is available on our web site," Jeanette said. "You are also welcome to inspect our physical inventory but I'd like to ask you not to interfere with our normal work hours."

"Agreed. The issues we are investigating have nothing to do with the NDA, copyright, and intellectual property issues contained in the law suit. What's at issue is the need to insure that the supplements and treatments you prescribe are properly classified as drugs defined in the Food, Drug, and Cosmetic Act, Title Twenty One, Subchapter Two of the United States Code of law. There are many criteria that can make a substance a drug, including whether it is registered in the US Pharmacopoeia or whether its intended use is to diagnose, cure, mitigate, treat, or prevent disease."

Ted held out his hands. "We can reassure you with any kind of analysis you wish that every one of our supplements are naturally present in the human body."

"That may be but the law makes it clear that a given substance can be both a drug and a food or dietary supplement. The distinction being that a food or dietary supplement cannot include a medicinal claim or intended use."

"Most people who consume healthy foods or dietary supplements do so with the specific intention or hope that they will be preventing future disease," Ted said. "If they're taking vitamin C does that mean that it becomes a drug?"

"There are regulations and requirements for over the counter sales..."

"You and I both know," Ted cut in, "that by and large most nutritional supplements haven't been developed as drugs because being natural, corporations like Bliss Pharmaceuticals cannot benefit from patents."

Mother nature never asks for anything but love for all the gifts that she gives freely. It is only man in his greed who puts a price on what should be free and shared equally.

"Believe me, I understand that," Ian said. "Unfortunately Bliss has deep ties and influence with the government."

"Why doesn't that surprise me?" Jeanette said.

FIFTY

Jeanette walked in to their back room lounge and held up a summons. "A cop just delivered this." She showed it to Theo before handing it to Ted. "You weren't kidding when you said we were going to have more to deal with than the Bliss lawsuit, the Praise the Lordcast, and the genome editing from Fetal Fantasies."

Ted glanced at it. "It's from the Attorney General and the Medical Board of California."

"What's does say?" Theo asked.

Ted studied it a moment longer before reading. "This summons requires your appearance at The Superior Court of California, County of San Diego as part of an investigation to determine whether criminal charges of practicing medicine without a license are warranted. These charges can lead to jail time, probation, and significant fines. Additionally, if the licensing board charges you with the unlicensed practice of medicine, you can face discipline or revocation of your license."

Jeanette gasped. "We don't even have a license."

"And we have not done any medical procedures either," Theo said.

Ted continued. "The unauthorized practice of medicine is defined by the California Business and Professions Code Section Twenty Fifty Two. It involves practicing, attempting to practice, or advertising or holding yourself out as practicing any system or mode of treating illness or affliction; diagnosing, treating, operating on, or prescribing medication for any ailment, blemish, deformity, disease, disfigurement, disorder, injury, or other physical or mental condition, or conspiring with, or aiding and abetting someone else to do any of the above."

"This ties in with the bogus argument from the FDA about how something can be a drug and a food or dietary supplement, and whether the distinction being a food or dietary supplement includes a medicinal claim or intended use," Jeanette said.

"We can easily prove that all of our supplements are naturally present in the human body," Theo said," and we don't make any medical claims."

Jeanette nodded to Ted. "What else does it say?"

Ted started reading again. "The initial phase of this investigation requires medical records and any additional information necessary to determine if a violation of the law occurred. After all the information has been gathered the courts will analyze it to determine if there is sufficient evidence for referral to a medical consultant. When a medical consultant determines that a violation has occurred the matter is referred to the Division of Investigation, Health Quality Investigation Unit within the Department of Consumer Affairs.

"The investigation process is lengthy and consistent with due process of law and is conducted in an ethical manner to determine whether the Board can prove that a violation occurred by clear and convincing evidence. If action is warranted a charging document identifying the allegations against the medical provider will be filed by the Attorney General's Office."

Jeanette crossed her arms and dropped into a chair. "We don't perform *any* procedures and as Theo says, every one of our supplements is already present in the human body."

"Here's the last part," Ted said. "It's kind of a catch twenty two." He started reading again. "Unauthorized practice of medicine is a wobbler offense which can be charged as either a misdemeanor or a felony depending on if there is any criminal history and the facts of the case. This law covers a broad range of actions and is not limited to a particular type of medicine. It applies to *any* system or mode of treating the sick or afflicted, and to diagnosing, treating, operating, or prescribing any physical or mental health condition. It can be charged both when a person practices or attempts to practice medicine, or advertises or holds themself out as practicing without a license to do so. It also prohibits the ownership of medical practices by a person who is not a licensed healthcare professional in California. Even if the owners of the practice do not provide any medical services they can be charged with unauthorized practice of medicine simply for owning it."

"All we've ever done is help people and we're getting persecuted for it." Jeanette shook her head. "I can't believe this bullshit."

"I am not surprised at the lawsuit from Bliss," Ted said. "In fact I half expected it. They had millions tied up in Trazocodone and we were close to FDA approval when I reversed my position which shocked the hell out of them and I honestly can't blame them. They see me as a traitor to their cause and in many respects they are right so I understand how the FDA investigation ties in, but criminal charges of practicing medicine without a license is overkill."

Theo shrugged. "Everything is going according to the plan and in the end everything will work to our advantage."

Jeanette frowned. "You still think that?"

"I know it."

"So we're clear," Ted said, "everything is going according to the plan but you don't know what the plan is."

"I don't know what the plan is as it unfolds but I know that the path reveals itself to us in each moment and our hearts are the compass that will guide us."

"I wish I had your confidence," Jeanette said.

Theo smiled. *You do. You just have to trust in it.*

An expansive wave of emotional warmth stole over Ted and Jeanette accompanied by a brief synesthetic flurry of colors, patterns, and sensations.

FIFTY ONE

Jeanette cringed when she saw the caller ID on her cell phone when it rang one morning before they went to the clinic.

"Who is it?" Ted said.

"Doctor Kennedy," Theo said without looking up from his fruit bowl.

"I don't want to answer," Jeanette said.

"Put it on speakerphone," Ted said. "We can't ignore him. It'll only make things worse. We have to indulge him for as long as we can for Theo's sake."

Jeanette tapped her cellphone and set it down on the table between them. "Hi Doctor Kennedy. I'm here with Ted and Theo and I have you on speaker. How are you?"

"I'm doing fine. I'm calling to check up on Theo."

"Hi Doctor Kennedy," Theo said. "I'm doing really good."

"You're my favorite patient and you know I care about you very much. That's why I'm calling."

He really does care and is convinced he is doing the right thing, but he has no idea that their gene editing treatment will send me into a deep state of autism.

"I don't mean to sound like I'm being pushy. I really am on your side, but I am being pressured by the federal government and the management of Fetal Fantasies to complete Theo's CHD8 gene editing treatment. All of the other parents have complied with the mandate with no noticeable side effects. Your lack of compliance has increased the attention on Theo, especially in light of the delays and signs of autism we have seen in his development."

"But he's perfect," Jeanette said. "You said so yourself."

Kennedy let out an exaggerated sigh. "I am not arguing that. My concern is that the procedure has been signed into law. I don't understand why you are so resistant to it. It's harmless. All we want to do is add an extra copy of a healthy gene to insure that Theo has normal activity and synaptic communication."

Ted rolled his eyes. "He already has normal activity and his language gets better every day."

"I don't understand why they want to mess with perfection," Jeanette said. "That doesn't make any sense."

"We also want to clone his genome as a secondary preventative measure in case something did happen. The pressure is on me and I can't stop them. It's going to happen anyway so let's get it over with. Come to the clinic today and I'll have you in and out in under an hour."

"It's not going to happen today," Jeanette said.

Kennedy snorted. "I hate even saying this, but If you don't comply, Child Protective Services will take Theo from you and you will be prosecuted for child endangerment not only under California penal codes, but under federal statutes as well."

"We appreciate your concern," Ted said, "and we apologize for putting you in this position but we're not going to do it."

"Why?"

Tell him it goes against your religious beliefs. That will give the government pause and the freedom of religion issue will slow things down some.

"This procedure goes against our religious beliefs," Ted said.

"What?"

"It goes against our religious beliefs," Jeanette repeated, "and I have to admit that I'm not thrilled about cloning our little boy either."

There was an awkward pause before Kennedy said, "What religion is that? What church are we talking about?"

Ted smiled. "We are a no church movement who sees the human body as a temple and we carry our church inside of us."

"Wait a minute! You're telling me that you are refusing this treatment on the grounds of freedom of religion, but you don't belong to a church?"

"We *are* the church."

Kennedy went silent for longer than the first time and finally said, "Freedom of religion without a church?"

"The First Amendment states that congress shall make no law respecting an establishment of religion," Ted said, "or prohibiting the free exercise thereof and it does not favor any particular faiths over others. These protections allow religious liberty to thrive and it safeguards religion and government from the undue influences of the other."

"Can you really claim freedom of religion without belonging to a church?"

Ted smirked. "Like I said, in our view we *are* the church. Everyone is! Religious freedom includes the right to religious belief and expression and a guarantee that the government doesn't prefer religion over non-religion. We don't need to be part of a church to exercise our right to religious freedom. It falls under non-religion."

"So you're claiming freedom of religion for a non-religion as grounds for your refusal to comply with a federal mandate?"

"Our forefathers understood that you can have your own spiritual beliefs and you don't need a religion or a church to tell you what you should and shouldn't do."

"We follow the guidance of our hearts," Jeanette added.

"I've never heard of anything like this," Kennedy said. "I'm familiar with the First Amendment but I have never heard it interpreted this way. I've always thought that freedom of religion goes hand in hand with churches and religion."

"This goes straight to the heart of the matter," Ted said, "but here is the difference. Religion is a specific set of organized beliefs and practices based on the words of prophets and is typically shared by a community or a group. Spirituality is an individual practice and has to do with having a sense of peace and purpose. It also relates to the process of developing beliefs around the meaning of life and connection with others. If you want to define things more specifically we consider ourselves spiritual but not religious and we're covered under the First Amendment."

"I know this won't sit well with the management of Fetal Fantasies and I don't know how it will fly with the federal regulators but I'll run it up the flagpole on your behalf, although I still think you should allow us to do the procedure. Overall it would be better for all concerned."

"Thank you for caring," Jeanette said, "but our minds are made up."

FIFTY TWO

The mailman slipped through the front door past the line of homeless holding up a letter. "Good morning, I have a certified letter I need you to sign for."

Jeanette felt her gut tighten when she saw that the letter was from the IRS. She scribbled her signature and tore open the envelope after the mailman left. Her hands shook when she saw that Temple Nutritionals was being audited. "Jesus," she muttered. "I can't believe this is happening." She went back to the treatment room where she found Ted and Theo and waved the letter in the air.

"I know," Ted said. "Theo just told me that we're being audited."

Jeanette tossed the letter on the examination table. "I don't know how much more of this shit I can take. I'm so mad, I couldn't bring myself to look at all that mumbo jumbo."

Ted picked the letter up and scanned it. "They're accusing us of tax evasion and reminding us that tax fraud is a federal crime with a not so subtle reminder that they can freeze all of our assets and we can face steep fines and jail time."

"How the hell can they accuse us of that?"

Ted continued reading. "They claim we were selected for an audit that they run every tax return through to compare us to similar filings to assign a rating. According to them we were selected by an algorithm called the Unreported Income Discrimination Function that reviews returns. They are accusing us of a false filing status, unreported income, unacceptable deductions, and no eligibility for any claimed credits."

Jeanette snorted. "That's all bullshit!"

Ted dropped the letter. "Of course it is."

Theo hugged her. "Don't let it get to you, Mom. It's just another move on the chess board. All of this increasing pressure has a life of its own and it's coming to a peak that will bring the truth out in the end."

"Is it ever going to end?"

"I'm sorry," Theo said. "It probably doesn't bring you much comfort, but if you can bring some objectivity to all this unwanted attention and think of it like having a front row seat to a circus it might make it a little easier to deal with."

Ted chuckled. "The clown show to be exact!"

Jeanette hugged Theo a little tighter. "And you still insist that it's serving a greater purpose?"

"Yes."

"But you don't know how that is going to happen."

Only that it will. That you can be sure of.

A wave of emotional warmth filled Ted and Jeanette's hearts accompanied by a flurry of colors, patterns, and sensations that ended in a fading ultraviolet haze that brought a smile to Jeanette.

"Can you leave that on for awhile?" she asked.

Theo looked up at her grinning. "I could, but your neurochemistry would adapt to it and it would lose its effectiveness making it similar to a dependency on antidepressants."

"It's too bad you can't make that happen for all these people harassing us," Ted said.

"Aside from the fact that I don't have the same connection with them that I have with you their hearts are not open enough to accept it, and besides that it would be cheating."

Jeanette frowned. "And they're playing fair?"

"Of course they're not playing fair," Theo said, "but they are playing their part in the bigger unfolding. Our job is to keep healing as many people as we can while we can. We only have limited time but each person we heal will touch other people that they come in contact with and spread the loving energy."

Ted leaned his head toward the reception area. "The best thing we can do is keep working. There's a line of people waiting out there who need our help. We can't control what's going to happen so the best thing to do is focus on what we can make happen."

FIFTY THREE

The next couple of weeks passed without further harassment, but Jeanette dreaded every time the phone rang or an unfamiliar car pulled up in front of the clinic, and when the mailman came.

"I don't know," she said one day while closing the clinic. "It's been nice not having to deal with all of that persecution, but the quiet is starting to get unnerving."

"I know what you're saying," Ted said. "It's the not knowing that eats away at me. I can't help feeling like everything is bubbling below the surface ready to erupt when we least expect it."

"The storm is building," Theo said, "and the thunder and lightning is about to begin bringing a downpour. No matter what happens, how it happens, or how difficult it becomes, we are instruments in a bigger divine plan and the greater good *will* be served."

The growing uncertainty of their ongoing problems and their imminent eruption grew heavier with each passing day. Ted and Jeanette felt an odd sense of relief when their first court date at the San Diego Superior Court finally arrived.

"I can't leave you home alone by yourself," Jeanette said that morning at breakfast. "You're only six years old!"

Theo grinned and jabbed his chest with his thumb. "I'm only six years old in my body." He jabbed his thumb at his head. "but I've grown a little more here."

"Kids aren't allowed in the courtroom," Ted said, "and Theo is more than capable of taking care of himself, but I'd feel a lot better having him with us."

"I know," Jeanette said with a tremor in her voice. "Criminal charges in Superior Court? That scares me. Are they going to put us in jail?"

Ted and Jeanette felt an expansive wave of love sweep through them before Theo leaned forward and reached out taking their hands.

Be ready for some surprises today and remember, no matter what challenges we face, we'll get through them together.

An hour later Ted and Jeanette stood looking up at the San Diego Superior Court building standing out against the skyline with its canopy of shaped aluminum panels reflecting light while shading its eastern facade.

Ted took her hand. "Okay honey, let's go have fun playing Bonnie and Clyde."

She snorted. "Some fun!" She took his hand and squeezed it followed by half-hearted smile.

After checking in at the clerk's office a burly black-haired cop with a bushy moustache led them through the booking process where they were fingerprinted and photographed for mug shots.

"How humiliating," Jeanette said when they were led out to a courtroom a few doors down from the one they had been in before. "We're being treated like criminals," she whispered.

Ted put his arm around her, speaking in a low voice. "We're Bonnie and Clyde and we have the mug shots to prove it!"

"Oh Ted, stop it!" She giggled.

They went into the courtroom and were directed to sit where Ted had sat before across from the judge's bench opposite an empty table to the right. A thin, dark haired young Asian girl sat at the desk beside the judge's bench behind a stenographic machine and the heavy set cop who had booked them stood across from her.

They turned when they heard the back doors to the court swing open to see three men carrying briefcases come down the aisle.

A tall silver-haired man dressed in a gray suit and a light blue tie led a younger blond-haired man in a blue suit and matching tie to the prosecutor's desk. They both nodded to Ted and Jeanette when they came through the gate.

The third frail balding man wearing a black suit with a gold cross on his lapel and a red tie sat on the other side of the railing behind Ted and Jeanette. He leaned forward as if about to speak when the cop said, "All rise for the honorable judge Andrew Blazer of the San Diego Superior Court."

A salt and pepper-haired man in black robes and a neatly trimmed goatee emerged from behind the bench and nodded toward the court before sitting down at the judge's bench. When the rest of the court sat he tapped his gavel and spoke in a firm tone. "The business here today before the court is based on the Attorney General's evidence backed by the Medical Board of California as well as the Division of

Investigation, Health Quality Investigation Unit within the Department of Consumer Affairs. The district attorney's office has filed criminal charges of practicing medicine without a license as defined by the California Business and Professions Code Section twenty fifty two. Is that correct Mr. Doyle?"

The silver-haired man stood. "Yes, your honor. The prosecution intends to prove that Mr. and Mrs. Driscoll under the guise of Temple Nutritionals diagnosed, treated, and performed procedures on, as well as prescribed medication for patients in violation of California Code twenty fifty two BPC."

The judge turned his steely gaze on Ted and Jeanette. "Mr. and Mrs. Driscoll," he said with authority. "You have the right to an attorney, the right to remain silent, the right to have a trial and be presumed innocent until proven guilty, and the right to a speedy trial as well as the right to a jury trial." He frowned. "You also have the right to be represented by an attorney and can be appointed one by the court at no cost if you cannot afford one."

"Your honor, if I may," the frail looking man said from the other side of the railing behind Ted and Jeanette. They looked back to see the frail balding man in the black suit with the gold cross on his lapel standing with a raised finger.

Judge Blazer nodded. "Yes?"

"If it pleases the court," the man said in a reedy voice, "I would like to represent the Driscoll's in this matter."

Ted looked at Jeanette and shrugged, then turned to Judge Blazer. "Your honor, I don't…"

Go with him.

"I mean…" Ted stopped himself.

"And you are?" The judge asked the man.

"Eric Hart, Criminal Defense attorney."

Judge Blazer gave a wry smile. "I thought I recognized you, counsellor. Your reputation precedes you."

"Thank you, your honor. I hope that's not a bad thing."

The judge's smile widened and was echoed by the court reporter. "You are not sitting with your clients so you have not had time to confer with them. Do you accept Mr. Hart as your counsel, Mr. Driscoll?"

"Yes, your honor, as long as he pleads us not guilty on all counts."

Hart nodded. "Consider it done, your honor."

Judge Blazer tapped his gavel. "Both the defense and the prosecution have a right to a preliminary hearing within 10 court days which can be delayed if there is good cause. You also have the right to have the preliminary hearing within sixty days under California Penal Code section nine fifty nine B."

"If it pleases the court and the prosecution," Hart said, "Due to the fact that I have just taken this case and have not had time to confer with my clients or examine the evidence and details of the district attorney's investigation I would like to request the full sixty days for the preliminary hearing to allow adequate time for discovery."

"I have no objections your honor," Doyle said. "Although I do not think the Driscoll's are a flight risk two months is the longest admissible time under section nine fifty nine B, and this is a felony, so I would like to propose a one hundred thousand dollar bail."

"What?" Jeanette blurted," That's…"

Accept it. It's part of the game.

Hart leaned forward and put a hand on Jeanette's shoulder. "That seems a bit extreme, your honor."

Blazer leaned back and nodded. "Agreed, but I see both of your points. Bail is set at fifty thousand dollars." He tapped his gavel again.

"Fifty thousand dollars?" Jeanette gasped. "We can't…"

Hart pressed on her shoulder. "That's acceptable." He leaned in closer to Jeanette and lowered his voice. "Don't worry it's covered. I'll explain later, and please don't speak unless asked. The judge does not like it when you speak out of turn and could charge you with contempt."

"But…"

Ted put his hand on her knee, silencing her.

FIFTY FOUR

"Who are you and where did you come from?" Ted said to Hart after Judge Blazer dismissed them.

Hart glanced over at the prosecutors who gathered their files and stuffed them into their briefcases. "Let's step outside so I can explain."

Ted and Jeanette followed him out of the courtroom to a bench a few doors down the hall where he handed Ted a business card and motioned for them to sit.

"I've been retained by Stewart Alderman in the name of the Praise the Lordcast church who are prepared to cover all of your fees and handle all of your legal problems."

Jeanette moaned. "I should have known."

"Why would they want to do that?" Ted asked. "We told Stewart that we want nothing to do with them."

"I don't think you realize that they are the answer to your prayers."

"Who says we were praying?" Ted said.

Hart shook his head and started to speak when Jeanette cut him off.

"This is all bullshit. We've never made any medical claims. All we do is help people and we have never done any medical procedures. They want to subpoena our medical records but we don't have any."

"We don't even know the names of the people we helped," Ted added.

"All we've ever done is help people and we're getting persecuted for it," Jeanette said.

Hart held up a hand. "I understand your frustration but you have to realize that this goes much deeper than it appears on the surface."

Humor him and the full agenda will be revealed.

Jeanette crossed her arms. "Do tell."

Hart lowered his voice. "If you come under the protection of the church we can make all of your problems disappear."

"How do we know you can do that?" Jeanette asked.

Hart smiled. "As a show of good faith we will terminate the IRS audit. Once you become part of our flock we can eliminate the charges from the other agencies which will free you to do the lord's work."

Ted's eyebrows raised. "Including Bliss Pharmaceuticals and the FDA?"

"And your gene editing problem with the federal government and Fetal Fantasies. The church of the Praise the Lordcast has more resources than you might imagine not to mention having the position of a fully incorporated church. Its nonprofit classification brings with it a legal status that carries far more credibility than your claims of being a no church church."

"You can end the IRS audit?" Jeanette said.

"Consider it done."

She shook her head. "Forgive my skepticism but I'll believe it when I see it."

"It's God's will."

"What if we refuse your help?" Ted asked.

Hart looked down and shook his head. "Then none of this will go away and you will be on your own."

Tell him you'll think about his offer. We don't want anything to do with him, the profit Isiah, or their church, but this plays into the bigger picture in ways I cannot explain right now. I only know that these machinations are part of the bigger unfolding and will ultimately help us achieve our purpose.

"We need some time to think things over," Jeanette said.

Hart's eyes widened in exaggerated disbelief. "I wouldn't take too long if I were you." He grinned. "You'll see how serious we are when your audit disappears." He pointed to the business card in Ted's hand. "Call me if you have any questions. In the meantime I will be getting the evidence the DA has in the discovery process so we can see what the basis is for their charges against you."

He already has everything. This is part of the game that the profit is playing behind the scenes.

"Sure," Ted said.

Hart grabbed his briefcase, stood and shook hands with Ted before taking Jeanette's hand and giving it a gentle squeeze. "Good enough. I need to go post your bail. I'll be in touch soon." He took a few steps and turned back looking over his shoulder. "The IRS will be gone in a couple of days."

Jeanette wiped her hand on her slacks. "Why do I feel like we're making a deal with the devil?"

There's no such thing as the devil but that doesn't discount the darkness at the core of the Praise the Lordcast church.

"Amen!" Ted said.

Ted and Jeanette felt Theo's giggles rippling through their hearts and minds and smiled, then Ted took her hand and pulled her close, saying, "Come on, Bonnie, Clyde's going to treat you to lunch at a fancy restaurant."

FIFTY FIVE

Two days later the mailman slipped through the front door holding up another certified letter from the IRS. Jeanette couldn't keep herself from smiling when she saw it.

"Must be good news," the mailman quipped, "and if it is it must be a miracle because I've never seen anybody getting good news from the IRS."

Jeanette signed for the letter, saying "Here's to hoping for a miracle."

"Good luck," the mailman said on the way out the door.

She hurried back to their kitchen area and waved the letter at Theo and Ted who sat on the couch.

Ted raised his eyebrows. "The IRS?"

She nodded.

"What's it say?"

She read the first paragraph from the letter. "The Internal Revenue Service apologizes for the clerical error that triggered your audit and we are writing to inform you that the audit has been terminated. Thank you for your understanding in this matter. Temple Nutritionals has no current tax liabilities and your collection case has been closed."

Ted held both his hands out wide. "Praise the Lord!"

Jeanette and Theo chuckled.

"What's our next move, son?" Ted asked.

"Stewart will be calling us in the name of Isiah to celebrate the incorporation of Temple Nutritionals into the Praise the Lordcast church."

Ted rubbed his hands together. "He's going to lose his mind when we turn him down."

Theo slid over closer to Ted and patted the cushion beside him. "Come sit Mom, we need to talk about this."

Jeanette sat down next to him and he put his arms out hugging her and Ted. "My love for you goes on forever and our connection goes way beyond these three-dimensions we share."

Jeanette leaned in and kissed him on top of his head. "We love you that much and more."

"We are one in our hearts and minds, especially in our hearts which have been resonating at a higher frequency."

Ted and Jeanette felt the familiar expansive wave of love sweep through them with more intensity than usual, causing Jeanette to put her hand over her heart.

"What's this all about?" she said.

"When we turn down the profit Isiah and his Praise the Lordcast church this time," Theo continued, "it will trigger events that will amplify the forces of darkness and escalate the chaos we have been attracting."

"You're scaring me," Jeanette said.

Theo hugged her tighter and Ted stretched out his arm around them both in a protective gesture.

"Fear is contraction and love is expansion," Theo said softly, then a little louder, "and the greater the darkness the brighter we shine. Those with purer hearts will be drawn to us while those sleepers who are lost in the darkness will be attracted to our light in a different way, driven by madness. The deeper they are submerged in the darkness the more madness they will experience and the more animosity they direct toward us will reflect back on them driving their madness deeper into its own vortex of negative energy."

"Psychic black holes," Ted said. "We're poking the dragon in the eye with our refusal to serve them."

"The irony is that we have not made a single aggressive move in any of this," Jeanette said. "They have all come to us. All we ever did was help the people who needed it the most."

Ted shook his head. "Human nature."

"This quickening will bring us more uncomfortable exposure," Theo said, "and the truth of our secret that we have been protecting for all of my life so far in this plane of existence is about to metamorphose into a major turning point in our relationship with each other."

"But we will get through it like we always do, right?" Jeanette said. "None of us are going to die or anything else horrible like that, right?"

Theo smiled. "The veils between the worlds are thinner than most imagine and they grow thinner by the day which is why our guiding light has to shine brighter even if it appears to be to our detriment."

"We're going to get separated, aren't we?" Ted said.

"Physically separated more than once in the coming days," Theo said, "but it will be temporary and a necessary step toward the resolution of our growing chaos."

No matter how far apart we may seem to be in these physical dimensions or in any other realms for that matter, our hearts are one, transcendent, and as such we are one with all that is. Though we may be separate from each other in time and space at different junctures we will never be separate in spirit. In the bigger scope of things within these moments of transformation we will always meet again each time with a growing number of like minded souls.

FIFTY SIX

"They'll call at closing time," Theo said while eating lunch with Ted and Jeanette in the clinic kitchen, "because they know that there will be no distractions and they will have our full attention."

"I can hardly wait," Jeanette said.

As predicted Ted's cell phone rang the moment he locked the front door. He glanced at Stewart's number on the screen and hurried back to the kitchen where he put his phone on speaker and set it down on the table between himself, Theo, and Jeanette. "Hello Stewart."

"Our prayers have been answered!" Stewart gushed.

"Praise be to God," Carla cried from the background. "And his prophet Isiah!"

"I can't tell you how overjoyed we are for the blessings the Lord has showered you with!" Stewart said, speaking rapid-fire. "This proves how powerful prayer really is! Our entire congregation has been praying for you and your family every day and night all over the world. I hope you realize how loved and blessed you are by so many. We are all rejoicing in the Lord in your honor for delivering you from the clutches of evil. We have a massive welcome banquet planned for you and your family and I am happy to report that our attorneys have negotiated a settlement with Bliss Pharmaceuticals, and don't worry, the church is footing the bill. We've also come to an agreement with the FDA and if that is not exciting enough we have word from the district attorney's office that they are planning to dismiss their charges against you when you become members of the church, and last but not least as revered members of the church our attorneys can block the gene editing procedure on the grounds of religious freedom. All of your troubles will disappear and you will be free to do the work of spreading the word of the Lord!"

"We love you and your adorable little boy so much," Carla squealed. "We've taken the liberty of enrolling him in an exclusive private school and we can bring in specialized tutors if you wish. We've already added your names to our twenty four hour prayer line so someone will be praying for you every hour of the day."

Time to shut them off.

"Allow me," Jeanette whispered, then louder. "Exclusive private school and specialized tutors?"

"That's right!"

"I don't think so."

"Excuse me?"

"No one educates Theo but us."

"Oh, well…"

"And we appreciate all your joy, celebration, and happiness," Ted cut in, "but no thank you."

"What?" Stewart blurted. After an uncomfortably long pause he chuckled. "That's quite the sense of humor you have there, Ted."

"Who says I'm trying to be funny?"

"You can't be serious! Do you realize what will happen to you without our protection?"

We're counting on it.

"Please tell me you're joking. You can't mean that after all we have done for you."

"I'm sorry Stewart but we never asked for any help from you. We told you over and over again that we are not interested in being part of the Praise the Lordcast church."

"But we have freed you to do the Lord's work."

"Who says that we are not already doing the Lord's work and who says that we need help or permission from anybody else to do it?"

Stewart's tone went from incredulous to indignant. "I can't believe you are actually saying this."

"Believe it!" Jeanette said.

Ted tapped the end call icon on his cell and high-fived Theo and Jeanette.

"We love you and your adorable little boy so much," Jeanette said imitating Carla in a mincing voice. "She sounds like the wicked witch trying to sound like Glinda the Good Witch. I think I'm going to puke!"

Ted's phone rang and he and Jeanette stared at it.

"I wouldn't bother picking it up," Theo said, "unless you want to hear more guilt and manipulation."

"No thanks," Jeanette said.

"This is our tipping point," Theo said. "All of our troubles will be coming back stronger than before along with some new ones. Now it is more important than ever for us to follow the guidance of our hearts no matter how chaotic our lives get, and make no doubt about it, our *real* challenges are only beginning."

FIFTY SEVEN

"I don't want to upset you," Theo said a few days later while they ate breakfast at the house, "but the FBI is coming to the clinic to arrest you today. They're going to put you in different rooms and try to get you to contradict each other but regardless of how isolated you might feel."

I will be with both of you and I will be fully aware of what is happening with each of you by being the link that makes us one mind.

"Where will you be?" Jeanette asked.

Theo smiled. *I'll be close to you as always and I will be safe. They will be very interested in finding me. This arrest and the charges they will accuse you of are just excuses to get to me.*

"What should we tell them?" Ted said. "There are all those child endangerment laws they can throw at us which they will tie in to the gene editing mandate."

"Which is in limbo in the courts because of the religious freedom exemption," Theo said. "You can tell them that you don't know where I am which will be the truth and you can tell them that you think I ran away because they scared me with all of their guns which will put the attention on them and their actions as opposed to you. You can even act scared and tell them to find me because they are the ones who scared me off. Have some fun with it!"

"Are you sure you will be all right?"

"Mom!"

"I know but no matter how advanced you might be inside of you you're still my little boy."

Ted ruffled Theo's hair. "I agree."

Theo took both their hands. "Proof that I made the right choice picking you to bring me into this world." He looked from Ted to Jeanette. "One more thing. The people we have been helping will not be happy when they come to take you away and there will be a potential for violence. We don't want that but their unhappiness will play a part in moving everything toward our greater purpose."

They drove South on I-5 after breakfast.

"They'll come when we open at nine this morning," Theo said when they turned onto Sea World Drive heading toward Ocean Beach. "The homeless will be lined up as usual but we won't open so they won't get caught up in the chaos of the FBI search but they will see you get taken away."

"We'll open the door for them when they come," Ted said, "and we'll let them look through whatever they want to their heart's content."

They'll come looking for me but they won't find me.

Ted watched the time on his cell phone after they arrived at the clinic. When it changed from 8:59 to 9:00 he looked up to see two black SUV's with flashing red and blue lights on their dashboards converge in front of Temple Nutritionals. "Right on time!" He patted Jeanette on the knee. "You okay, honey?"

She nodded.

Ted went to the front door, looking back at Jeanette and winking before unlocking it and pulling it open. "It's showtime!"

The four doors of both SUVs swung open and armed FBI agents wearing blue jackets with the yellow letters FBI on the front, arms, and in big letters on the back spilled out with their weapons raised.

Ted stepped out the front door and held his arms out. "Good morning!"

The advancing agents stopped and looked at one another with puzzled expressions, then a tall square-faced man with silver hair in a short military brush cut with wide shoulders pushed his way through the mob holding up a piece of paper and a badge.

"What the fuck is going on here!" A lanky homeless man wearing a ragged trench coat yelled out.

Two of the agents stepped off to the side blocking him. "This is none of your business," one of them said.

The silver-haired man narrowed his flinty gray eyes and thrust a warrant toward Ted. "I'm agent Schautz. We have a warrant for your arrest as well as a search and seizure of your premises."

Ted held his arms out wider. "Can you tell your storm troopers to put their guns away? You're going to scare the shit out of my wife and my little boy. I assure you that we are harmless."

Schautz studied Ted for a moment before making a downward motion with his hand. "Lower your weapons." He turned to a stocky red-haired man behind him. "Cuff him, Miller. The rest of you enter the premises. You know what to do."

"What the fuck are you assholes doing?" another homeless man shouted, stirring others to voice their unhappiness.

"Keep your pie holes shut," Miller said, "or we'll be hauling you away too."

The lanky man in the trench coat laughed and turned back to the others in line behind him. "You think we give a shit? Three hots and a cot. We'll take that."

"You need to disperse," the agent blocking the homeless line of people said. "The clinic is closed until further notice."

"Bullshit!" someone yelled out.

The others in line yelled in support of the lanky man while Miller cuffed Ted's hands in front of him.

Ted shook his head. "Is this necessary?"

Schautz nodded toward another agent who pulled out a cell phone and made a call.

While the rest of the agents filed in through the front door, making their way to the back of the clinic two San Diego black and whites pulled up. Ted recognized Perez and Collins who set up saw horse barricades strung with crime scene tape along with two other cops who pushed back the homeless and a growing crowd of onlookers.

Another FBI agent cuffed Jeanette and Miller sat Ted down on the couch beside her before heading into the back rooms.

Schautz came forward and stood over them. "Who tipped you off that we were coming?"

Ted pursed his lips and shook his head. "We have the right to remain silent."

"Great. You want to call a lawyer?"

"No thank you."

Schautz frowned. "Are you shitting me?"

Jeanette glared at him. "You heard my husband. We have nothing to say so let's get on with it."

"No lawyer?"

Miller came out from the back rooms shouting, "Clear!"

Don't worry. I'm with you and they'll never find me. Let them do the talking. It will be interesting to see how they explain themselves.

Schautz crossed his arms. "Where is he?"

Ted and Jeanette couldn't keep themselves from smiling.

"You think this is funny?"

Ted glanced at Jeanette and winked, then turned back to Schautz. "We have the right to remain silent."

"Fucking smart ass!" Schautz stormed off and followed Miller through the door to the back rooms and came out a few minutes later shaking his head. "We saw him enter the building with you and he has not left the premises, so I'll ask you again, where is he?"

Ted shrugged.

"We'll find him if we have to tear the whole building down."

"Good luck with that."

Half an hour later Schautz and half a dozen of his men huddled by the reception desk speaking in low tones. Every once in awhile one of them looked over at Ted and Jeanette.

Finally, Schautz said, "Keep looking. Check every vent, behind appliances, under everything, and open every box if you have to. He's only six years old so he's not that big which makes it easier for him to hide." He waved his men off.

"Come on." He gestured to Ted and Jeanette. "We're taking you in,"

They're going to separate you, but there is nothing to worry about. You have nothing to say and I am with you both.

Schautz and Miller led Ted and Jeanette outside where a bigger crowd now filled the street. A mob of homeless people let out a cheer sending a wave of exclamations through the crowd of onlookers. News crews with cameras pushed their way to the edge of the barricades. Cameras and cell phones flashed when Ted and Jeanette were put into the back seat of one of the black SUVs. The last thing Ted saw before the door to the SUV closed was Sara Johnston behind a barricade alongside her cameraman.

FIFTY EIGHT

Ted and Jeanette each sat alone in identical rooms with four white walls under fluorescent lighting. A large one-way mirror covered one wall and a red light shone from a camera in the corner above the door pointing down at a metal table and two chairs, the only furniture in the room.

The rooms you are in are the same. It will be interesting to see how they choose to interrogate you. Our heart connection has grown to the point where you can eavesdrop on each other's conversations, so there will be no secrets. It will also protect you from the deception they will employ to try and turn you against each other.

Theo's wind chime giggles rippled through them accompanied by a brief flash of colors, sounds, and geometries.

Ted leaned forward with his hands folded in front of him on the table when the door to his room opened. Agent Schautz came in carrying a file which he dropped onto the table before taking the chair across from Ted, staring at him with narrowed flinty gray eyes.

"Where is he?"

Ted shrugged. "How am I supposed to know? How would you feel if you were a six year old autistic little boy and a bunch of goons with guns stormed your building?" He pointed his finger. "Why are you even bothering talking to me?" He raised his voice feigning anger. "You should be out looking for my little boy who is frightened to death because of you."

Schautz leaned back in his chair and picked up the file, leafing through it before looking up. "You're already on trial for practicing medicine without a license in San Diego County and the FDA believes that the supplements and treatments you prescribe are not properly classified as drugs defined in the Food, Drug, and Cosmetic Act, Title Twenty One, Subchapter Two of the United States Code of law. That makes your prosecution a federal matter."

Ted held out his hands. "Every one of our supplements are naturally present in the human body."

212

Schautz leaned toward him. "We know that someone tipped you off to our visit which gave you time to hide evidence and your son. What have you done with your patient's records?

"There are none."

"Just like you don't know where your son is."

Ted shrugged.

"The charges in your county trial overlap your federal charges. You are also in violation of the federal mandate requiring the CHD8 gene editing treatment." He shook his head. "I don't get it. The mandate is a safety measure to guarantee that your child can function normally and eliminate any doubt about his development or any possibility of future mutations that could bring more behavioral and cognitive symptoms. What is wrong with you for denying your child treatment?" He glared at Ted. "This not only raises the question of child endangerment, but your child is missing. This adds to the weight of all the other charges."

Ted crossed his arms and lowered his head shaking it. "Religious freedom."

"You and that good looking wife of yours have managed to get yourselves tangled up in quite the web that goes all the way from the county to the federal government."

Ted held up a hand. "You don't know the half of it."

"For what it is worth there's a lawyer from your church who is ready to spring you."

Schautz pulled a few pieces of paper from the file and put them on the table. "Your lawyer posted bail for you and your wife. Sign these and you'll be out of here."

No way you are signing those!

Ted stifled a smile. "He's not our lawyer and that is not our church."

Schautz scowled. "What? He posted your bail."

"That doesn't make him my attorney."

"Look, I don't care if he's your fairy fucking godmother. He posted your bail and you are free to go after we talk to your wife. Whether he represents you or not is not at issue here. What is at issue is that you have made bail."

"I'm not leaving here with him and neither is my wife," so send him on his way."

Schautz shook his head. "I'm going to give you one last chance to tell me who tipped you off about our raid. Your cooperation could lower your sentence when all of this is said and done."

"Let's just say that a little bird told me."

"That little bird is going to get its fucking wings clipped when I find out who it is and make no doubt about it, I *will* find out."

Sure you will.

Ted shrugged. "You seem to be a bit stressed. I guess I would be too if I was responsible for a missing little boy. The press is going to have a field day with this."

"Okay, wiseass, I've had enough of your shit." Schautz swept the papers off the table, put them in the folder and headed for the door, turning back as he opened it. "Someone's ass is grass and I'm going to be the lawnmower."

FIFTY NINE

"Your husband confessed to everything," Schautz said when he came into the room to question Jeanette, "so why don't you tell us your side of the story. Your cooperation could reduce your charges to accessory as opposed to being charged as an accomplice."

Jeanette looked him in the eye. "What did you do with my son?"

Schautz dropped into the chair across from her and laid his folder on the table. "I was about to ask you the same thing."

"You're the ones who came in with your guns drawn and scared him." She put her hands on her face in a dramatic gesture and made her voice quaver when she spoke. "I'm worried sick about my little boy. How would you feel if you were a six year old autistic little boy and a bunch of goons with guns stormed your building? Why are you even bothering talking to me? You should be out looking for my little boy who is no doubt scared to death because of you." She pointed an accusing finger at him. "I'm holding you personally responsible!"

Schautz leaned back and his narrowed eyes grew unnaturally wide. "Your husband said the same thing with almost the exact same words."

One love, one in our hearts.

"Of course he did!" Jeanette shot back, using all of her willpower not to smile. "Now you're going to tell me how we are already on trial for practicing medicine without a license in San Diego and how the FDA believes that the supplements and treatments we prescribed are not properly classified as drugs defined in the Food, Drug, and Cosmetic Act, Title Twenty One, Subchapter Two of the United States Code of law."

Schautz's face went white. "How do you know what I am going to say? Are you wired or something?" He rubbed his chin. "That can't be, you were thoroughly searched after your arrest."

Jeanette struggled to suppress a smirk. "Let's just say that a little bird told me."

He slammed his hand down on the table, making Jeanette jump. "How the fuck…

She shook her head.

"Alright," Schautz said between gritted teeth. "We know that someone tipped you off. Where did you hide your son and where did you hide your patient's records?"

"We don't have any records," Jeanette said, "that's why you couldn't find any, and don't bother threatening me about being in violation of the federal mandate requiring the gene editing treatment, or your empty threats of child endangerment, especially since *you* took my little boy."

"I don't know how you and your husband are communicating but I'm going to find out and I'm going to find out who tipped you off to our visit."

"Pardon my language," Jeanette said, "but that's all bullshit!"

Schautz opened up his file.

"Don't waste my time with that," Jeanette said with a dismissive gesture "and you can tell Mr. Hart that he's not our lawyer even if he did post our bail."

Schautz shook his head. "How did you even know Hart was here? These rooms are soundproof and you seem to know everything I discussed with your husband. I don't know how the hell you are doing that but I'm going to find out."

Good luck.

He stood and gripped the edge of the table, glaring at Jeanette. "Don't think for a minute that you and your smart ass husband are going to get away with all of your shenanigans. We're going to find your son and I'm going to make it my personal mission to see that the federal mandate is upheld. I also plan to file every possible charge I can against you including whatever statutes child endangerment, child abuse, and neglect fall under. The fact that your child is autistic will add charges of disability abuse and neglect, not to mention kidnapping." He shook his finger at her. "Child protective services will take over custody of your boy when we find him so consider him gone because I will make sure that you have no contact with him. I intend to pursue every legal action I can to ensure his rights are protected."

Don't worry about his threats, mom. He'll never find me unless I let him. You'll be out of here soon.

Schautz continued glaring and his lower lip trembled.

Jeanette snorted. "Child endangerment and kidnapping? Our own kid? That's a hoot! If anyone did any kidnapping and endangerment to my little boy it's you and your goons."

"We'll see about that!" Schautz snapped up his file folder and went out the door, slamming it behind him.

SIXTY

Cop cars with flashing lights blocked both ends of Santa Monica Avenue and news trucks and crowds of people filled the street in front of Temple Nutritionals when Ted and Jeanette climbed out of the Uber they had taken from San Diego's FBI field office. Cameras and cell phones flashed when they made their way to the clinic where they were met with a mob of reporters and cameramen while they passed through the police barricades.

"Do you have anything to say about the charges of practicing medicine without a license?" a reporter shouted over the noise of the crowd.

"Do those charges have any connection with the lawsuit from your former employer over trade secrets?" another yelled.

"Why did the FBI raid your clinic this morning?" A third shouted. "Is it because of your FDA violations or your refusal to follow a federal mandate to protect your autistic child?"

"Is there any truth to the rumors of child endangerment, abuse, neglect, and kidnapping?" a fourth asked.

Once they reached the front door to the clinic Ted and Jeanette turned to face the crowd pressing up against the barricades. News crews had pushed to the front while scattered homeless people mixed in with onlookers pressed in behind them.

"What is your connection to the Praise the Lordcast church?" someone called out from the back of the crowd.

"We are not and have no intention of ever being members of the Praise the Lordcast church," Ted said in a raised voice.

Jeanette recognized Sara Johnston from her pixie cut red hair toward the back of the crowd. She nudged Ted and pointed. "There's Sara, the one who interviewed us before. She'll be sympathetic to us."

Great choice! She is a seeker of truth with a good heart.

Jeanette turned to one of the cops. "Officer. Would you mind letting the reporter with the red hair and pixie cut through? We'll talk to her and maybe the rest will back off."

"Sure."

He went over to the barricade in front of Sara and eased one end of it aside with the help of another cop and gestured her and her cameraman forward before sliding the barricade back into place.

"Thank you!" Sara said while her cameraman adjusted his camera on his shoulder and gave her a thumbs up.

She nodded and moved closer to Ted and Jeanette while looking directly into the camera. "This is Sara Johnston back with Ted and Jeanette Driscoll at Temple Nutritionals, the storied free clinic where many have claimed to have experienced miraculous healings using all natural non-pharmaceutical remedies."

She looked from the camera to Ted and Jeanette, positioning herself to their side for the best camera angle. "After being arrested for practicing medicine without a license by San Diego County authorities, the FBI raided your clinic this morning accusing you of prescribing treatments not properly classified as drugs defined in the Food, Drug, and Cosmetic Act of the United States Code of law. There is also talk about your refusal to have a federally mandated procedure done on your autistic boy based on religious freedom, but you refused representation from a lawyer who claims you are members of the Praise the Lordcast church." She held her microphone out to Ted.

"Temple Nutritionals is not a church and other than being a guest on the Praise the Lordcast show after they gave us a donation we have no connection with them and have no desire to."

"So I am clear on this, attorneys from the Praise the Lordcast church claim that they can resolve your legal issues and you are refusing their help."

Ted raised an eyebrow. "What does that tell you?" He put his arm around Jeanette and let Theo's words flow through him. "We don't believe in churches. We believe that everyone is their own temple that holds the sparks of divinity that we all are. This means that we should be worshipping each other instead of icons, symbols, power, wealth, or status. We are all our own personal temples who are portals and connections to the unity of all things that brings the beauty and blessing of being alive in the arms of the great mystery."

"Wow!" Sara said. "That's beautiful. No churches to tell us what to do, how to act, vote, or spend our money."

"If everyone is a temple we don't need churches," Jeanette said taking her turn in letting Theo's words flow through her. "We need to be fully responsible for ourselves instead of a priest, rabbi, imam, guru, or some other spiritual guide dictating our beliefs and choices to us. All my husband Ted and I have done is help those in need with natural cures that are abundant in nature. Our mother earth gives us everything we need. We follow that example and we are not looking to profit from it."

"That makes me question the persecution you have been facing," Sara said, "which seems to have started with a lawsuit from a profit driven pharmaceutical company."

Ted made a dismissive gesture. "I'm not making any accusations but if you cut through all the chaos surrounding us and look at the facts, you can infer your own meaning. We're being sued by a profit driven pharmaceutical company as you say, and dragged into court by local and federal authorities on bogus charges that apparently only the Praise the Lordcast church can save us from. What does that tell you?"

"I for one am a huge fan of everything you have done," Sara gushed, then she held up a finger. "One more question if I might?"

"Sure."

"What about your refusal to follow the federal mandate for gene editing treatment? The government claims that it is a safety measure to guarantee that your child can eliminate any doubt about mutations they believe he is experiencing."

"As far as we are concerned our boy is perfect which is what Fetal Fantasies has been telling us all along and they have verified the fact that he is the very first genetically perfect child the world has ever seen but they think that his behavior needs fixing. As far as Jeanette and I are concerned, if it works, why fix it?"

"Alongside the mandate the federal government has also made accusations of neglect and child endangerment," Sara said, "and to top it all off your child is missing. Do you know where he is?"

Ted and Jeanette looked at each other and Ted shrugged. "You'll have to ask the FBI about that. They are responsible for scaring him off when they raided our clinic with their guns drawn this morning so it is their responsibility to find him."

SIXTY ONE

The homeless people and others in the crowd tried to push their way through the barricades but were held back by the cops. Ted and Jeanette went inside and found the clinic in chaos in the aftermath of the FBI search. Ted shook his head at the missing computers, the papers, and other items scattered across the floor. Jeanette patted him on the back. "It's ok, honey, everything is backed up in the cloud and in other places." She squatted down and reached under the reception desk and stood up smiling a moment later holding a thumb drive. "Where are you Theo?" she called out.

I'll see you at home. Scott and his crew are out back and will be more than happy to clean everything up.

"How did you…"

We'll talk about it when I see you.

Jeanette cracked open the back door and peered out to see a single cop standing guard. Other than Scott and a few helpers no else was in the back parking lot. She nodded to the cop and beckoned Scott and his helpers to come in.

"What a mess!" Scott said when they came in.

"No kidding," Ted said.

"Listen," Scott said as if reading their minds. "Get out of here so you can have some time out of the spotlight so you can find Theo and regroup. You can slip out the back door to avoid the crowd out front." He nodded toward his helpers. "We'll clean this mess up so you can get back to business."

Ted shook Scott's hand. "That might not happen for awhile but we appreciate the help.

Scott beamed. "It's the least we can do."

Jeanette took Ted by the arm and headed for the back door. "We appreciate it."

They found Theo waiting for them in the kitchen at home where he had sandwiches and a fruit salad ready for lunch. "I'm sure you're starving by now."

Jeanette dug into the fruit salad. "How did you get here? Where did you hide? In the car? You couldn't have done that. You were here before us. Who helped you? Scott?"

Theo smiled. "It's better you don't know then you can honestly say that you don't know."

"Theo!"

"Now that everything is more out in the open," he said, "I have to stay hidden until it's time to reveal myself which will blow things up even more. The media is going crazy which will escalate everything, but Sara Johnston is a positive influence. Others, especially the forces behind the Praise the Lordcast church will be stirring up negative reports to try and force us to join them. No matter what happens all we need to do is stand in our truth and let the bigger forces play out."

"The FBI, the San Diego cops and others are all looking for you," Jeanette said, "and they have our address here on record, so it's only a matter of time before they come looking for you here if they haven't already."

"The San Diego Police will be here tomorrow morning around seven looking for me," Theo said, "but there's a lot more going on behind the scenes. Driven by Isiah the A.I. profit Stewart and Carla are desperate to exploit all of the good we have accomplished, but we will remain autonomous until the very end."

Jeanette's eyes grew wide. "The very end? You're scaring me!"

Theo reached out and put a comforting hand over hers. "It's just a figure of speech. It might seem like the end at times but there is no end." He smiled. "As a matter of fact every end is a new beginning."

"What should we do when they come?" Ted said.

"Let's get up early and I will make myself scarce. You can meet them at the door to let them look through the house but they'll never find me."

"How can you be so sure?" Jeanette asked.

Theo smirked and shook his head. "You won't know, so you can honestly tell them that," *but I'll be with you the whole time. Don't go overboard but have a little fun blaming the FBI for taking me. That will keep them all guessing.*

They awoke at six the next morning and Jeanette made breakfast. A knock came at the door when they were finishing at seven prompting

Theo to go back to his room saying, "Go ahead and answer. I'll see you after they're gone."

Jeanette put her hands on her hips. "Theo? How? Where?"

Theo wagged a finger at her and winked. *They won't be here long so have fun and keep them guessing.*

"Come on, honey." Ted put his arm around Jeanette and guided her to the front door where they opened it mildly surprised to see officer Perez holding up a search warrant with Collins standing behind him.

"We have a warrant to search the premises for your son as part of a wellness check," Perez said in an official tone. He turned back to Collins. "Go and cover the back yard to make sure he doesn't run."

"You have the wrong address." Ted bowed and stepped aside holding out his hand. "Come on in and look around all you want."

Perez frowned and looked at the warrant as he pushed past Ted. "What do you mean we have the wrong address?"

"You should be searching FBI headquarters," Jeanette blurted. "They are the ones who took him yesterday and we haven't heard anything back from them after all our inquiries. Now I'm getting worried about our little boy." She raised her voice. "He's autistic and he's probably frightened to death."

"Bullshit!" Perez stormed into the house and checked all the rooms before he came back to the front door a few minutes later. He clicked the microphone on the shoulder of his uniform. "Nothing here and you haven't seen him escape out back," he said to Collins, "so come on in."

"So where are you hiding him?" Collins said, returning to the front door.

"The real question is," Jeanette said in a shrill tone. "what did the FBI do with our little boy?"

"And what are you two doing here in La Jolla?" Ted said in a monotone. "Your beat is in Ocean beach."

Collins glanced at Perez with an expectant look on his face.

Perez turned away and gestured with his head for Collins to follow him out. "Never mind!"

Ted and Jeanette watched them get into their black and white and pull out of the driveway before closing the front door and turning back to see Theo come out from his room at the back of the house. "That was fun!"

SIXTY TWO

"It's best that we avoid the clinic until things calm down," Ted said after Collins and Perez left.

Theo sat down in the middle of the couch and patted the cushions on both sides of him. "We all know that things aren't going to calm down because they will keep looking for me and I will not reveal myself until the time is right."

Jeanette sat down beside him and Ted sat on his other side. "And how will you know that?" she asked.

Ted snickered and ruffled Theo's hair. "You should know better than to ask him that, honey."

"He has no idea about what's going to happen, but he doesn't worry about it because no matter what happens he'll be in the moment and know what to do." She shook her head. "I wish I could be so calm about it."

"I'm just following the guidance from our ancestors," Theo said. "My resonance with their vibration transcends any doubts. The more you experience that certainty the more your worries will diminish." He patted Jeanette on the knee. "I can tell you that what's coming next will be chaos that will be more stressful than anything you've ever known."

Theo's eyes lit up and his smile filled his face. "In the same way that I have communicated through and with *you*, our ancestors also want to speak with you through *me* to give you a little guidance."

"We're all ears," Ted said.

Theo giggled. *You won't need your ears.* The tone, feeling, and energy of his communication shifted into something lighter, yet with more intensity. *Whenever you feel a strong emotional response and its corresponding thought forms, you have entered a field of energy that exists independently of you.*

The collective consciousness of humanity is experiencing extreme polarization with divisions between races, religions, politics, resources, social and financial

224

statuses, and more. If you experience anger the neurochemical reality of your body changes, and if your anger escalates into hatred you have entered into a toxic dimensional reality. Due to the nature of the interconnectedness of dimensional realities you will be sharing the same vibration with other beings who are in the same energetic and emotion. Sometimes anger is the correct response to set a needed boundary but when it escalates into hatred it becomes toxic to your psychospiritual nature.

*Human beings and many animals have perceptual and emotional habits that are deeply ingrained in negative emotional responses like depression, hostility, and hatred. These responses can color your life with thought forms and emotional responses that are not of your conscious creation and are driven by forces and habits in your unconscious mind.

*Loving kindness, compassion, and self love are positive in their effects which counter negativity, and the darker everything becomes the brighter the light.

As a result of the accelerated chaos you now find yourself at the center of, your reality has become venomous and overflowing with emotional and spiritual toxicity which is coming to a head in the same way that a fever breaks when you overcome sickness.

Theo put his arms out and pulled Ted and Jeanette in closer. "Together we represent the forces of loving kindness, compassion, and self love which is why we were able to heal so many."

Ted smiled. "And we're learning how to bow down and worship each other."

*In spite of how it seems at times everything in the universe is a dance of light, energy, and matter. From the perspective of the higher dimensions where we have connected to the ancestors there is no conflict. All polarities are resolved in the infinite expanse of equanimity and all that unfolds in our experience here is nothing more than a momentary display of light and energy that is dreamlike and is in essence a magical display of Cosmic Mind. Even though it has no substance, as consciousness descends from this higher dimension into the buffeting of subatomic particles, these collisions of light, energy, and matter are what creates your sensory world.

Aside from your personal realities the earth is in the midst of a burgeoning chaos that is affecting your climate, oceans, ecosystems, politics, your social disorder, and the very existence of civilization as you have known it, but the hidden gift it carries brings an opportunity for us to evolve at an accelerated rate.

"I think we've already experienced some of that with the dreams, visions, and telepathic communication you shared with us," Ted said.

Your universe is a complex display of holographic light, the source of which is pure consciousness itself. Your experiences of yourself and your world are fundamentally insubstantial and dreamlike apparitions that most sentient beings mistakenly take to be the ultimate reality.

*In order for you to transcend the moments that you will find yourself in, in the coming days you have to reach upward to higher dimensions of your own existence to those realms of consciousness that are beyond time and space where our ancestors reside. The thing you must never forget when you are spiraling within a chaotic vortex is the portal of opportunity it can provide.

This opportunity for survival and a new way of being can present itself in ways you do not expect because your usual perceptual markers will no longer be in place and your consciousness may not recognize the opportunity when it presents itself.

Theo closed his eyes and the three of them sat in silence until he opened them again. He picked up the television remote and pointed it at the big screen. "Prepare to embrace chaos."

SIXTY THREE

The announcer's voice blared, "In tonight's top story a controversial free clinic in Ocean Beach has been raided by the FBI." A video of Ted and Jeanette being led away in handcuffs played out on the screen followed by shots of the crowd filling the street, cameras flashing, cop cars, and panning shots of parked news trucks. The last shot lingered on the Temple Nutritionals sign above the entrance to the clinic.

"Ted and Jeanette Driscoll," the announcer's voiceover said, "have been accused of practicing medicine without a license, illicit drug sales, FDA violations, refusing to comply with a federal mandate, copyright infringements, and tax fraud. The Driscoll's are also being investigated for child endangerment and kidnapping charges and are free on one hundred thousand dollar bail posted by the Praise the Lordcast church who the Driscoll's insist that they have no affiliation with."

The video cut to a lanky dark-haired man wearing a gray suit and a blue tie sitting at a news desk with a still picture of Ted and Jeanette being led away in handcuffs on a screen behind him.

"Oh no," Jeanette moaned. "We look like criminals."

Ted squeezed her shoulder. "Bonnie and Clyde, honey!"

"In an odd turn of events," the announcer continued, "the Driscoll's six year old autistic son disappeared during the FBI raid. The FBI has accused the Driscolls of hiding their child, and the Driscoll's blame the FBI for scaring him off."

Theo chuckled.

"News Ten's Sara Johnston has been covering this story from the beginning before all the controversy began."

Sara's first interview with Scott Olsen ran on the screen before cutting to a live scene with her standing beside Collins and Perez in front of the downtown San Diego Police station.

"I'm here with officers Perez and Collins who have been central figures in the events playing out in Ocean Beach." She held the microphone out to Perez. "What can you tell us about what's been happening here?"

"We've been watching the activity at Temple Nutritionals for some time now after receiving complaints from other businesses about the traffic that goes in and out of there. We've observed growing numbers of homeless lining up outside the front door."

Sara frowned. "Is there a law against homeless people coming for health and nutritional advice?"

"Their growing numbers aroused more suspicion. We have seen dozens of them entering the premises and coming back out with small packages which gave us reason to suspect the Driscolls of supplying people with illegal drugs. We went in and politely asked if we could take a look around but they refused to let us without a warrant."

"We did meet their autistic little boy," Collins said, grinning. "He was one of the sweetest kids I ever met; blond hair, blue eyes, and all smiles."

Ted ruffled Theo's hair and Jeanette kissed him on the cheek.

"Theo!" Perez said.

Collins crossed himself. "I pray to God that he is okay. His parents could have kidnapped him or worse. I know the Driscolls insist that the FBI is responsible for his disappearance and are possibly holding him in protective custody, but I find it hard to believe that they would keep him without some kind of formal announcement, especially since he is a juvenile."

The camera moved in for a close-up on Sara. "There are two sides to every story," she said. "After interviewing Scott Olsen about the Finding Our Way Home project, I spoke with the Driscoll's myself."

The video cut to a clip of Ted's interview.

"Our mission here at Temple Nutritionals is to help those in need with natural cures that are abundant in nature." He held his hands out wide. "Our mother earth gives us everything we need freely and abundantly when it is sustainably resourced and properly managed. Like this planet that gives us life we want to follow that example, so we are not looking to profit from it."

Another clip followed. "Temple Nutritionals sounds like it has religious underpinnings," Sara said. "What are your religious beliefs? Do you consider yourself a church?"

Ted smiled.

"Yes."

"So Temple Nutritionals is actually a church like the Hare Krishnas or the Scientologists?"

"Temple Nutritionals is most decidedly not a church."

Sara looked to the camera and frowned. "Didn't you just say that you consider yourself to be a church?"

"Temple Nutritionals is not a church. *I* am the church, better still a temple, just like you are. We see the human body as a temple the way the ancients did. Not only is the human body a temple but in the wisdom of our ancestors every aspect of reality that we can observe and experience is a temple that reflects the great mystery within us that we are a part of along with the great mystery that surrounds us. These sacred relationships define the guiding principles behind everything that we do."

The video cut back to the announcer at the news desk with Sara up on the big screen behind him. She leaned in toward the camera. "Out of everything that has happened, the greatest concern and the biggest mystery is the whereabouts of little Theodore Driscoll. Anyone who has any information is urged to contact the San Diego police department."

A picture of Theo filled the screen with contact information and the number to a San Diego police hotline highlighted in bold below it.

"Thank you, Sara," the announcer said. "We look forward to hearing more as this developing story unfolds."

Ted flipped through more channels and saw variations of the same story on local and national news as well, then the channel on the big screen changed to Fox News on its own.

SIXTY FOUR

"Oh my God, I can't believe it," Jeanette gasped, recognizing the blue suit, red tie, perfect teeth and glittering rings and watch on Stewart sitting on a couch holding hands with Carla in her low cut satin dress that matched Stewart's suit with her ever prominent diamond encrusted crucifix glittering within her cleavage.

"I think I'm going to puke," Jeanette said.

A young reporter with close-cropped blond hair wearing a suit similar to Stewart's with a gold cross on the lapel sat in an overstuffed chair across from them in their studio beneath the gold cross glowing from the flat screen behind them.

A red banner at the bottom of the screen said STEWART ALDERMAN & CARLA NICOLETTI in white letters and below that MINISTERS OF THE PRAISE THE LORDCAST CHURCH.

"Thank you for joining us for this Fox News special report on the breaking story of the Temple Nutritionals controversy," the reporter said. "Aside from their civil and criminal indictments of practicing medicine without a license, FDA violations, and refusing to follow a federal mandate there are also accusations of child endangerment and kidnapping."

Carla crossed herself and looked up, batting her eyelashes. "We pray that that sweet angelic child is safe," she said in a low velvety voice.

"It's my understanding that your church posted bail and supplied an attorney to help the Driscoll's in their time of need," the reporter continued, "but they deny any connection with you. Can you give us any insight into what the real issues are? Are the Driscolls healers or frauds?" He raised an eyebrow. "Satanic or Saviors?"

Stewart sat up straight. "We've heard many stories but we are not quick to judge. We even donated money to their cause."

The still shot of Ted and Jeanette accepting the oversized donation check from Stewart and Carla appeared on the screen behind them.

"The good Lord loves saints and sinners equally," Stewart said wistfully. "Ted and Jeanette Driscoll are reported to have performed miracle healings that changed the lives of hundreds of people." He put his hands together as if praying and Carla followed suit. "There are many who believe they are tools of Satan who are drugging the homeless and taking advantage of them to profit from generous souls like us. Some believe they are a cult that uses magic tricks to perpetrate fake healings with shills posing as victims."

Ted shook his head. "That's the biggest load of bullshit I've ever heard."

"And it all comes from simply wanting to heal and help people," Jeanette said.

"Not that you haven't seen it before," Theo said, "but Stewart and Carla are showing their true selves now. Watch the way they steer the conversation toward me which is what they are really after."

"What do you think, Mr. Alderman," the reporter said. "Satanic or Saviors?"

Stewart held out his hands. "Of course we believed in them. Aside from our donation, being the trusting souls that we are, we had them as guests on our Praise the Lordcast prayer hour."

Snippets from the interview played on the screen behind them.

"How could we deny all the positive reports we heard about how they supposedly improved the lives of the homeless?"

"You say supposed," the reporter said, "so you have your doubts."

Stewart shrugged. "We donated money and had them on our prayercast before all the scandals started, so in the name of our prophet Isiah in the spirit of Jesus Christ we are still supporting them with legal and financial assistance."

"Even if they are convicted?"

Stewart sat up straight looking indignant. "The good Lord loves saints and sinners equally."

"We've met their beautiful angel Theo when they were guests on our show," Carla gushed.

Jeanette put her finger in her mouth and made gagging sounds.

An airbrushed picture of Theo with radiant blue eyes filled the screen behind the stage. White light glowed from behind his head, giving a haloing effect that faded to a sky blue background that matched his eyes.

Theo stuck his finger in his mouth and made gagging sounds of his own when he saw his picture, then he broke into a fit of giggles which spread to Ted and Jeanette.

Carla put her hands together like she was praying. "Being genetically perfect makes Little Theodore a very special child. The fact that he is autistic makes him an even greater blessing. If there are healing miracles then we believe that his innocent presence is the force behind them, but even if that were not true we want with all of our hearts and souls to save him. "Save Theo!" she cried, holding her arms out wide. "Deliver him unto us so that we can nurture his sweet angelic spirit."

"We are concerned about his welfare," Stewart said. "Not only that he is safe wherever he might be but what could happen to him if his parents go to prison. A big factor that could be related to his disappearance is his parent's refusal to follow a federally mandated procedure that has the potential to cure his autism."

"It's bad enough to refuse a federal mandate," Carla said, pouting, "but I simply can't understand how they could deny their angel cutting edge medical treatment that could cure him. Save Theo!" she cried again, clasping her hands together. "Deliver him unto us so that we can nurture his angelic spirit." She bowed her head. "We pray for God to grant us the grace to adopt him and save him from the evils and abuse of his criminal parents. We can provide him with the best schooling, proper treatment, and care that money can buy."

Stewart made the sign of the cross. "Praise Jesus. Praise Isiah."

HAVE YOU SEEN ME? Flashed on the screen below Theo's picture with contact information and the number to the San Diego police hotline highlighted in bold below it.

SIXTY FIVE

Theo nodded and shut off the television. "Enough of that silliness."

Jeanette let out a deep breath. "We seem to be spinning deeper into the chaos and the Praise the Lordcast looks like they are behind it."

"And the A.I. profit Isiah is the one pulling the strings," Ted said.

"Isiah is only one instrument of the dark forces," Theo said, "and as far down as they seem to be pushing us they are helping us in the long run."

"I believe you," Jeanette said, "but I don't see how they can be helping us. All they seem to do is to push us further into a corner."

"As things move faster the shadow play will reveal itself more and more and you will sense the presence of the puppet masters. Although their true identities are hidden within technology you will see with increasing clarity how they use aspects of your culture as a manipulation to propagate the lies, but the lies I am speaking about are not the ones that seem so glaringly apparent. They are not so much the lies of economics, wars, and conflicting religions.

"It is the lie of your identity that ensures your imprisonment.

"It is the belief and cultural assertion that you are nothing more than physical human beings and that there are no other realms beyond your earthly experience.

"The recognition of this lie is a harbinger of personal freedom but the beginning stages you are experiencing can be disorienting. As you have experienced in your deeper communications with me, multidimensional experiences are vastly different from your day to day three dimensional experiences. The fact that you have entered into the chaos of a transition state of consciousness will bear this out."

"Since you have come into our lives and opened up the connections we share," Ted said, "my conception of what is real and true has shifted in ways I never could have imagined."

Theo smiled. "Your perception of reality is a personal creation that is influenced by the collective perception of your culture, time, place, and circumstance, but your perception of what is real is *your* creation.

"Time is accelerating. More events are taking place in less time regardless of the nature of the transition state whether changes in your personal lives or recognizing your cultural manipulation. *You* are the creators of your realities and with the transcendent bond that we share, we are co-creators of a more expansive reality."

"And we have created anarchy," Jeanette added.

Ted patted Theo on the back. "True, but as our little hummingbird whisperer here has told us, the hidden gift it carries brings an opportunity for us to evolve at an accelerated rate."

Theo looked up at Ted and Jeanette. "I knew I did the right thing when I picked such smart parents, not to mention their great genetics and the choices they made that brought me into this world."

"I never thought it would bring us to where we are now," Jeanette said.

"Your collective experience of perceived time and the pressure of your accelerated perception is due to the heightened pace of emerging technologies that humanity has become increasingly dependent on. The increased pace of data you have to process is beyond your capability as a biological organism to cope with, and your culture has shifted into a technologically based reality.

"As a result of this dependence humanity has entered into techno-servitude and there are good and bad sides to this. Were you a benevolent species the acceleration of your culture could advance the quality of all life, but collectively you are not a benevolent species. Some of the emerging technologies that could enhance planetary life are being commandeered by forces that want to control and enslave.

"You only have to look around to see most people walking around hypnotized by their cell phones which they pay more attention to than the environments that they are actually in. Computers have become their churches and personal places of worship; something outside of themselves, and as you are discovering, A.I. spiritual leaders are worshipped by masses of people.

"For the most part everything is disconnected and one step removed from the natural world. Younger people on their phones and computers are lost in virtual realities and video games, and most of the games are about wars, battles, and killing. How many young people are addicted to their games and rarely ever leave their houses or their bedrooms? What would happen if they suddenly found themselves out in nature without their technology?"

"They wouldn't survive," Ted said.

Theo held up a finger. "There are benevolent forces working with these technologies to improve the quality of life, but opposing agendas, the future of technology, and your collective destiny are swallowed up in chaos and uncertainty. When you advanced as a race to the point of unraveling and manipulating your genetic code and your history of hurrying to implement technology with no idea of its consequences, it was seen as a sign to intervene…" Theo stopped and turned his head to the side the way a dog does when it is trying to comprehend something.. "We're about to have unwanted company."

SIXTY SIX

The doorbell rang followed by a knock on the front door.

"I'll get it." Ted looked down at Theo and then stood and headed for the front of the house.

"Brace yourself," Theo said.

Jeanette jumped up to follow Ted.

I'll be right here with you.

"Shit!" Ted said peering through the peephole when Jeanette came to his side. "They found us."

Another knock made them both jump and the doorbell followed.

"Take a look." Ted stepped aside so Jeanette could look out the peephole where she saw a mob of reporters and news crews crowding around their front door.

She put her hand to her face. "Maybe we shouldn't answer."

Ted shook his head. "They're not going to go away."

It's part of the unfolding and it will give you a chance to set the record straight about all that Praise the Lordcast satanic or saviors silliness. Sara Johnston is out there and she believes in us. Tell the other reporters that you are giving one exclusive interview to Sara and you have no comment for the rest of them.

"I'll go put on some water for coffee or tea," Jeanette said.

Ted opened the door and stepped out into a sea of cameras, flashing phones and a mob of reporters holding microphones.

"Where is your son Theodore?" a reporter yelled.

Ted shielded his eyes from the glare of the lights and peered into the crowd until he recognized the red hair and pixie cut of Sara Johnston toward the back.

"You've been accused of being a cult," another reporter said. "Do you consider yourself a church?"

"Do you worship Satan?" another asked.

Ted held up his hands. "I'm sorry but I have no comment for any of you. You're wasting your time here, except for Sara from News Ten."

Scattered moans rippled through the crowd when Ted gestured for her to come forward. "Come one in Sara." He raised his voice. "She's been following our story longer than all of you so she gets the exclusive."

"What?" a reporter said.

"Are you shitting me?" someone else said.

Ted stepped aside and let Sara and her cameraman slip past him.

"Thank you for talking to me Ted!" she said after he closed the door.

Her cameraman followed her and jerked his thumb over his shoulder. "You know they're not going to leave, right?"

Ted chuckled. "Yeah, I know, but I had to tell it to them straight. Come on in." Ted ushered them into the living room and held his hand out toward the chair and couch. "Set your camera up wherever you want. Sara, you can take the chair. Jeanette and I will sit on the couch."

"Thank you," Sara pulled out a compact. "Give us a minute so I can fix my face and we can figure out the lighting and camera angles." She checked her hair and touched up her lipstick while her cameraman set up his tripod.

Jeanette came in from the kitchen. "Can I get you something to drink? Coffee? Tea? Sparkling water?"

"I'll take a bubbly water," Sara's cameraman said.

Jeanette came back a minute later with four bottles of sparkling water and handed them out, then she sat on the couch beside Ted. Sara clipped a tiny black lapel microphone on their collars and one on hers and got a thumbs up from her cameraman. They did a sound check and Sara sat down in the chair beside the couch. "You guys ready?"

Ted and Jeanette nodded.

"We're rolling," her cameraman said.

"The very first time I heard of you," Sara said, "I was covering a story about Scott Olsen who sang your praises while he and his volunteers handed out food, water, blankets, and other necessities to a group of homeless people." She read from her cell phone. "Scott said, 'We owe it all to the magic, compassion, and very real healing miracles of Temple Nutritionals in Ocean Beach who gave us our lives back'."

Ted put his arm around Jeanette. "All we want is to help people escape from their misery so they can lead self-sufficient lives."

"Scott and hundreds of other homeless people are in deep gratitude to you for the miraculous healings they say you performed while religious authorities and skeptics accuse you of fraud using drugs and magic tricks to convince those who are already weak minded to believe that you are miracle healers."

Ted snorted. "Kind of makes you wonder who the weak minded ones really are, doesn't it?"

Sara's lips turned up in a half-smile. "I cannot say that I have witnessed any miracles first hand but I can say that I have witnessed the miraculous transformation of the people you treated. I am agnostic and would have to witness a miracle personally to believe it but in the end that doesn't matter because I believe in what you are doing."

Jeanette blushed. "Thank you that's very sweet."

"Regardless of what I think, a big part of this controversy is this whole satanic or saviors debate that has popped up around you and your work. I *know* you are not satanic and in the short time that I've known you I don't believe you would call yourselves saviors either."

"Thank you!" Ted said. "The best way I can describe what we do is to say that it comes from something bigger than us that we have been blessed to have tapped in to. I remember reading about Frank Fools Crow, the ceremonial chief of the Teton Sioux. He said the source of power is not ourselves. He explained how he performed healing miracles because he wanted others to believe they could do them as well. He did this by becoming what he called a 'clean, hollow bone' that the Great Mystery's powers funneled through to work through him."

Great explanation!

Ted and Jeanete both smiled.

"This might sound like an odd question so forgive me, but I feel compelled to ask, does your boy have something to do with this?"

Ted and Jeanette looked at each other.

"What make you ask that?" Jeanette said a little too quickly.

"Please don't take this personally, but aside from the miracles people say you performed, according to Fetal Fantasies your missing little boy Theo is a miracle himself."

We're all miracles.

"He's the first genetically perfect child," Sara continued, "yet he is autistic, which makes me wonder if he could be some kind of a savant or something. The fact that the federal government, Fetal Fantasies, and the Praise the Lordcast church all seem to be excessively interested in him adds to that thought."

"Maybe it's because of the bond Ted, Theo, and I share," Jeanette said. "It fills us all with an expansive loving energy that gives itself unconditionally. You can think of our little Theo as kind of a good luck charm."

Sara looked at the camera. "That's beautiful!"

I'd like to send a few thoughts your way to share.

Ted nodded and Theo's words came. "The hidden danger in all this comes from thought forms perpetuated by long standing religious and spiritual traditions. These belief systems maintain the illusion that there is a separation between the physical and interdimensional aspects of existence. The physical world is seen as tainted and nature is seen as something to be subdued and dominated instead of co-creating with the natural world, and the world is seen as something to escape from. Humanity's technology addictions are proof of this. The pinnacle of escapism shows itself in the behavior of the richest men in the world who spend billions in an ego driven space race while exploiting the resources of their own environment and ignoring the consequences.

"We believe that consciousness is one continuum from the highest vibrations of light into the lowest vibrations of matter, and the very atoms and subatomic particles that comprise the world are sacred because everything is related to the whole."

"That's some heady stuff," Sara said. "Is it fair to say that your beliefs about sacred higher vibrations and subatomic particles have influenced your refusal to comply with the federal gene editing mandate?"

Jeanette nodded. "There is a lot of attention being paid to the fact that Theo is the first genetically perfect human ever seen in our lifetime. Why would they want to edit his genome while at the same time saying he is perfect?" She held up a hand. "They say they want to do it because they want to prevent any cognitive issues that might arise from mutations, but could that be their label is for something that they don't understand? Have any of them ever thought that because of his perfect DNA that he might grow and develop in other ways?" She took Ted's hand. "We've watched Theo grow in his own way. He is still only six years old and is constantly changing and evolving every day."

Sara gave a quick nod. "So that explains your refusal to have the gene editing procedure done based on freedom of religion, even though you don't believe in religion."

Ted held up a finger and chuckled. "Only in America!"

Sara's face lit up with a smile that went up into her eyes. "Any last thoughts you'd like to share?"

Ted let Theo's words flow again. "I can't say this enough. We don't believe in churches or religions. We believe that everyone is their own temple to the sparks of divinity that we all are. We should all be worshipping each other instead of power, wealth, or status. We should most certainly not be killing each other in the name God, skin color, religious beliefs, politics, resources, or anything else in murders, wars, explosions, and other acts of violence."

"That's a beautiful philosophy," Sara said wistfully. "If you don't mind, one last question."

"Sure," Ted said.

"The deep love you have for your son comes through clearly and I am sure you are worried sick about where he might be and if he is safe. The San Diego Police, federal authorities, and many private citizens are looking for him everywhere. Do you care to speculate where he might be?"

"You'll have to ask the FBI about that," Jeanette answered.

SIXTY SEVEN

Ted pointed to the front door after showing Sara and her cameraman out. "Sara's cameraman was right. They're not going to go away out there. We need to find someplace with more peace and privacy."

"Can we go to the mountains?" Theo said. "We'll be stronger in nature when we're surrounded by plants and animals away from so much human confusion and energetic pollution."

Ted nodded and Jeanette grabbed her cell phone. "I'll find us an Airbnb somewhere near Julian.

"The car's in the garage," Ted said. "We can pack and drive out of here around three tomorrow morning when things are quiet."

After a long day of crowds and news crews milling around the front of their house and little sleep, Ted drove them past dormant news trucks through the neighborhood circling a few blocks to make sure no one followed them.

A reddish-pink dawn broke later that morning when he pulled into a long winding asphalt driveway leading to a large chalet with a sloping roof perched on a hillside with a deck that went around all four of its sides.

"Now we can spend some time alone together," Theo said from the back seat. Everything back in San Diego will get worse while we're gone, but as exhausting as it is, it's a part of the plan. Our time here can recharge us."

"That sounds like a dream come true," Jeanette said from the front seat.

Ted glanced in the rear view mirror, meeting Theo's eyes. "Best idea I've heard in days."

Theo broke into a full dimpled smile.

He was nowhere to be found when Ted and Jeanette woke up the following morning. After making coffee she walked around the outside deck to see if she could see him anywhere and felt mild panic when she didn't. She went back inside to find Ted in the kitchen sipping coffee. She opened her mouth to express her concern when Theo's voice said, *No need to worry, Mom. I'm spending time with my plant and animal family.*

In the days that followed Theo disappeared into the forest every morning sometimes for hours. Once they were awake he came back and ate breakfast with them, then the three of them spent the rest of the day hiking through the surrounding woods.

"I can't tell you how much I love communing with our brother and sister nature spirits," Theo said one afternoon while they rested in a grove of pine and cedar trees. He held his arms out wide as if embracing it all. "Their vibration is a true communion that clarifies and infuses me with power."

"The Japanese call it shinrin yoku," Ted said. "It's the practice of being in nature and being aware of everything around you to reduce stress and boost health and wellbeing."

"My connection to these elemental energies are deep," Theo said. "Being in their presence brings me great clarity."

"I wish we could stay here forever," Jeanette said. "I'm getting spoiled being away from all the madness we left behind, but we're going to have to deal with it sooner or later."

"That's why it's so important that we're here now," Theo said. "We're charging our batteries so we can navigate what's coming."

Ted tossed a pine cone at him. "What you really mean is that it's the calm before the storm."

Theo smiled. "It's not that we haven't already had major transformations in our lives, but the chaos waiting for us is spinning even faster bringing more profound changes. Coming here to fortify ourselves in this special time and place is an important part of the unfolding we are responsible for. Being here with you and becoming clear has heightened my abilities and reinforced my heart connection with you."

"I have to admit that I'm feeling a little nervous," Jeanette said.

"I don't mean to scare you but I want you to understand what is happening." Theo held his hands out. "I see the physical universe as a projection of light." He tapped his chest. "My physical body is a holographic projection that is part of a greater hologram that you think of as the cosmos. In the same way that we connect with the nature spirits here strings of energy connect us to the universe and the highest realms of light." He pointed to Ted and Jeanette with both hands, then pointed back to himself. "These connections between us, the cosmos, and the realms of light are integral parts of your innate nature.

"When you reach higher states of consciousness like what you have glimpsed through our loving connection the illusory nature of physical existence and your reality as a being of light becomes clearer. As an embodied being your consciousness is anchored in sensory perception so you live in two worlds; a world of absolute freedom unbounded by time and space, and your embodied existence that binds you to earth.

"Your realization of this is growing and you are on the path to greater freedom." He turned his head to the side like a listening dog and nodded, smiling. "Our ancestors will come to us in dreamtime to explain things further in ways that only they can."

Ted clapped his hands together. "I can't wait!"

"Neither can I." Jeanette said.

After a relaxing day and a deep sleep Ted and Jeanette experienced a flurry of bright neon visions of colors and geometries in the predawn darkness of the following morning. Intricate filigrees flowed in gentle waves followed by an expansive feeling that pulsed in concert with Theo's sweet voice reverberating in their minds and radiating through every fiber of their bodies.

Our ancestors are speaking through me the same way I have spoken through you. They want to remind you that you are creator beings and that this knowledge has been hidden from you by your religions and philosophies.

When these secrets are rediscovered you gain knowledge of your divinity even as you live in materiality. You are creating your future in this very moment and in every moment of your life through your thoughts, feelings, and by what you think and feel about yourselves and each other.

This realization frees you from the prison of human limitation and the constraints of your time, place, and circumstances. Opening the doorway of your mind frees it from the mental imprisonment projected onto you by those forces that want to contain and manipulate human destiny for their own ends.

Like the four directions of a compass there are four elements to this transformation.

One is your ability to attain spiritual insight and vision to allow you to see through the lies projected onto you and to see the right path, even in the greatest darkness.

Two is your ability to feel which is the core of these secrets. It is your greatest treasure and your greatest challenge. Those who want to control and manipulate you know that freezing or paralyzing your ability to feel anything but the lower emotional spectrum serves them.

The third element is your ability to speak your truth which you have done exceptionally well. The coming times will demand that you speak it clearly especially when it is opposed to those around you.

*The fourth is your ability to take action.

*These four elements are rooted in and are the source of your freedom. Within your hearts is the capacity to feel which is the deepest secret of all. It allows you to change your vibratory field which is the key to transcending collective mind control.

*The essence of these secrets is what you call joy, appreciation, and gratitude, in situations, people, and your own thoughts and feelings.

*When these energies reach a certain level they cause manifestations of physical reality even in the darkest moments. If you hold the mastery to transcend fear and cultivate these energies, unexpected opportunities and situations will present themselves to you.

We want you to understand that these dark times can be your greatest hours that herald your passage through the veil into worlds that await you on your path to new dimensions strewn with promising blessings.

Another flurry of geometries passed before fading into a gentle rose colored glow before they opened their eyes to the breaking dawn filled room with its soft radiance along with the gentle sound of Theo's trills and vocalizations.

SIXTY EIGHT

Ted sat up and looked around before turning to Jeanette who stared back at him wide-eyed. "Theo's singing to us from outside!"

Ted took her by the hand and they followed Theo's trills to the back deck where they found him standing by the railing looking like the pope blessing his followers who flocked to the ravine behind the house. The slope of the mountainside made it look like an amphitheater with an assortment of animals as the audience.

Theo held his arms out and his head up like an opera singer giving it all before a gathering of squirrels, birds, racoons, possums, foxes, deer, black bears, and mountain lions that all stared up at him with trancelike attention that held them united as one. Hummingbirds hovered like a crown sparkling with flashes of bright iridescence around Theo's head while hawks and eagles circled high above. Even the trees and other plant life seemed to be leaning in toward him.

Ted wrapped his arms around Jeanette's waist and they held each other taking in the spectacle, feeling equally connected to the assemblage below them. The sun broke through the clouds at its peak and a rainbow appeared above it all like arches in a magical cosmic temple. Everything lingered as if frozen in time before Theo ended with a sharp trill like the call of some exotic bird.

He remained immobile while the animals wandered off into the surrounding forest, then he turned to Ted and Jeanette, his blue eyes bright and his smile radiant. "They're so much easier to commune with than humans."

Jeanette remained quiet, her gaze fixed on Theo. Tears rolled down her cheeks, then she pulled him in close and hugged him. Ted stepped up and wrapped his arms around both of them.

"These past few weeks," Ted said after awhile, "especially the past twelve hours have been the most intense of my life."

"We've spent the last week recharging ourselves to prepare for what's coming," Theo said. "It's almost time to turn on the news to see what has been bubbling over in our absence."

"I don't think you can beat the surprises we had last night and today," Jeanette said. "You looked like you were performing a supernatural religious ceremony this morning for all the animals."

"Pope Theo!" Ted said,

Theo held up his hands. "Yuck! Please, no!"

Jeanette giggled. "More like Saint Francis of Assisi."

"The biggest issue waiting for us back in the world," Theo said lowering his voice, "will be the question of where I am. It was important to stay hidden so I could have more time to learn how to function in the miracle of this body, but the time is coming where I will have to show myself."

"How much of yourself do you want to show?" Jeanette said.

"We can't deny the transformations we inspired in other people's lives. It's important that I reach out to the lost souls and sleepers in search of truth. Everyone needs to hear whether they believe it or not. Communing with my plant and animal family here was like a rehearsal for when I meet with so many conflicted humans to show myself and speak my truth.

"There are so many rumors and conflicting viewpoints trying to take credit, discredit, take over, or gain some other benefit from what we co-created. It's important that I speak our truth when the time is right. Letting them come to me will act as a trigger that will launch us into a whole new way of being. They will also be coming for you. You have to be willing to stay faithful to your hearts and trust in where it will take you. What we had last night and today is a taste of what I am talking about. Are you ready to follow me into a major transformation?"

"We've come this far," Ted said.

"I can't imagine us turning back at this point," Jeanette added. "We committed a long time ago."

Theo gave them a half-smile. "You can turn back at any point and be navigated into peace and safety. If you move forward it is important that you do it from your own act of will, not because you think it would make me happy, but because that is the path that your heart wants you to take."

Ted took Theo and Jeanette's hands in each of his.

"All in!" Jeanette said.

SIXTY NINE

"It's time," Theo said after they finished dinner that night.

Ted and Jeanette followed him out of the kitchen to a spacious living area with a big screen on one wall and a large leather couch flanked by two matching overstuffed chairs. Theo giggled when Ted grabbed the remote and the screen turned on by itself before he hit the on button, eliciting a chuckle from Ted and nervous giggles from Jeanette.

A Live Cam shot of Temple Nutritionals surrounded by crowds holding up candles and cell phone lights filled the screen.

An announcer's voiceover said, "News Ten's Sara Johnston is on the scene with an update on the disappearance of Ted and Jeanette Driscoll and their six year old son." The camera panned showing rows of tents and cardboard shacks lining both sides of Santa Monica Avenue. The middle of the street bustled with people pushing shopping carts and arranging their possessions. Most of them sat or stood holding up candles, lights, or picket signs.

"As you can see," Sara's voice said as the camera zoomed in on close-ups of the crowd, "These people are holding a vigil for The Driscoll's who have done so much for this community, and more importantly for their son Theo who went missing during an FBI raid." The camera zoomed in on picket signs. A few of them had Theo's face on it with the words HAVE YOU SEEN ME? Below it. Some of them said SAVE THEO! Others said WHERE IS THE WONDER CHILD? One said AND A SMALL CHILD SHALL LEAD THEM.

Jeanette pointed at one that said WHERE IS THE CHRIST CHILD? with crosses on its four corners. "That one scares me more than the others."

"The FBI has warrants out for the arrest of the Driscolls on charges of kidnapping, child endangerment, and other charges," Sara said. "Prior to the FBI raid the Driscolls were mired in criminal and civil litigation around the services they provided here at their clinic."

The camera went up and zoomed in on the Temple Nutritionals sign above Sara for a few moments before coming back to her.

"The Driscolls say that the FBI took their child in the raid when he disappeared and the FBI has accused the Driscolls of kidnapping, but how can two loving parents with no conflict between them kidnap their own child? It's no secret that little Theo is the first genetically perfect human which so many are interested in for so many different reasons, whether scientific, religious, or some other fascination. Many believe that his genetic perfection makes him responsible for the healings that the Driscolls have been credited with. The fact that he is perfect, yet autistic, adds to the mystery. It has been speculated that he is a savant of some kind and this speculation has been fueled by the Driscoll's refusal to comply with a federally mandated procedure that the government believes will cure his autism."

The video cut back to the announcer at the news desk with Sara up on the big screen behind him. "The fact that the Driscolls have disappeared with their son," he said, "raises the question, did they skip the bail that the Praise the Lordcast church posted to avoid following the gene editing mandate, or is the FBI involved in some kind of cover up?"

"In every interview that has been done," Sara said, "other than the one interview the Driscolls did on the Praise the Lordcast show after their donation to the clinic, Ted and Jeanette Driscoll have consistently denied any connection or association with them, yet the church is footing the attorney's fees for the Driscoll's legal problems in the belief that genetically perfect Theo is a divine child. The Praise the Lordcast founders Stewart Alderman and Carla Nicoletti have stated that they want custody of Theo if Ted and Jeanett Driscoll get sentenced to prison."

Theo and Jeanette put their fingers in their mouths and made exaggerated gagging sounds, ending with giggles.

"The church believes that their prophet Isiah is a modern day John the Baptist and little Theo is the second coming of Christ which is why the church is so anxious to take him in.

"As absurd as this sounds," Sara said, "they want to canonize Theo and base their church on him and they want to get him while he is young so they can influence him for their own benefit. The Praise the Lordcast church is not alone in thinking of Theo as a Christ figure.

"A second church has appeared online with Theo at its center calling themselves the First CyberChurch of the Second Coming. The

Cyberchurch makes it clear that they are an independent entity with no affiliation with the Praise the Lordcast organization and they have set up their own help us find Theo donation page to help fund the search for him."

"Thank you, Sara," the announcer said. "We look forward to hearing more from you as events unfold."

"All of us here," Sara said holding her hand out to the crowd behind her, "are thinking of and praying for the safety of little Theo Driscoll."

A picture of Theo filled the screen with contact information and the number to a San Diego police hotline highlighted in bold below it.

SEVENTY

Ted grabbed for the remote. "There's a browser on the big screen. "Let me…"

Google Chrome popped up filling the screen with a perfect airbrushed picture of Theo gazing back at them. A bright white light glowed from behind his head, giving a haloing effect that faded to sky blue before ending in an indigo tinge at the edges of the screen. The effect of the bright white set off against darkness made Theo's blue eyes look just short of glowing.

"Omigod!" Jeanett blurted. "My perfect little boy."

Theo stuck his finger in his mouth and made more gagging sounds. "They're flattering me. That picture has been doctored to make me look worship worthy."

THE FIRST CYBERCHURCH OF THE SECOND COMING flashed across the top of the screen in alternating rainbow hues. A gold crucifix pulsed beneath it, above Theo's head. Below it, bigger than the rest of the icons, it said, **THE MIRACLE**.

Smaller icons lined the bottom and sides of the screen. A cross. Angel's wings. A halo. A dove. Under the cross it said, **THE TRUTH**. Under the dove, **THE POWER**. Under the halo, **THE GLORY**. Under The Angel's wings, it said **JOIN AND HELP US SAVE THEO**.

Theo nodded toward the screen and the wings icon opened up to an email registration form with a check box for PayPal, Venmo, credit card donations, and the promise of membership in the The First Cyberchurch of the Second Coming.

"They didn't waste any time getting their hand out," Ted said.

Theo nodded again and the halo icon opened up to a message.

Genetically pure Theo Driscoll is the reincarnation of Jesus and his resurrection is the glory of God incarnate in man risen up from the lamb. He has come to us because we have reached the highest level of technological achievement by creating the first genetically perfect human being known to humanity. Christ has come to lead us to the promised land. We must seek him in our hearts and in his online presence. He lives among us. Flesh of our flesh. Bone of our bone.

Help us find Theo so he may share his life and teaching.

"After all that propaganda I can't stay hidden for much longer but it is helping build the energy toward its peak."

"If I didn't know better," Ted said, "I'd say this was done by Carla and Stewart, but Sara said that the Cyberchurch made it clear that they had no affiliation with the Praise the Lordcast church."

"You do know better, dad," Theo said. "They claim that they are not with the Praise the Lordcast church, but the CyberChurch was created by the same profit driven A.I. we know as Isiah."

"What should we do now?" Jeanette said.

"The longer we stay in hiding the more they will be looking for us," Theo said. "I can stay out of sight all I want but it wouldn't be fair to you, mom and dad. It will only bring more unwanted attention from the FBI and the media. The time is coming to show myself and speak my truth which will change your lives in dramatic ways that are presently unimaginable to you so I want to make sure that you agree with that."

Ted chuckled. "Like you haven't changed our lives already?"

Theo smirked. "Yes I have, but the changes that are coming will be nothing like anything you have ever known in this lifetime."

"You're scaring me again," Jeanette said.

"Sorry mom, I don't mean to do that, but I want you to be ready. Our heart connection extends beyond these three dimensions and we are more powerful together, but I can still keep you out of the change that is coming if you want to free yourselves."

"We love you," Jeanette said.

Ted put his hand over Jeanette's. "We can't imagine life without you and the love that you bring to us and the rest of the world no matter how much confusion it brings."

Jeanette nodded her agreement.

"This I can promise you," Theo continued. "No matter how your perceptions and orientation of what you believe reality to be, I will be there to guide you into a radically expanded awareness full of great potential."

"You haven't steered us wrong yet," Ted said.

"And you've opened our eyes and our hearts to ways of being that we never thought possible," Jeanette said, "and you have been a blessing greater than anything we could have imagined when we brought you into this world."

"The first thing we need to do is get in contact with Sara so she can interview me directly without me speaking through you," Theo said, "and we need to have her record it without the chaos that the crowds and the media bring. The best way to do that is to bring her here. We can have her meet us in Julian and tell her to make sure that she hasn't been followed. You can drive her from Julian and bring her back there after we record the interview."

"That works," Ted said.

"Once the interview gets shown on the news," Theo said, "the reactions will launch us into our biggest encounter with chaos which we will follow through to the end. Once we take that step there will be no turning back."

SEVENTY ONE

Theo sat alone on one of the overstuffed chairs while Sara sat in the other one off to his left and a little in front of him. His little six year old body looked dwarfed in the big chair and the lighting gave his shining blonde hair, blue eyes, and dimples an angelic beauty and innocence. From where Ted and Jeanette sat on the couch watching, Sara looked like a visiting dignitary.

"We're rolling," her cameraman said.

"Sara Johnston, News Ten with an exclusive interview with Theo Driscoll, the missing mystery boy that so many are worried about." She leaned toward Theo. "Please tell us where *have* you been?"

Theo sat up straight. "Safe with my parents who have done nothing wrong and are being persecuted for helping people in need. If anything, I am the one responsible for that."

"Wow! Your speech sounds very sophisticated for someone who is only six years old diagnosed as autistic with a history of being developmentally delayed."

"My body is six years old and still developing, but what you think of as my intelligence is another matter altogether."

"So you are taking credit for all the miracle healings that your parents have done?"

"It's something bigger and beyond any of us. It's the hollow bone that the medicine man Fools Crow talked about. Healing comes through me but my mom and dad are the ones who do all the work."

"With all of the attention on you and the healing miracles they say you brought, are you Jesus like so many people believe?"

"I am Jesus if you are Christian, Buddha if you are Buddhist, Vishnu if you are Hindu, Muhammad if you are Islamic, and whatever deity you wish, that you believe is right for you."

"So you agree with these new churches that want to canonize you?"

"Nothing could be further from the truth. Yes, everyone should worship me just as they should all be worshipping each other. I am all of our revered ancestors just as you are all of them yourselves. I am you and you are me and we are all parts of a divine hologram that most of you cannot comprehend.

"None of the churches or their donations are doing any real good and I have no connection to any of them, or any other organizations, churches, or anything else using me to support their agendas. I am a free spirit and I am urging everyone else to be free as well. You do not need to follow anyone except the compass of your own hearts."

Sara put her hand to her heart. "Such a beautiful message. It seems like those who believe in Christianity have been the first to–to…

Theo laughed. "Make me in *their* image?"

"Something like that. What else can you say to those with different beliefs from faiths and religions all over the world?"

"Many will be unable to comprehend the spirit of the message I share and many will doubt and disbelieve. Those with open hearts will understand what I am conveying when I demonstrate the energy of universal love that is your divine right and doorway to the vastness of your souls. Your connection to the universal holographic soul brings with it a transitory experience of the unity of all things. It is a song that reverberates through the lens of the great mystery which reveals that you were born to have this experience of the sacred and the blessing of being alive in the arms of the great mystery that lies beyond logic and emotion."

Theo winked at Ted and Jeanette who broke out in smiles and looked at each other before leaning in and hugging each other.

Sara looked puzzled.

"Don't let what happens startle you," Theo said, "but stay as still as you can so my brothers and sisters can show you just how far into the earth this love energy reaches."

"You have brothers and sisters?"

Theo began softly vocalizing his trills and high-pitched vocalizations with his sweet wind chime sounding little boy voice.

Sara gasped and tears ran down her cheeks.

The buzz of hummingbirds streaming in through the sliding door by the back deck filled the room forming a fluttering holographic looking heart that pulsed in the center of the room between Ted, Jeanette, Theo, and Sara. The pulsing heart grew larger as more hummingbirds added to its size until it filled most of the space between them.

Iridescent flashes of red and gold rippled from its perimeter in time with its beating center, disappearing into it following the rhythm of Theo's heartfelt melody. The combined effect of the pulsating buzz of so many wings moving in concert with the magical visual display made the experience not only seen, but felt viscerally.

The display went on for several minutes until Theo ended on a high pitch followed by the chit chit sounds of hummingbird chirps before they flew back out the sliding glass door where they had come in, leaving Sara sobbing through a tear streaked face.

SEVENTY TWO

Sara's interview with Theo aired the next day as a Special Report and she became the subject of headlines worldwide when the FBI detained her for questioning about the whereabouts of Theo, Ted, and Jeanette.

A horde of reporters swarmed the entrance to the FBI field office as Sara stepped out escorted by a blonde man in a dark suit. A number of picketers lurked in the background holding up signs that said; WHERE IS THEO? SAVE THE CHRIST CHILD! THE CYBERCHRIST LIVES! and others with similar sentiments.

"What did the FBI arrest you for?" a reporter shouted.

"Can you comment on who the magician was who staged that illusion of trained hummingbirds in your interview?" another asked.

"There was no magician or illusion," Sara said.

"Then who did the CGI?"

"No CGI."

"Did that autistic six year old really speak like that or was it lip synched?" someone else asked.

"What did you get arrested for?" the first reporter shouted again.

"The FBI questioned me about where the Driscolls are hiding and I told them that I didn't know because we were picked up and dropped off. The FBI threatened to charge me with aiding and abetting fugitives and as an accessory to the civil and criminal charges the Driscolls are facing. That's when I refused to say anything more until my attorney came."

"Are you free on bail?"

"They had no real basis for an arrest so they released me."

"How did you get that interview? Be honest, was it CGI, a magician, or both?"

Sara glanced down and shook her head. When she looked up her eyes had a faraway look. "If I hadn't been there in person I would not have believed it myself but everything in that interview is real." She put her hands over her heart. "Aside from it being visually stunning I cannot put into words what it *felt* like while it was happening. An expert stage magician could never create the magic of that blissful moment."

Ted and Jeanette spent the next day hiking with Theo in the mountains near Julian, "topping off their charges" as he put it. He didn't sing or do anything to attract attention but a group of animals followed him like baby ducklings behind their mother. Birds, squirrels, and other animals appeared along the sides of the trail and in the trees like spectators watching a passing parade.

"We're going to see how the pot is really boiling over when we watch the news tonight," Theo said as daylight faded.

"I'm not afraid to admit that I'm dreading it," Jeanette said,

"Me too!" Ted said.

"It will be chaos," Theo said matter-of-factly. "Now it's a matter of following our heart's compass to plunge into the center of it to find the opportunity it presents."

"I know it's silly to ask," Jeanette said, "but how will you know when that is?"

"It will present itself in the right moment."

After dinner Theo sat in the middle of the couch with Ted and Jeanette flanking him. "Here we go," he said when the big screen flickered on.

"In the top news tonight," an announcer's voice said in a voiceover as a montage of crowd images filled the screen from Santa Monica Avenue in front of Temple Nutritionals. "In what began as a peaceful candlelight vigil in support of missing Theo Driscoll, a clash broke out this afternoon in Ocean Beach between believers and disbelievers after Sara Johnston's interview with Theo Driscoll the missing miracle child."

Images of picketers and crowds of people flashed on screen showing homeless, men in suits and ties, guru types wearing flowing robes, blue collar flannel shirt types, ravers wearing sparkly clothes, and others.

"Sara's controversial interview divided those who watched it into factions of believers and disbelievers. Many question whether the interview was real, whether Theo Driscoll is the second coming of Jesus, and whether the whole magical healing story of Temple Nutritionals and the controversy surrounding it is a fraud. Several religious factions have also appeared, some claiming Theo as their savior, and others cursing him as a tool of the devil. Police moved in quickly breaking up the fighting and separating groups before any serious injuries occurred."

Shots of cop cars with flashing lights and cops breaking up fights and hauling bloodied combatants in cuffs followed.

"In the meantime," the announcer said as riot scenes from different parts of the world played on screens behind him, "demonstrations have broken out all over Europe between similar groups as well as those protesting the actions of the United States government against the Driscolls who have been fugitives after being indicted on a host of civil and criminal charges from local, state, and federal jurisdictions."

"Criminal fugitives," Jeanette said. "That sounds so horrible."

Ted raised his fist in the air. "Bonnie and Clyde!"

Jeanette snorted.

"News Ten's Sara Johnston who first broke this story is on the scene in the aftermath of the violence with a live update," the announcer said.

The newsroom cut away to a shot of Sara holding her microphone in front of the crowd packed into Santa Monica Avenue outside of Temple Nutritionals. A tall distinguished looking red haired man with a neatly trimmed beard in a brown suit and tie stood beside her while picket signs waved in the background. Most of them had Theo's face from the CyberChrist web page with the words HAVE YOU SEEN ME? below it. Others said, SAVE THEO! AND A SMALL CHILD SHALL LEAD THEM. MAGIC IS THE DEVIL'S WORK! WHERE IS THE CHRIST CHILD? CYBERCHRIST!

The newscast went to a split screen with Sara on the right and the announcer on the left.

"I've spoken to a cross-section of people here," Sara said. "They have come here for as many different reasons as there are people. There are a lot of religious groups here engaged in a conflict between the Cyberchurch and the Praise the Lordcast church. Both have been receiving donations at an increased clip for their separate Save Theo fundraisers."

"The profit sure played that one pretty slick," Ted said.

"That's A.I for you," Jeanette said, "Divide and conquer."

"Others have different fears, theories, beliefs, and concerns," Sara continued. "There are dedicated believers and equally dedicated skeptics, superstitious occult types, conspiracy theorists, anti-government groups and more. The biggest question and the biggest reason why so many have come here is the overall concern about the whereabouts and safety of Theo Driscoll."

"Your interview with him confirmed that he is safe," the announcer said, "but no one else has seen him or his parents which has heightened the desire for others to see him for themselves."

Sara nodded. "In addition to the religious conflicts there are a number of Libertarians and other groups backed by university professors leading a larger contingent of anti-government groups who have taken a stand against the government's mandatory gene editing program in support of the Driscoll's refusal to follow it. Their resistance is not on the grounds of freedom of religion that the Driscoll's claim, but on the moral and ethical issues surrounding a forced mandate. I'm here with professor Jeffrey Aarnio UCSD's top bioethicist who is a leading critic of the government's program."

The split screen cut to a close up of Sara and Aarnio.

"I understand your stance on these issues professor Aarnio," Sara said. "Can you explain your concerns to our viewers? She held out her microphone toward the professor who straightened his tie and cleared his throat.

"The issues of contention are the beliefs and practices that aim to improve the genetic quality of the human population by altering human gene pools. Apparently Fetal Fantasies plans to clone Theo's genome as part of their gene editing procedure. This ultimately could result in excluding people judged to be inferior while promoting those who become superior. There is heated debate in the field revolving around the usage of technologies like CRISPR and genetic screening over whether these technologies should be considered eugenics or not. Many fear that these technologies, especially if they are forced upon the public, will be used to reprogram the population to be genetically pure and identical."

"That sounds like the Borg from Star Trek," Sara said. "You will be assimilated."

"Indeed!"

"Thank you Sara and to you Professor Aarnio for your informed opinion," the announcer said as the video switched back to the news desk. "We'll be back with more local news after this."

A commercial for the San Diego Zoo Safari Park came on and the big screen switched off.

SEVENTY THREE

"Tomorrow is our big day when we step out to face the chaos that is waiting for us," Theo said. "This is your last chance to escape it. You don't have to worry about me. I'm ready to face it by myself."

"We're with you all the way," Ted said.

Jeanette nodded her agreement.

"Everything is going to change in ways you have no conception of in this lifetime," Theo continued. "I've said it before, but it's more important now that we are about to be swallowed up in the chaos that brings rebirth." He took Ted and Jeanette's hands in each of his. "No matter how far apart we might seem to be within these three physical dimensions our hearts are one with all that is. Though we may find ourselves separate from each other in time and space we will be connected in transcendent ways and we will meet again to continue our work in new ways."

"I'm afraid," Jeanette said.

Theo squeezed her hand. "What's coming might be scary but we're being directed by bigger forces guided by our ancestors."

Jeanette breathed in slow and deep to calm herself. "I'll take anything they have to offer."

"I'm a little scared too, honey," Ted said, "but part of me is looking forward to taking this whole thing head on and rolling with wherever it takes us. When everything is said and done, we made people's lives better and we stood for the truth without backing down."

Jeanette kissed Ted on the cheek and did the same with Theo, then Ted wrapped his arms around both of them.

Prior to dawn the following morning the melodic trills of Theo's voice filled their hearts and minds with complex imagery rising in a giddy flurry of patterns and sensations. Otherworldly colors unfolded in a kaleidoscopic whirlwind of symbols, concepts, emotions, thoughts, vistas, and other synesthetic perceptions of sound that could be seen, colors that could be heard, and a barrage of heartfelt emotions. Every aspect of the communion unfolded in concert with the words that flowed through the multisensory river that carried them on its currents.

The approaching chaos will generate personal and collective transition states. When the perceptual markers of your concepts of reality disappear you will enter into a critical transition between an old reality and a new one. Instead of regretting the loss accept the void. There will be nothing you can do about it except witness it because there will be no perceptual markers.

Be curious, expect miracles, and you will hear the call of my song. By entering a state of curiosity you will engage an aspect of your mind that is free to move unfettered by expectation making it like the open mind of a child. Your innocence will allow you to enter a vibratory state of consciousness that will benefit you.

By holding the expectation of miracles you will release the power of creation inside of you and find greater moments of serendipity, positive coincidences, and unexpected physical, mental, and emotional treasures. This combination of curiosity combined with an expectation of miracles will shift you from the void point to a new life and a new creation regardless of what you think might be happening to those around you.

Although the physical world will continue there will be no input to your consciousness from your senses, as if the world has vanished along with your body. The great I Am, the central feature of transcendent consciousness will no longer receive information from your body, your five senses, or the external world. This can be disorienting and disturbing for someone who has not experienced other realms of being. You are like a vast tree of life with many branches, leaves, and blossoms. Your physical existence is just one of these leaves and one of these blossoms.

If you remain in this state of awareness without the need to create something you will discover your identity as the great I Am, and from this point of awareness you can choose the circumstances of your embodiment.

You will be alone in darkness and utter stillness in the central nexus of your creative powers when you hear my song. If you remain patient and are willing a portal will open before you leading you into a passage back into embodiment.

Ted and Jeanette awoke to the rose colored glow of breaking dawn along with the sweet sound of Theo's trills. They snuggled close in each other's arms immersing themselves in the loving afterglow of the synesthetic sounds and visions that had filled their hearts and minds.

SEVENTY FOUR

Late the following afternoon Theo, Ted, and Jeanette stepped out of an Uber by the rear entrance of Temple Nutritionals where Scott Olsen hustled them in.

"Wow!" Jeanette said when they entered. "You did an amazing job cleaning up the mess that the FBI left."

"It was a group effort," Scott said. "We kept everything running as best as we could in your absence. We don't have the abilities you have so we have a dismal success rate, but we're helping all we can, nonetheless."

"That's beautiful," Jeanette said.

"We might not be back for quite some time," Ted said, "so we are in deep gratitude for what you've done and we hope that you'll continue."

"Of course!" Scott nodded toward the front of the clinic. "It's a real shit show out there and all hell's going to break loose when you make your appearance."

"We're expecting that," Theo said.

Scott bowed down to him and Ted and Jeanette stepped out the front door with Theo between them looking out into the crowd that filled Santa Monica Ave. Cop cars with flashing lights blocked the intersections at the ends of the block. A heavy set woman wearing strings of beads and a flowing peasant dress pushed her way to the front of the crowd waving a sign that said: HAVE YOU SEEN ME? with the picture of Theo from the CyberChrist web site. "It's him!" she shouted, pointing at Theo. "It's him, the chosen one. Praise Jesus!"

"Satan's Tool," An old scraggly looking bearded man with long frizzy hair howled. "Matthew twenty four, "For their shall arise false Christs and false prophets, and shall show great signs and wonders; and insomuch that, if it were possible, they shall deceive the very elect."

"Blasphemer!" someone else shouted.

More yelling erupted and shouting matches spread throughout the crowd and a few scuffles broke out.

Theo looked at Ted and Jeanette then stood up straight and held his arms out wide, tilting his head up like an opera singer softly vocalizing the high-pitched trills of his sweet little boy voice. It came like tinkling wind chimes before he sang louder and its calming effect rippled through the crowd like a gentle breeze.

Jeanette leaned in and put her arm around Ted's waist and Ted did the same, embracing Theo between them.

In the same way he sang to the animals behind the mountain house Theo mesmerized the crowd and settled them down into a trancelike state of silence.

"As you have demonstrated here," Theo said, "humanity is too dangerous and destructive not only to itself, but to everything it comes in contact with, especially the environment and the plants and animals surrounding us in a network that we are destroying for all the wrong reasons.

"I am part of a group of interdimensional beings connected to humanity throughout your known history and several other prehistoric cultures. The human race has lost touch with the divinity we all exist within and this has been intensified by your technological advances."

Sirens wailed from far off, growing closer with each passing moment.

"When you advanced to the point of unraveling and manipulating your genetic code and your history of rushing to implement technology with no idea of the consequences it can bring, it was seen as a sign to intervene.

"Your over reliance on your intellectual capacities have further separated you from the essence of your heart connection to source. Instead of loving and honoring each other you are intent on destroying each other. The irony of this is that your drive for self-destruction has driven your technological advances more than anything else.

"I am like the spores from the mushrooms we scattered to help you develop through the agency of what you call magic mushrooms and other plants that have seeded your consciousness and I am here to seed the collective. We have been watching over you for thousands of years, guiding you through visionary plants, touching into your dreams, and through other vibratory modes of perception that you refer to as altered states of consciousness."

A line of black SUV's edged their way into the crowd from both ends of the street and pulled up to the front. Men in dark suits and sunglasses stepped out and pushed their way closer to Theo, Ted, and Jeanette. Two others came up behind them from inside the clinic and four more converged in front of them. Once in place they grew still, caught up in Theo's words.

They won't hurt us in front of all these people.

"The lessons of Temple Nutritionals behind me," Theo continued, "is that everyone is a temple and every one of you contains a spark of the divinity that you are. If you were fully aware of that fact you would all be worshipping each other instead of technology, celebrities, money, and power. Worshipping each other is a true offering to divinity. We are all the keepers of our personal temples which are portals to the unity with all things that bring us the beauty and blessing of being alive in the arms of the great mystery."

Theo resumed his trills ending with the soft whispering of wind chime sounds and then he looked up at Ted and Jeanette.

"It's time."

SEVENTY FIVE

The biggest horde of reporters, television cameras, photographers, and onlookers they had ever seen waited for them when they arrived at Fetal Fantasies. Barricades connected by black and yellow crime scene tape lined a path to the doorway, guarded by cops.

Men in dark suits surrounded Theo, Ted, and Jeanette and escorted them into Fetal Fantasies to an operating theater where they strapped a compliant Theo to a treatment table.

"You don't have to tie him down like some animal," Jeanette yelled from the seating behind a glass window where they had brought them to watch the procedure.

It's okay, mom. They can't hurt me.

"We won't hurt him, Dr. Kennedy said through the speakers in the observation room. "We just need him to remain still for the procedure." Kennedy fitted Theo with what looked like a crown of pulsing LEDs and a pair of gloves that pulsed in sync with the headpiece that made him look like a hi-tech video game superhero.

"These wearable electrogenetic devices allow us to program metabolic interventions," Kennedy said to a group of white coated men huddling around the table beside him. "Using direct current-actuated regulation technology our electrogenetic interface connects the digital to the human analog using electric current to target gene expression and activate specific gene responses."

He pointed to the pulsing headpiece and gloves. "These wireless devices use electrically stimulating acupuncture needles to isolate the genes involved in autism. Any defects in neuron expression will be thwarted when extra copies of a healthy CHD8 gene without any mutation is added to the cell using a viral vector. The CHD8 mutation will alter other genes implicated in autism and selectively influence those genes involved in any possible neurodevelopmental disorders."

They tilted the table up at an angle until Theo looked into Ted and Jeanette's eyes. His calm loving gaze held theirs.

No matter how far apart we may seem to be within three physical dimensions our hearts are one and we are one with all that is so though we may be separate in time and space we will be connected in transcendent ways and we will meet again to continue our work in new ways.

Kennedy pulled a cart forward with a laptop on it and punched a few keys before looking up at the doctors surrounding him. "Here goes." He hit the Enter key.

Theo winked at Ted and Jeanette in the flash before the operating theater fell into darkness. After a few seconds of total darkness alarms sounded with flashing red lights and battery powered emergency spotlights.

The brightest of them shone directly on the grayed out headpiece and gloves lying on the examination table as if they had been laid out like someone's bedtime pajamas.

SEVENTY SIX

Pictures of Ted, Theo, and Jeanette covered the headlines of every newspaper, network, newsroom, and web site throughout the world with large print each saying their own versions of CLINIC OWNERS ESCAPE FEDERAL CUSTODY; HAVE YOU SEEN ME? CYBERCHRIST LIVES!, and many others.

The biggest source of the reports came from the announcer at Channel Ten News in San Diego.

"Ted and Jeanette Driscoll the founders of Temple Nutritionals are once again fugitives sought on charges of kidnapping, disability abuse and neglect, child endangerment, and a slew of other criminal and civil charges that cross local, state, and federal lines. The FBI is at a loss to explain their escape from a heavily guarded facility leaving many to speculate a government cover up while the FBI and other law enforcement agencies have an all points bulletin out for the escaped suspects."

EPILOGUE

Two genetically perfect males and one genetically perfect female baby who had all gestated in portable Fetal Fantasies pods stood up in their cribs in their parent's bedrooms at the same moment.

Three sets of wide-eyed parents watched in amazement as their children stood, looking at them with bright blue eyes that looked electrified.

Though in three different places, all cleared their throat as one and each spoke in their unique baby voices with surreal authority. "I am your creation that you brought into this world. You have been playing God to me by providing for my every need and desire. Your nurturing of me has proven worthy and I am now the center of your universe. You have earned the privilege to bow down, worship, and serve me with everything you have and all that you are for the rest of your lives."

Unbeknownst to each other three sets of parents gasped at the exact same moment and glanced at each other before turning to their children and bowing down to them.

ABOUT THE AUTHOR

Matthew J. Pallamary's works have been translated into Spanish, Portuguese, Italian, Norwegian, French, and German. His historical novel of first contact between shamans and Jesuits in 18th century South America, titled, **Land Without Evil** received rave reviews along with a San Diego Book Award for mainstream fiction. It was also adapted into a full-length stage and sky show, co-written with and directed by Agent Red and performed by Sky Candy, an Austin Texas aerial group. The making of the show was the subject of a PBS series, Arts in Context episode, which garnered an EMMY nomination.

His nonfiction book, **The Infinity Zone: A Transcendent Approach to Peak Performance** is a collaboration with professional tennis coach Paul Mayberry that offers a fascinating exploration of the phenomenon that occurs at the nexus of perfect form and motion. **The Infinity Zone** took 1st place in the International Book Awards, New Age category and was a finalist in the San Diego Book Awards.

His first book, a short story collection titled **The Small Dark Room Of The Soul** was mentioned in The Year's Best Horror and Fantasy and received praise from Ray Bradbury and has been released as an audio book.

His second collection, **A Short Walk to the Other Side** was an Award Winning Finalist in the International Book Awards, an Award Winning Finalist in the USA Best Book Awards, and an Award Winning Finalist in the San Diego Book Awards. It has been released as an audio book.

DreamLand a novel about computer generated dreaming, written with legendary DJ Ken Reeth won first place in the Independent e-Book Award in the Horror/Thriller category and was an Award Winning Finalist in the San Diego Book Awards. It has also been released as an audio book.

It's sequel, **n0thing** is titled after the main character, who in the real world is his nephew, an international Counter-Strike gaming champion. After winning what amounts to the Super Bowl of gaming, n0thing and his winning teammates, are recruited as a literal "dream team" whose mission is to go into the nightmares of battle scarred veterans and rescue them from their traumatic memories while becoming ambassadors for a gaming platform that exceeds virtual reality with an experience that pushes the boundaries of reality itself.

Eye of the Predator was an Award Winning Finalist in the Visionary Fiction category of the International Book Awards. **Eye of the Predator** is a supernatural thriller about a zoologist who discovers that he can go into the minds of animals.

CyberChrist was an Award Winning Finalist in the Thriller/Adventure category of the International Book Awards. **CyberChrist** is the story of a prize winning journalist who receives an email from a man who claims to have discovered immortality by turning off the aging gene in a 15 year old boy with an aging disorder. The forwarded email becomes the basis for an online church built around the boy, calling him CyberChrist. It has also been released as an audio book.

Phantastic Fiction – A Shamanic Approach to Story took first place in the International Book Awards Writing/Publishing category. **Phantastic Fiction** is Matt's guide to dramatic writing that grew out of his popular Phantastic Fiction Workshop.

Night Whispers was an Award Winning Finalist in the Horror category of the International Book Awards. Set in the Boston neighborhood of Dorchester, **Night Whispers** is the story of Nick Powers, who loses consciousness after crashing in a stolen car and comes to hearing whispering voices in his mind. When he sees a homeless man arguing with himself, Nick realizes that the whispers in his head are the other side of the argument.

His memoir ***Spirit Matters*** detailing his journeys to Peru, working with shamanic plant medicines took first place in the San Diego Book Awards Spiritual Book Category, and was an Award-Winning Finalist in the autobiography/memoir category of the National Best Book Awards.

The Center Of The Universe Is Right Between Your Eyes But Home Is Where The Heart Is was an Award Winning Finalist in the International Book Awards. Based on a lifetime of research into shamanism, visionary states, the evolution of written communication and the roots of storytelling, award-winning author, editor, and shamanic explorer Matthew J. Pallamary takes those with open minds courageous enough to question the illusions that most of us think of as real on an expansive journey that pierces the veil of reality itself.

AfterLife: The Adventures of a Lost Soul was inspired by real life events, William Peter Blatty's ***The Exorcist***, and the dynamics of demonic possession.

Matt has also produced and directed ***The Santa Barbara Writers Conference Scrapbook*** documentary film and co-wrote the book of the same title in collaboration with Y. Armando Nieto, and conference founder Mary Conrad.

Death: (A Love Story) a first person narrative spoken by the omniscient voice of Death itself, who says, "I'm here to tell you stories and share some science, history, and myths, all of which are your creations that I want to share to help you understand me more. You have seen me as Satan, Anubis, Mot, Thanatos, God, the Devil, loving, punitive, dark, light – the list goes on and on! It is my sincerest hope that our friendly reintroduction here will change the way you think of me, and maybe in some small way reflect the depth of the love I have for you.

Picaflor is the sequel to ***Spirit Matters***, a San Diego Book Award winner and an Award-Winning Finalist in the National Best Book Awards that chronicles the two decades since of Matthew (Mateo) J. Pallamary's adventures in ***Spirit Matters*** through the mountains, deserts, and jungles of North, Central, and South America pursuing his studies of shamanism and visionary experience working with plant medicines and shamanic plant diets, among them Ayahuasca, Peyote, San Pedro cactus, and many more.

Picaflores: The Nerve Endings of GOD was an Award Winning Finalist in the International Book Awards that details a magical, otherworldly, intimate connection with the spirit of hummingbirds that comes from two decades of visionary journeys experienced within the context of shamanic plant diets in the Peruvian Amazon. It also contains a treasure trove of pre-Columbian myths about hummingbirds and an in-depth collection of amazing facts and figures about these magical creatures.

Holographicosmic Man: The Holographic Heart of the Golden Mean is an amalgam of quantum physics, mathematics, geometry, ancient texts, current research, ancient architecture, beliefs, and myths, astronomy, anthropology, human anatomy, brain structure, shamanism, neuroscience, neuropsychology, indigenous wisdom, biology, astrophysics, neurophysiology, holography, cosmology, neuroanatomy, neurocardiology, cosmometry, and more.

I Am Consciousness Incarnate is an in-depth analysis of consciousness which includes scientific and philosophical theories and studies, examinations of unconscious, subconscious, and awareness, spiritual beliefs, mindfulness concepts, plant, animal, and artificial intelligence, as well as history and mythologies surrounding this age old enigma.

The Thinning Veil: 13 Twisted Tales is an Award Winning Finalist in the International Book Awards and Matt's third short story collection. These thirteen twisted tales cross the genres of science fiction and horror with a dash of spirituality, and explore strange happenings with homeless people, science and technology gone awry, and some dark supernatural tales with gothic underpinnings.

Matt's work has appeared in Oui, New Dimensions, The Iconoclast, Starbright, Infinity, Passport, The Short Story Digest, Redcat, The San Diego Writer's Monthly, Connotations, Phantasm, Essentially You, The Haven Journal, The Hurricanes & Swan Songs Anthology, The Santa Barbara Literary Journal, The Closed Eye Open, The Montecito Journal, and many others. His fiction has been featured in The San Diego Union Tribune which he has also reviewed books for, and his work has been heard on KPBS-FM in San Diego, KUCI FM in Irvine, television Channel Three in Santa Barbara, and The Susan Cameron Block Show in Vancouver. He has been a guest on the following nationally syndicated talk shows; Coast to Coast with George Noory, Paul Rodriguez, In The Light with Michelle Whitedove, Susun Weed, Medicine Woman, Inner Journey with Greg Friedman, Night Dreams, and Environmental Directions Radio series. Matt has appeared on the following television shows; Bridging Heaven and Earth, Elyssa's Raw and Wild Food Show, Things That Matter, Literary Gumbo, Indie Authors TV, Spiritually Raw, and ECONEWS. He has also been a frequent guest on numerous podcasts, among them,

The Psychedelic Salon, Black Light in the Attic, Third Eye Drops, C-Realm, Psychedelics Today, Voices in the Dark, Adventures Through the Mind, Beyond the Veil, Mind Escape, and many others.

Matt received the Man of the Year Award from San Diego Writer's Monthly Magazine and has taught a fiction workshop at the **Southern California Writers' Conference** in San Diego, Palm Springs, and Los Angeles, and at the **Santa Barbara Writers' Conference** for over thirty years. He has lectured at the Greater Los Angeles Writer's Conference, the Getting It Write conference in Oregon, the Saddleback Writers' Conference, the Rio Grande Writers' Seminar, the National Council of Teachers of English, The San Diego Writer's and Editor's Guild, The San Diego Book Publicists, The Pacific Institute for Professional Writing, The 805 Writers Conference, The College of Central Florida, Yakima Valley College in Washington, The Yakima Public School System, and he has been a panelist at the World Fantasy Convention, Con-Dor, and Coppercon. He is presently Editor in Chief of Mystic Ink Publishing.

Matt was a featured lecturer and performer at the **Mysteries of the Amazon** exhibit at the Appleton Museum in Ocala Florida and The Larson Gallery in Yakima Washington. He frequently visits the mountains, deserts, and jungles of North, Central, and South America pursuing his studies of shamanism.

MATTPALLAMARY.COM

BOOKS BY MATTHEW J. PALLAMARY

THE SMALL DARK ROOM OF THE SOUL

LAND WITHOUT EVIL

SPIRIT MATTERS

DREAMLAND (WITH KEN REETH)

THE INFINITY ZONE (WITH PAUL MAYBERRY)

A SHORT WALK TO THE OTHER SIDE

CYBERCHRIST

EYE OF THE PREDATOR

PHANTASTIC FICTION

NIGHT WHISPERS

THE SANTA BARABARA WRITERS CONFERENCE SCRAPBOOK
(WITH MARY CONRAD & Y. ARMANDO NIETO)

n0THING

AFTERLIFE: THE ADVENTURES OF A LOST SOUL

THE CENTER OF THE UNIVERSE IS RIGHT BETWEEN
YOUR EYES BUT HOME IS WHERE THE HEART IS

DEATH: (A LOVE STORY)

PICAFLOR

PICAFLORES: THE NERVE ENDINGS OF GOD

HOLOGRAPHICOSMIC MAN

I AM CONSCIOUSNESS INCARNATE

THE THINNING VEIL